MW01088674

a thriller

Silenced **to Death**

a novel of life lost and found

Donna Graham

ISBN 978-1-937391-46-1

Cover images by Jason Mowry - Unsplash
Designed and distributed by Romeii, LLC.
Visit our website at ebooks.romeii.com

Revised July 2023

This book is dedicated to my loving husband, Jim, who has always supported me with my crazy ambitions and has never, ever forgotten how to make me laugh.

Contents

"Courage is grace under pressure."

By Ernest Hemingway

Silenced **to Death**

chapter
one

Monday, June 4, 7:00 a.m.

Winckowski Farm, 49 Calico Fields Road,
Blanchard, Minnesota

Over the years, the house on Calico Fields Road was not properly maintained and, at times, abused, much like the family inside, who called it home.

The heavily burdened farmhouse slumped in the overgrown yard, peppered with broken glass, a rusted mailbox, broken toys, spent cartridge shell casings, and a well-worn overstuffed armchair. The dirty windows resisted the sunshine and left the impression of a blank stare. As if signaling for help, a TV cable tapped non-stop on the window of the cock-eyed dormer, which was losing its grip on the roof. Trying to escape, the tri-colored squares of siding swung side to side, resembling a fluid patchwork quilt.

The front door was stuck open; the knob plunged deep inside the sheetrock wall behind it. Aqua, a surprising pop of color, brightened the wooden storm door, with its eight windows, two broken. The storm door blasted open as a terrified little girl flew out, leaped off the stoop, and scrambled underneath the front steps. Gulping for air, nine-year-old Annabelle wedged herself firmly against the backside of the wooden stairs, tightly wrapping her arms around her stomach where her dad had landed a painful punch. Tired and hungry, Annabelle's sin was walking between the TV and her father, Wayne Winckowski, especially mean after drinking and popping pills all night.

The storm door was stuck open, caught on the overhang, and she could hear their cat, Kitty meowing from inside. Annabelle prayed her family had hidden away from the house because they would be in trouble if they were still inside. Shivering, she realized the house had become dangerously quiet.

Hiding this close to the house Annabelle worried Wayne would find her. She hoped her older brother, Harley, had hidden somewhere safe. He was one year older, but they shared the same birthday, July 7th. When they needed to hide from their father during one of his rampages, Harley was his sister's guide to the farm's best spots. Usually they hid together, but she would have to find a better hideout alone.

An ear-splitting explosion startled Annabelle, and she hit her head on the underside of the splintered floorboard. Someone had pulled the trigger on Wayne's shotgun... except no one uses it but him. The truth banged at her as she quivered like an arrow. Refusing to believe until the smell of burnt gunpowder floated down through the cracks of the steps, stinging her nose.

Another blast cracked the quiet of the house wide open. Annabelle cowered, hearing shrieks, bare feet pounding, and woeful pleading. Over the hysteria, her dad shrieked over and over again, "Shut up! Quit making me mad!"

Annabelle slid, shaky hands over her ears, hoping to block out the horrific sounds. Squirming deeper into the tiny hideout, she wanted to be gone, to blink and be invisible. Tears rolled steadily off her bent bare knees.

A shrill scream was shut down by another blast. The deafening sound echoed off the living room walls as Annabelle tucked her head between her knees, trying to smother the painful clash. Her mind swung like a possessed pendulum from one petrifying thought to another. Trying to become as small as possible, she locked her hands around her legs and pinned her elbows against her ribcage.

Silence descended again. Its eeriness prickled Annabelle's arms. Over the hot smell of gunpowder, an unknown metallic odor curdled her stomach with its gagging sweetness.

Annabelle whispered over and over, *I'm tough, I'm tough…*

Two more shots shattered the air as Annabelle bucked, smashing her nose on the top of a knee. Her useless hands were unable to muffle the terrifying sounds as her toes curled inside the sweaty borrowed shoes.

That's four shots. Who? No, no, I don't want to know. God, don't let this be happening, please! Dad told me I was his favorite, so God, he wouldn't kill me, right? Please help me hide better.

As fast as the click of a trigger, the echoing stopped. A hush blanketed the stillness slowing, the passing of time as each millisecond bumped into the next. Annabelle released her hands, praying to hear any sounds of life. Wiping her tear-streaked face, she felt a sharp pain tapping inside her chest. Squirming around, she felt it ease up.

She heard her dad's heavy footsteps as he stumbled through the living room, kicking the appliance-box bedrooms out of the way as he moved toward the back of the house. Being drunk was his mean, usual self, but never this crazy.

Feeling cold and unable to move, Annabelle was startled when she heard her dad returning to the living room.

The TV volume went up, and the whoosh of his recliner as he dropped into it. A loud thunk spooked her, but it was the footrest being released.

Stillness had once again darkened her home. Annabelle's confusion moved to a familiar memory of the day her dad had brought home the brand-new recliner. The family had all been so excited.

Annabelle had been standing with her two brothers and two sisters as they watched their father pull the large camouflage chair out of the bed of his pickup truck. The fabric was beautifully covered with leaves, trees, and deer. That recliner was big enough to fit all five kids.

Lifting the chair with ease, Wayne carried it straight through the front door. The kids followed him in, watching as he carefully positioned the new chair in front of his large screen TV. Turning quickly, he pointed his fat finger at his children and said, "This is your only warning: no one is to sit in my chair." Leaning into his voice, he shouted, "Ever!"

Hearing his scary voice, Annabelle yipped, jamming her fists to her mouth, and quickly stepped back. Wayne knew they would obey him, and he was right.

Quite pleased with the ensuing silence, he smirked, turned to his chair, and sat down. Releasing the footrest, he used the remote to turn on the TV. Then Wayne pulled a beer from the case that sat on the floor next to him. Snapping the tab, he guzzled it down, burped, dropped the empty onto the floor, and pulled out another one. He began flipping through his favorite creepy TV shows, *The Devil Chose You*, *Hydrating Your Way to Sobering Up*, *A Night Out for a Murderer*, and *Snakes in the Bayou*. Along with his endless adult cartoon list.

Disheartened, Annabelle and her siblings looked at each other. The new recliner was the only usable piece of furniture in the living room.

Lost in thought, Annabelle twitched as she heard the shotgun being pumped. Her dad was reloading! Her mind screamed, *Get out! Get out now, or you will be next!*

Quickly Annabelle started wiggling out of the tiny space. As she slid her back along the underside of the wooden landing, pain tore through her as a protruding nail sliced deep into her flesh. Annabelle gasped, and her hand muffled the agonized mewing sounds that tried to escape. Her head dropped as tears rained onto the dry dirt below.

Holding her breath, Annabelle lowered herself off the piercing nail. The pain was unbearable, but it needed to be ignored. Peeking out from underneath the steps, her blurry eyes zeroed in on the dilapidated garage just yards away. Counting to three, she duck-walked quickly underneath the living room windows. Holding her thick, dark braid, the tiny girl cleared the corner of the house and then ran flat-out until she cut into the trees on the side of the new hideout.

The one-stall garage was wrapped with dingy white clapboards, and spring-green moss overlaid the old roof shingles, securing them together. Gnarly trees grew too close to the sides, slowly squeezing the walls inward. The pressure from the trees' mighty trunks forced the front of the roof to pitch downward, permanently blocking the two pullout car doors.

Fighting through the weeds alongside the battered building, Annabelle reached the dark backside of the garage and stooped, searching for the gap. Ducking under an enormous pine bough, she found the red squirrel hole toward the bottom, which Annabelle and Harley had been making larger over the years to accommodate their growing sizes.

Crawling army-style, she poked through the hole and slid onto the oil-soaked dirt floor, knowing the dark den was home to several small animals and many big spiders. Hating spiders, Annabelle unconsciously shuddered. Pulling a heavy cardboard box behind her, she closed off the sunlight from the entrance. Kneeling, she looked around, seeing black on black, waiting for her eyes to adjust. Annabelle whispered, "Harley, you in here?" No response.

Harley was her best friend and the hiding champion teacher, showing Annabelle where to hide and the tricks of how not to be found. They knew someday their dad would go nuts. Behind Wayne's back, they would snicker using their dad's nickname, "TBoom," short for timebomb. For the past two years, the duo had worked on their escape plan.

Someday had arrived, and Annabelle was alone, without her Harley. She sniffed, praying that he was all right.

Finally, able to see through the dusky garage, Annabelle was ready to use one of Harley's radical ideas to become invisible. She ran to the workbench, held onto the edge, shucked off her sister Gail's shoes along with her tee-shirt, shorts, and Winnie the Pooh panties. Standing on her tiptoes and reaching high across the bench, Annabelle dug into a red Folgers coffee can and carefully lifted out one plastic grocery bag. Opening it, she stuffed her clothes inside, then dropped the bag behind three old coal shovels in the corner.

Back at the workbench, Annabelle bent over, trying to cram her sweaty feet back into the black strap shoes. A wave of dizziness made Annabelle swoon. She shut her eyes and held onto the edge of the workbench. Fearing her dad would find her made the wait agonizing and wasted precious time. Straining her ears, she listened for sounds from outside but heard nothing.

Her head cleared, and opening her eyes, she spotted the old, mucky can of axle grease. Taking off the cover, she pulled it out and set it on the dirt floor. Harley had given

her the idea of using the thick, black, oily substance to camouflage herself.

Annabelle's thick, long hair had never been cut, and the
heavy braid always seemed to be in the way. Whipping her
head, the nuisance plait was tossed back. Squatting in front
of the can, she scooped out handfuls of the dead dinosaur–
smelling goop and began smearing it over her body.

Blackened top to bottom, Annabelle looked down,
checking for light spots, and dabbed more goop on them.
Dropping to the cold, dank soil, Annabelle rolled around,
squirming on all sides, hoping the oil-soaked dirt would
darken any skin she had missed.

The cut on Annabelle's back had been forgotten until
grit rolled into the open wound. Feeling pain radiate
through her, she hopped up, holding her hand to her back,
and marched in place, hoping to ease the throbbing that
crawled up and down her back. She whimpered as the pain
lingered.

"I'm a tough chick. I'm a tough chick," Annabelle muttered over and over as she picked up the grease can to
put it away but immediately dropped it when she heard a
shotgun blast. It was the fifth… and there was no scream
before it. Her hand still in the air, Annabelle turned numb
as her lower lip trembled. Her leg muscles released, and she
dropped to the ground.

There was no scream! *Maybe I can't hear this far from the
house? But what if Dad found Harley? No, that would not happen.
Harley is the champion hider!*

Annabelle sniffled, knowing Harley couldn't scream. He
was mute.

God, make me wrong. Make me wrong! Make Harley okay, please?

Annabelle looked at the closed garage doors trying to see
beyond them, wanting to know, but not. She knew Wayne
would now start hunting for his youngest. If he found

Annabelle, she would not only be next, but she would be the last one.

Out of time, Annabelle leaped up, leaving the grease can on the floor. Running to the side of the workbench, Annabelle ducked down onto the lower shelf slithering through the lineup of blackened boxes, tins, and buckets that would camouflage her soot-colored body. Settling down with her back to the outside wall, she felt a slight tug as her heavy braid fell, touching the ground. Afraid that spiders might climb into her hair Annabelle grabbed the messy braid, tucked it under her shoulder, and laid back down facing the interior.

Trying to close her eyes, as they fought against not seeing. Annabelle forced them to shut so tight, she worried they might pop.

Someone began pulling on the garage doors; becoming rigid, she listened. Wayne was yanking and swearing furiously. Then as quick as a snap, Wayne turned on the charm. He called out to her sweetly, using her dreaded nickname, "AnnieBelly! Come out! Something has happened." Terror-stricken, Annabelle knew that syrupy voice. It was his rattle before he struck, and the snake had found her hideout.

Wayne pushed and pulled, fighting as the pullout door flailed against his brute strength. Annabelle knew the door was blocked by the bent roofline and could not be opened. She felt safe for the time being.

That feeling didn't last long. Annabelle tensed when she heard wood cracking. The door was being forced open! Fearing her hideout was no longer safe, Annabelle debated if she had enough time to run back out of the squirrel hole. Maybe she could convince her dad not to hurt her. Her heart was thumping so hard, Annabelle was afraid Wayne might hear it.

Finally pushing the door open, Wayne dragged it across the overgrown tire ruts, snapping chunks off from the bottom of the door. Splinters, moss, and broken shingles fell off the bent roofline, raining down over his head. He took no notice as he continued forcing the door open wider and wider. Annabelle felt sunlight washing over her closed eyes as fear strained her muscles.

Wayne scanned the garage for his favorite kid—and the only witness to his killing. Sunlight exposed the center of the trash-filled shed, leaving the sides of the building dim. Picking up his shotgun from the doorjamb, he held it ready, pausing to listen. Getting rid of Annabelle was Wayne's only option, although, in his mind, she was the only one who loved him. He called out again, "AnnieBelly! I'm here to save you. Where are you, honey?"

Wayne walked closer to the workbench. Hearing him so close jolted every cell in Annabelle's body, urging her to scream. She swallowed it down. Her terror-ridden mind smothered all thoughts. Stumbling by, Wayne accidentally kicked the grease can.

"Get out here now!" Wayne raged with his scary voice. He stopped screaming, and listened. Annabelle quieted her breathing. Wayne heard a sound and twisted himself to face the open door. Those were sirens far off in the distance. Disregarding them, he got back to the job at hand. Hearing a noise near the back wall, he quickly raised his shotgun, shooting twice. Lurching forward, Wayne knelt down to poke at a raccoon, which had been blasted to smithereens. The shot opened a good-sized hole into the wall, emitting more light into the gloomy hideout.

Standing up quickly, he stumbled and shouted, "Damn it! Get out here, you little bitch!" Annabelle tightened further as Wayne drew closer. He couldn't see his grimy daughter lying on a shelf, below his sightline, only two feet away.

Running to the front corner of the garage, he toppled a huge metal shelf, kicking at cans and boxes as they landed, continuing to kick until he fell. Wayne had always been a clumsy drunk.

Lying and panting, he rolled onto all fours and lifted himself up with a grunt, and grabbed the gun. Staggering out of the garage, he slammed the drifting door against the wall. Whipping around, Wayne faced the dusty interior of the garage and swore.

Walking back toward the house through the overgrown yard, Wayne stepped up on the front steps and turned around, staring at the litter-strewn yard. His maternal grandfather, Wydell Winckowski, Sr., had unwittingly given the farm to his only grandson years ago when Wayne convinced him that they should become business partners. The property would become a successful truck farm, and they would be rich.

Wayne moved into the farmhouse and used the business loan to buy his souped-up personal truck, ATVs, clothes, and liquor for his dark parties. When Wayne made no attempt to create the business, make payments, or return the loan, a vicious dispute erupted between them. The argument ended when Wydell died of a heart attack while screaming foul words at his grandson. The farm became Wayne's by default.

Wayne initially made big plans for fixing up the farmhouse, but the needed property repairs just got bigger and bigger. The farm slowly began to crumble.

Furious that he was being forced to leave his home, Wayne pulled the front door out from under the overhang and slammed it back, again and again, breaking out the rest of the windowpanes. Breathing hard, he held onto the edge of the quivering door. Shoving it back it caught under the overhang, and he entered the house.

Annabelle listened from the garage, trying to track her dad's movements. She couldn't hear anything but then caught the far-off wail of sirens.

Hurry, hurry! Annabelle cried in silence, laying her head back down.

Hearing sounds from outside, like something really heavy was dropped onto metal, Annabelle realized Wayne was loading the bed of his pickup truck. Was he leaving?

Annabelle braced herself when she heard his thunderous footsteps approaching the garage, but they stumbled past. The driveway ran to the back of the property. More outbuildings were located there, but some had fallen into piles of rubble.

Towering over the other buildings was the two-story hay barn, which stood straight and tall, and was Annabelle's favorite. Faded to a rose-gray color, the big barn's knotholes were tinged with the original brilliant red stain. She thought the old barn might have been painted years ago with a Coca-Cola red. Stone walls made up the ground level, set up for cattle to settle in for the night. Above, the loft stored several bales of moldy hay.

The cash bag! Annabelle's brain snapped to the present as she understood why her dad had run to the back of the property. It was to get the money from one of his many hiding places. Wayne returned a few minutes later. He didn't seem to be in a hurry. The pipes on his Ford suddenly came to life and rapped twice before he tore off in his souped-up truck.

The roar faded, leaving Annabelle alone in the eerie silence. Shaking engulfed her, so violent, it caused the cans to bang around her. Struggling to breathe, Annabelle tried to pull a full breath, but her lungs felt shut off. Panicking, her heart raced on.

Suddenly Annabelle was able to breathe. Still shaking, she began whispering, "one, two, three." She stopped at two hundred and thirteen when she heard crying from outside the garage. Lifting her head she strained to hear, but dropped it back down. It was their cat, Kitty, yowling loud and long.

Should I go into the house and see if they're okay? Annabelle wondered. *Did Dad really leave, or is he trying to trick me into coming out? Should I find a better hiding spot? God, I don't know what to do.*

Annabelle's fears had become a reality. Heaving with emotion, tears skittered down her greasy black face.

chapter
two

Two Streams Police Department
Two Streams, Minnesota

*L*eading the morning briefing was Roger Jorgenson, Chief of Police for the city of Two Streams. During the chief's election, Roger had towered over the other candidates, and the running joke was the tallest man won. The truth was the victory was bagged by the smartest and most honest man, and his stern, dark good looks didn't do him any harm either.

Roger started speaking in his low, Russell Crowe–type voice as the room quieted. "Good morning. We have a couple of essential items to cover today. Just a reminder that next week starts our DARE program at the elementary school. Also, Hank, the school's crossing guard, is out sick today, so we'll need someone over there at 3:00 p.m. The principal is covering this morning's shift, and volunteers are to check with Liza. Speaking of Liza, today is her twentieth anniversary as our dispatcher. She's at her desk, so let's give her a hand!" The room whistled and clapped.

Liza shouted back to the group from her office, "Thank you all for the flowers, and whoever left me the apple fritter, I love you!"

Smiling, the chief began again. "Next, we have a lost blind dog, Wilbur. It's Mattie Karnik's, and neighbors looked all over town last night, but no luck. So, keep your eyes peeled. Mattie has offered a reward that whoever finds Wilbur will get free breakfasts at her Goulash Cafe for a month."

The deputies shouted their approval. Deputy Tommy Johnson, one of the new guys, stood and said, "Those free meals are mine!"

The group booed him down. He quickly countered with a huge smile and said, "Hey, I'm starving here!" He threw his arms wide, exposing a tight khaki shirt stretched over his drum-sized chest. The young triathlete had gained his strength through the physical workout that came with growing up on a farm. He was much stronger than any gym rat, but his build contradicted his Norwegian cuteness and flaxen hair.

The room filled with groans. Donut pieces flew straight at the smart-alecky deputy. His talent was catching mid-air dunkers, and he did not disappoint. Sitting down, his cheeks distended, he chewed slowly, as his blue eyes twinkled.

Chief Roger was wrapping up the week's instructions when Liza rushed into the room with a printout, which she handed to the chief, and whispered urgently to him. Roger's emotions showed with the reddening tips of his ears. The officers knew their boss, and the situation was serious.

Liza finished and ran from the room as Roger said to her back, "You know what to do."

The chief shouted to the room of now-standing deputies, "There have been several shots fired inside a house at the Winckowski's' farm. Someone driving by called it in." Dropping his eyes to the sheet of paper, he read, "49 Calico Fields Road, in Blanchard. Tommy, grab the extra guns, ammo, and flak jackets. I don't know what we're going to find, but let's be ready."

The officers moved before the period had landed from the chief's directive. "Hilde, with me!" he shouted over the din to Hilda Crosby, his second in command as chief deputy of police.

Deputy Paul Nelson shouted out to the group, "That's the old Calico Fields Farm."

Hilde rerouted herself out the door to the chief's car, climbing into the passenger seat and buckled herself in. The driver's door flew open as Roger took off his hat, threw himself in, turned on the lights and siren while putting on his seat belt. The patrol car lurched forward so quickly that Hilde hadn't noticed Roger had turned the car on. The chief's powerful V8 roared out in front of a line of his deputies, heading west of town.

Roger glanced at Hilde and said, "Tell me everything you know about the Winckowskis. We've got about forty-five minutes to that farm." Crosby had been on the small side as a new deputy, but she had added muscle over the years, defining her strength. Hilde's Danish-blonde hair was always twisted under her hat. She was ever the professional, but her blue eyes relayed her true feelings. Roger knew Hilde was his best asset on the force, quick and intuitive with her assessments.

He was ever so grateful Hilde was alive. Years ago, while on night patrol, they almost lost her after she was severely beaten and raped by a stranger. The daily reminder was evident, a deep half-moon scar curled around the outside of her left eye. The case had gone cold, and thankfully, Hilde's memories of that night were cloudy.

The chief deputy replied to Roger's question, "Wayne Winckowski, the dad—and believe me, I'm using that term very loosely—is and will always be a slimeball. The Winckowski farm has been in the family for a long time, but after lawsuits and death, it finally landed in Wayne's hands. He runs his own vending machine business and, from what I hear, pretty much ignores the farm.

"Seeing his dumpy place, you would think no money ever came into that household. Wayne is a big-shot drinker, and he provides very little to his family. Hey, didn't you pick him up on a DUI just a couple of years back?"

Roger replied, "Yeah. He's a big guy. He was drunk off his butt, and it took three of us to get that dirty fighter into a cell. Stan Pickens lost a molar from a punch that Wayne threw. That drunk is one nasty son of a bitch."

Having heard those rumors, Hilde was not surprised. Continuing, she said, "Last month, I had a chat with Doris Dickens because she was concerned about the welfare of the children. Doris and Jim, her husband, have the farm right behind Wayne's place. The Winckowski kids would periodically walk through the fields to their farmhouse and beg for food.

"Doris emphasized that she did not mind feeding the kids, enjoying them immensely, but her main concern was that they always had some type of injury, and she was fairly certain that Wayne was the abuser."

Roger cut in, "She didn't think it was the mother?"

Hilde paused before speaking. "No, I'm pretty sure she doesn't hurt them. I met with Letty right after I talked with Doris, and she doesn't have the strength to beat her kids, literally. She is just a tiny, frail woman, but looks ten years older."

"So, what does Wayne do with all of his money? Having his own vending machine business is a cash cow." The chief quickly looked over at Hilde, who was chewing on the cap of her Bic pen, thinking.

"I wondered that, too, so I called Mary at Blanchard State Bank. She told me that Wayne would bring in tons of coins, exchanging them for bills. He would stack them into a canvas bag right in front of her. Only a hundred dollars was deposited into the joint account with Letty. Mary told me Wayne never left the bank without winking at her while licking his lips. It gave her the creeps."

Roger took that in and said, "You went over to see Winckowski?"

"Yup. Wayne's place had broken furniture all over the yard, and the house had cracked windows and a burnt-out sunroom. There are lots of outbuildings too. It's an okay-sized farm, maybe fifty acres, but he doesn't do anything with it other than pile junk on it.

"Anyway, I drove into their yard and parked, leaving my window open. Locking myself out of my own squad car has already been done, so I won't let that happen again. Check!" Hilde drew an invisible checkmark in the air.

Roger nodded in agreement.

Hilde continued, "There was a little red car in the yard, alongside a rusted beige Ford pickup. I checked the truck's registration, and it was Wayne's. It had the biggest set of dual exhaust straight pipes I have ever seen. Those things are expensive.

Anyway, Letty must have seen me drive in and opened the front door for me with a small smile that showed a couple of teeth missing. I met Letty long ago, and she used to be pretty. But the day I stopped by, Letty looked almost unrecognizable. Deep, dark circles around her eyes and her light brown hair hung in clumps. And thin, oh my gosh, Letty was so thin. I can't imagine she weighs over a hundred pounds, and from what Mary said, Letty might be twenty-nine, maybe thirty years old at the most.

"Walking in, I realized there was nowhere to sit. There was an oversized recliner in the living room, but a cat had that one. The room was filled with large cardboard appliance boxes with dirty pillows and blankets stuffed inside. The couch was missing cushions and listed to one side, so I decided my best bet was to stand.

"In the kitchen, I spotted a huge, overflowing garbage can filled with liter-sized booze bottles. I don't think Wayne stopped drinking," she said grimly.

"Letty moved back around to her ironing board and ironed some pretty nice men's shirts." Hilde took a breath and looked out her window as the spring green pastoral view flew by.

Roger's fast V8 was still leading the way, but he was frustrated that it would take them so long to reach the farm. Blanchard's little town was huge in landmass, but the population was too small to have their own police force. The Two Streams Police Department covered not only Blanchard but several other outlying towns.

Continuing, Hilde said, "I tried engaging Letty in conversation, but she stammered and paused before answering the most basic of questions. It's as if she was terrified of giving a wrong answer. I asked her how she was, and she just shrugged."

"I then asked to see Wayne, and Letty said he was in the barn on the back of the property. I thanked her and let myself out.

"The two-story barn was way behind the house. Once I reached it; I let myself in. Wayne's at the work bench, and he jerked when he saw me, and his eyes almost popped out of his head. I couldn't see what he was doing, but he just about turned himself inside out, hiding whatever it was. I assumed he was counting money.

"Anyway, when he turned back to me, Wayne had this big nervous smile on his face. I explained I was out making courtesy calls, letting people know I was around in case they ever needed my services."

Hilde raised her hand, flipped it, and said, "Right before my eyes, his whole persona changed into this charming prince of a guy. He walked toward me, shook my hand with both of his, and told me what a great idea it was for me to get to know the community."

Hilde paused; she would not disclose what had happened next. When Wayne had grabbed her hand to shake it, she felt a flutter of fear. Her eyesight went blank for a split second but that passed when Hilde jerked her hand out from Wayne's grasp, wiped it on her pant leg, and stepped back. With a smirk, Wayne lowered his head but continued to leer at her. A sweet smell of cologne surrounded him and crimped her long-buried memories. Then normalcy returned.

Clearing her throat, Hilde continued her story to the chief. "Then Wayne hijacked the conversation, talking about his wonderful family, and spoke lovingly of his wife. He bragged about his vending machine business, and that traveling on the road was so exhausting, blah, blah, blah."

Hilde turned to Roger, lowering her voice, rotated both pointer fingers, and snidely said, "My eyeballs rolled up into my head and spun around several times until they finally dropped back down into their sockets." The chief chuckled.

Hilde cleared her throat again and said, "As you may have guessed, I was not impressed with Wayne, even though he is Satan handsome. He was clean, even for being in that filthy barn, and wore a crisp white long-sleeved shirt.

"Just then, a teenage boy entered the barn, and within a nanosecond, I could feel Wayne's friendly demeanor turn into something dark and seething. The boy quickly looked at his dad, then looked to me and said, 'I hate to bother you,

Chief Deputy, but our cat just jumped into your car. I didn't want to go in after Kitty without your permission."

"The boy was Wayne's son, Mattson, and the boy said he was thirteen—"

The chief glanced over to her, interrupting her with a question. "Didn't you just say that Letty was twenty-nine or thirty?"

The chief deputy looked like she had just smelled poop and said, "Ewww, icky. So, let's see, Letty might have been fifteen when Wayne knocked her up, and he was around thirty-two?"

Under his breath, Roger said, "Predator."

Hilde nodded. "Anyway, back to the barn. Wayne once again changed his persona into 'Father of the Year' and went over to Mattson, raising his hand, guessing he was about to give him a pat on the head, but Mattson ducked. I assumed this was a natural instinct for Mattson, dodging his father's huge hands.

"I had had enough. I thanked Wayne and walked out with Mattson, hoping the cat hadn't peed in my car.

"Mattson really charmed me. We talked a lot about Kitty, and I asked him how he knew I was a chief deputy. Mattson said that his dream was to go into law enforcement, and he had been reading up on the police department rankings. Mattson really impressed me for a kid of his age.

"We walked back to the squad, and sure enough, Kitty was lying on the driver's seat, sunning herself. I opened the door for him, and Mattson slowly, gently picked her up. It's a beautiful cat, fluffy and black, with a white ring around its nose." Smiling, Hilde was using her hands to explain further. "Mattson stretched the cat across his shoulders and let the cat chew on his hair. They were so cute together. We talked a bit longer, and then I left."

"There was barely enough to file a report. I only saw Mattson. He was small, but so was Letty, and he didn't have any visible bruising on him. I should have waited to see the other kids to check them out." Hilde's mind wandered to what they might find at the farm.

Just as the chief was going to speak, Hilde spoke up once again. "This is what I think: Wayne is a mean drunk, but sober, he can be very charming."

The chief asked, "Do you think he would hurt his family?"

Hilde paused longer than usual, chewing on the end of her pen cap. Finally, in a low voice, she said, "Wayne gave me the willies. Thinking someone is truly evil is not like me. But…" She wagged her finger. "He made me nervous, but I don't know why. Actually, I kept my hand on the butt of my gun the entire time I was talking to him. It was an unconscious act. Walking to my car with Mattson, my arms swung freely. I didn't need my hand on the gun."

Hilde swallowed, realizing the implication of what she had just said.

She turned and looked at Roger.

He didn't need to see her face; he felt her fear. The chief stepped on the gas, flying dangerously over the gravel roads while they sat in silence.

chapter
three

Monday, June 4, 8:45 a.m.

Winckowski Farm, Blanchard, Minnesota

A breeze fluttered across the fifty acres of barren farmland that surrounded the Winckowski home. Roaring into the yard, Chief Roger Jorgenson hadn't noticed the rusted gray mailbox on the side of the driveway, the name "Winckowski" written across its side in a child's handwriting. He clipped the metal mailbox sending it spinning out of the way.

Several blaring squad cars followed into the yard. One by one, the officers cut their engines and sirens. The red and blue lights sliced a nerve across the silence of the farm. Their climactic arrival had gone unnoticed.

The chief looked toward the quiet house. The multiple colors of siding protected the home against the weather, but from a distance, the house had the look of a menacing toothless grin, widening as each of the shingles shook loose.

The aqua window trim had oxidized; slivers of paint pulled away from the wood, curling into ribbons before flaking off and falling to the ground. A loose coil of antenna wire hung free, occasionally rapping a warning against the remaining shards of glass in an upstairs window. The chief noticed the charred shell of a sunroom, probably struck by lightning. The useless addition desperately hung onto the front of the home while the melted lace curtains waved urgently from the airy windows.

No one would move until the chief signaled. He stood silently, studying the area. Tall prairie grasses covered the yard, and a broken tree swing hung limp. All Roger heard was the blood whooshing through his ears. Then he felt the tiny hairs prickle on the back of his neck.

Never taking his eyes off of the front door, he released his gun from his holster and nodded to the others to do the same. Guns were drawn, the *swish* from the stiff leather holsters echoed.

Swiping his neck, the chief started moving slowly toward the house. The farm was just as Hilde had described. He passed a rusted folding chair in the middle of the yard, a boy's bike with only one wheel, a dangerously rusted propane tank, and a dirty, overstuffed floral chair. A small red car with a flat tire was the only vehicle in the driveway. The trees were crawling with Woodbine, a noxious climbing vine. The innocent green tendrils were joyfully strangling the tree to death.

The house's front door yawned open, the glass from the broken windows littered the stoop, as the shards glistened in the full June sun. Approaching the front of the house, Roger selected one officer, Deputy Belinda Jackson, to stand guard at the front of the house. The chief signaled to two other rookies, Deputies Tommy Johnson and Howard Mason, to search the outbuildings and the surrounding area. Tapping his heart twice, he expressed his concern meaning "be careful." The rookies slowly made their way towards the back of the property.

Roger and Hilde stepped up onto the porch, followed by their senior team, Stan Pickens and Paul Nelson, with a recent transfer, Caroline Stephanek, bringing up the rear. The broken glass crunched under their feet, sounding like a crackling campfire. As Roger entered the house, he could see the living room was littered with overturned furniture, broken liquor bottles, and empty beer cans.

He shouted, "Police!"

Hilde, her gun ready, moved in tandem with Roger. Her head swiveled, as she followed him through the living room and finding three doorways, one with its yellow door closed. The team moved to the left, toward the colored door, and the chief signaled his men to fall back, away from the yellow door.

Again, "Police!" shouted the chief. Silence was returned.

Roger threw the door open as they all flattened themselves against the wall, hoping to avoid a barrage of bullets. None came.

The chief took a quick peek inside before stepping into the rose-pink bathroom, his two hands holding the gun leading the way. He stopped just past the open door. Looking down to the left, his solid body seemed to melt.

Blinking, he paused momentarily, regained his stance, and holstered his gun.

In the bathtub, still clutching the moldy-gray shower curtain, was a teenage boy covered in blood. A young pre-teen girl in a long dress was wedged behind him, her hand flat on his back. Her face was tucked behind the boy, and her long, light brown hair splayed over both of them. Squatting next to the tub, the chief lifted the boy's hand and checked his pulse. Then, leaning slightly forward, Roger gently lifted the little girl's wrist, but again found no life. From the wounds, it appeared a shotgun had been used to kill them. The children were small and would not have survived the blast even if the police had arrived earlier. At least, that's what Roger prayed was his correct assumption.

Walking out, Roger looked at Hilde and shook his head. She blinked, took a breath, and entered the bathroom, scrutinizing the room before turning her eyes to the tub. Her lips peeled inward. Her throat constricted and she coughed to release it.

Exiting, Hilde did not look up but shook her head and whispered a name to Roger in a croaky voice so low that she had to repeat it. "Mattson."

The chief saw her pinch her wrist. It was Hilde's way of reminding herself that her emotions would be dealt with later. Roger quickly pinched the itchy red tip of his left ear. Pointing to Deputy Stephanek to secure the bathroom, the group moved to the next door.

The door hung open, exposing a collapsed staircase that once led to the dormered second floor. A black cat with a white ring around its nose sat on top of the jackstraw pile of stairway rubble. The cat mewed softly, walking in circles.

Hilde stared dumbly at the cat and whispered, "Kitty." Roger did a double-take at Hilde, seeing her storm cloud–blue eyes fixed upon the animal. He softly nudged her. Hilde jerked as if awakening from a trance and blinked. Nodding, Hilde rolled her shoulders and pinched her wrist again.

They moved to the doorway of the kitchen. Upended bowls of soggy cereal had spilled milk over the tabletop and onto the floor, where it pooled with fresh blood, creating a repugnant concoction. One milky puddle dripped onto the bare arm of a woman lying underneath the table.

Hilde whispered, "Letty."

Roger had surmised it was the kids' mother. Letty's light brown hair was partially released from a pug on the nape of her neck. The apron she wore over her faded sleeveless shirt and shorts was pasted with children's stickers. Her feet were bare. She had gone through a lot recently, the chief noted, seeing the ripe bruising on her arms, neck, and face. One of her big toes was dark blue and crooked.

Partially hidden by her mother's body was a small girl lying on her back, with her hand still twisted inside the bow on the back of her mother's apron. The little girl wore a yellow and pink patterned dress. Her feet were also bare.

Again, the chief checked the victims' pulses, knowing what the results would be. Dead.

Silently the chief tapped Deputy Pickens to stand guard over the mother and daughter who had innocently begun their day by sitting down to breakfast.

The chief, Hilde, and remaining Deputy Nelson quietly made their way to the closed door in the kitchen. Repeating the routine of knocking, announcing their presence, and then quickly opening the door. Roger peeked around the doorway and assessed the room, guessing it was the parents' bedroom.

The small room was filthy, and its function was lost among the trash that had been dropped around it. One unwashed blanket lay bunched on the bare, stained mattress, with two dirty pillows completing the set. So many booze bottles were scattered across the floor that the cops couldn't avoid clinking them together as they walked through. The window blinds hung broken and bent, and dresser drawers stood open as if that was their original intent. Oddly enough, inside the closet hung several neatly pressed men's shirts and jeans. Some shirts hung partially off their hangers but held on by the shoulders, stiff with starch.

With guns drawn, the deputies checked the closet and under the bed but found no weapons and no suspect. An upended cardboard TV box stood next to the bed, looking like it might have been used as a nightstand. Lying on the floor next to it was a lamp. The yellowed shade had a burn mark, apparently from the glowing bulb that hadn't been turned off.

Deputy Paul Nelson stood closest to the box. Wordlessly, the chief signaled with this gun for the deputy to lift the box. Paul holstered his weapon, braced his feet, grabbed the sides of the box, and pulled straight up, lifting it high over his head, exposing a small boy.

The officers gasped at the sight. The blood-stained child was curled into a fetal position. Barefooted, he wore a thin white tee shirt and shorts that had patch pockets bulging with his treasures. He might have been about ten or eleven years old, Roger guessed. The chief knelt down, trying to avoid the sticky blood, and for the fifth time, he checked for a pulse, finding the soft skin cool to his warm touch. A fourth child was dead.

Apparently, the young boy tried to hide under the box, but the killer had found him. The group stood motionless, not understanding who could massacre children. Their faces pale, they cleared their throats and pinched their ears or wrists. Deputy Paul set the box aside, leaving the newest victim uncovered. Swaying ever so slightly, Paul stood with his hands folded, looking down at the child.

Hilde spoke under her breath, "I'll finish checking the rest of the house." She quickly left the room, unintentionally kicking glass bottles.

Paul softly called to the chief, "Roger, I'll stay here with the little guy." The chief's face unconsciously twitched, hearing the tender words. He looked over at Paul, gave him a slight nod, and Roger left the house.

Standing in the yard taking cleansing breaths of the fresh spring air, the chief clenched his fists, trying to calm his sizzling nerves. He watched a red Case tractor plow the fields behind the Winckowki farm. The monotony of the motion calmed his mind. Then the silent questions began: Did

Wayne Winckowski do this? Where is he? Who would be able to identify the unnamed victims? Is there anyone else that would want this family dead? Where's Wayne's truck?

Roger's thoughts were disrupted by running footsteps coming out of the house. Looking over his shoulder, he spotted one of the rookies, Howard, running into the yard just in time to puke. He and Hilde worried about him, not knowing if he could handle the multiple layers of police work. The new deputy was a big, fleshy kid who barely passed the police physical and was really nosey. Roger wondered if Howard had finished searching the outbuildings before allowing his piqued curiosity to see the murder scene.

In the last few years, Two Streams' Police department had lost two officers to retirement and one to poor health. Now the chief and Hilde were saddled with three newly hired pups, two men and one woman. This crime scene would stain their minds forever. Murders were far and few between around Two Streams.

Hilde joined the chief in looking over the fields and said, "I think Wayne Winckowski killed his family." Unsurprised, Roger glanced down at her. "I found a gun case in the back hall," she said, "and next to it were several shells that looked to be a match to the shotgun shell casings we found near the bodies. Also, Tommy and Howard reported that they could not find Wayne's Ford pickup anywhere on the farm. I'm assuming that was his getaway vehicle."

The chief turned back to watch the slow-moving tractor. "Did you put out the APB for him and set up roadblocks?"

"Yes, but in this vast county, the roadblocks won't even cover a tiny percent of the area."

Nodding, the chief knew exactly the ineffectiveness of that plan, but he needed to start tracking down Wayne Winckowski. "Call Liza and have her call every local and state police department that can lend us a hand. We're too small a department to try to catch this guy. He probably knows every back road around Blanchard better than the mailman."

chapter four

Monday, June 4, 11:00 a.m.
Winckowski Farm, Blanchard, Minnesota

Roger saw Deputy Tommy Johnson down in the ditch, checking for evidence when a woman walked out of the fields, making her way toward him. Tommy clambered out of the trench to meet her. She looked to be in her mid-fifties and wore jeans and a short-sleeved plaid camp shirt. The humidity had sprung a few stray white curls around her unlined, freckled face. While talking with Tommy, the woman stroked the white braid that hung over her shoulder continuously as if it was a string of worry beads.

Roger walked over, and Tommy introduced the woman as Doris Dickens as Tommy took a couple steps back, allowing the woman to speak with the chief. She stood with her back to the Winckowski house and nervously restated her name. "Hi, I'm Doris Dickens. Jim Dickens is my husband. We... we farm over there, just over that rise." She pointed over her shoulder to a white farmhouse above the fields, where Roger saw full clotheslines waving in the breeze. "I don't mean to interrupt you, but I was wondering, why are you here? Are the kids okay?"

Looking beyond the neighbor, Roger once again saw the moving tractor, but this time with a flock of birds behind it diving for seeds. He figured the driver was Jim Dickens. The chief asked her very quietly, "Doris, were you home this morning?"

Hilde joined Roger, taking her notebook from one of her many pants pockets. Nodding to the neighbor, Hilde was poised to take notes. Doris looked to them both, cleared her throat, and said, "I was gone for a while helping my neighbor, Bertha Camp. I washed her hair. I do that every now and again; she's ninety-two. I go over once or twice a week before seven o'clock and normally stay to have coffee, but this morning it was such a nice day I wanted to get back so I could hang out the wash. I got home around eight."

"I'll need the address of Bertha Camp. Also, where was your husband this morning?"

Nodding toward the fields, Doris said, "Jim has been plowing the fields since before seven. Bertha's house is just a mile north of here, 26 Finger Lake Trail."

Hilde took the address down while the chief looked at the neighbor, trying to gauge how much he should tell her. Roger decided a distraction was best, avoiding details and asking questions only.

"Do you know how many people live in the Winckowski home?"

Doris got goosebumps with that question. Rubbing her arms, she counted using her fingers, not trusting her troubled mind.

"Yes, seven. The parents and five children."

Roger's neck prickled. One child was missing. His instincts were to get away from Doris and start searching the property for the missing kid.

Doris surprised them when she loudly said, "I'm going to be completely up-front with you. Wayne Winckowski is a mean bastard. He tortured his family by not providing them with very basic needs, such as food and clothing. Letty didn't even have a decent car!"

Pointing to the field, she continued, "Those sweet kids walk through those fields, politely knock on our door, and ask if we could spare any extra food. How embarrassing for those children to have to do that!"

Fury had made Doris's face cherry red, and the color-splashed down her neck. "They are welcome in our home anytime. They each have their favorite cartoon glass for juice or milk. Love those kids.

"Our only child, Sarah, has moved out." Doris dropped her head as if that was a sore subject.

Doris continued prattling, fingering her braid. Looking up at Roger, she continued. "Actually, they were over just a couple of days ago, and we are so comfortable with them now. Occasionally, Jim would see them traipsing through the fields, and he'd turn off the tractor to join us for lunch."

Doris could avoid the chief's eyes but not the sensations she was getting from the officers. Something wasn't right. Doris's voice rose, and she smiled, telling a story about the kids.

"When they first started stopping by, they would go after the food like animals, until Mattson, the oldest, would knock *once* on the kitchen table. The kids would stop, look to Mattson, and put their hands in their laps. Letty does a good job raising those kids, other than keeping that monster of a husband.

"When the kids finish eating and are ready to walk back, I give them as much food as they can carry. It is mostly fresh vegetables, a watermelon or muskmelon, sweets, and books." She waved her hand as if it was nothing,

Her voice broke. "Watching them stumble over the fields makes me feel so dang helpless. I know Wayne is mean to those sweet kids. But I don't know…" A small *click* noise came out of her throat. "What else can I do?"

Turning to Hilde, Doris said, "Thanks, Hilde, for coming over that day. I tend to over-worry and then overthink my over-worrying." She sputtered a nervous laugh.

"Anytime, Doris."

Doris's nervousness was apparent, and she continued babbling. "I feel bad for Letty. She is really in a bad spot. Being so young and then having all those kids five years in a row, well, the last time I visited, I thought she looked strung out." Doris shook her head and started again, "Oh, dear, I shouldn't have used that term because I can't imagine that she uses drugs. She normally just looks horrible."

Doris's hands flew over her face, embarrassed. Quickly dropping them, she continued, "Oh, gosh, I am not speaking very well of Letty. I'm sorry. What I'm trying to say is that Letty seems to have a weakness over her whole body. She always looks sick and has a perpetual look of despair, or maybe it's fear. I don't know. But whenever I stop by, she is a gracious hostess and makes coffee for us. We'll sit at the kitchen table as I prattle on, trying to cover the silence. Periodically I'll catch her smiling when I compliment her on how well she is raising her children."

She finally paused. "Is everyone okay? The family, I mean?" Doris asked, not looking at the chief, fearful of seeing the truth in his eyes.

"Is your husband driving the red tractor over there?" Roger asked, tipping his head toward their land.

"Yes, he's planting peas, but he's been at it for a few hours now."

"Excuse me for just a moment, please." Roger turned as Hilde sidestepped, taking Roger's place next to Doris. The two women talked about the weather.

The chief took a few steps over to Officer Tommy. Placing a hand on Tommy's shoulder, Roger pointed to the red tractor in the field and quietly said, "I want you to run through those fields to get Jim Dickens. He's driving the tractor, and I want you to bring him back here immediately. His wife is going to need him. Okay?" Tommy nodded and sprinted off into the fields, stumbling on the overturned clumps of fertile soil.

The chief walked back to Doris and took her elbow, guiding her to a picnic table under a huge maple tree. Doris sat with her back to the house, wiggling as she tried to release the goosebumps that crawled over her.

chapter five

Monday, June 4, 11:30 a.m.

Winckowski Farm, Blanchard, Minnesota

Hilde turned her attention to a gold Cadillac driving into the yard. She knew it was Muriel Friechs, a reporter from the *Blanchard News* who had the most repellent personality she had ever encountered. The reporter was also the mayor's wife, and their characters complemented each other in the worst way.

She knew that once again, Muriel had received a tip from someone inside their police department. When things simmered down, Hilde's first order of business would be to find out who was leaking information to the news media and take them down a stripe or two. The chief deputy signaled to Deputy Stan Pickens, and together they walked over to the Caddy. The driver's-side door was just opening when Hilde slammed it shut. Stooping low, Hilde looked through the open window.

The liquid foundation on Muriel's face was two shades darker than her naturally pale face, and the application ended at her jawline, highlighting the white swinging turkey neck. Her wrinkles broke through the dried foundation and cracked every time she spoke. The old woman's rheumy eyes were outlined in black eyeliner and circles of bubble gum pink accentuating Muriel's high cheekbones, adding to her creepiness. Several applications of hairspray kept the woman's dark gray beehive perfectly round.

Muriel said, her voice raspy, with an empty smile, "Why, Hilde, I didn't expect to see you here. I thought you'd be downtown trying to track down Wilbur."

Hilde explained with her own empty smile, "No, no, I had more important things to attend to. I am Chief Jorgenson's chief deputy, remember?"

"Well, I had always hoped that a man would have been chosen to assist our nice chief. But I'm sure Roger likes to dally with you on occasion." Hilde crossed her arms.

"I would suggest you watch what you say because the chief has quite a temper." Hilde's face and neck had gone crimson.

Muriel said as she shook her middle finger at Hilde, "Oh, now look at you! You're blushing—what a girlie-girl thing to do. You're in the wrong business, missy, and I've told you this before. Now tell me, what is going on here?"

"No comment. You must leave the premises, Ms. Friechs."

"Oh, my gosh! Is that the coroner wearing a hazmat suit?" Muriel whipped out her phone, stretched her arms through the open window, and started taking pictures. Hilde snapped Muriel's phone from her blue-veined hands and stepped back.

The old reporter tried to open her door, but Stan had stepped in, shutting it each time Muriel opened it. Hilde studied Muriel's phone and quickly deleted the pictures that had just been taken. She quietly said, "No more picture taking. I will keep this safely at the office until later." She passed the phone to Stan, who pocketed it.

Muriel was still grabbing for her phone but clearly had the disadvantage of being shut in the car, her arms flailing out the window. Stan had quietly locked her car door.

Muriel screeched, "Let me out of my car! How dare you!" Pointing a long yellow fingernail at Stan, she said, "I will have you off this force with a snap of my finger. I'll tell my husband that you stole my phone! That is against the law!"

Hilde said calmly but firmly, "Ms. Friechs, you must leave now."

Muriel slung more insults. "You sons of bitches." Looking Stan and Hilde straight in the eyes, she slammed her car in reverse. Flying backward, she almost clipped the new deputy, Belinda Jackson, who was directing traffic on the road. Putting the car in drive, Muriel then tore off, driving like a maniac and leaving a trail of dust devils.

Hilde shouted at Belinda, "You okay?"

Dusting off her pants, Deputy Belinda gave a thumbs up to Hilde.

Stan said drily to Hilde, "Muriel is homely enough, but adding that disgusting personality is a real insult to mankind."

Nodding with a slight smirk, Hilde said, "Thanks, Stan, for the help."

"Yes, ma'am." He strolled down into the ditch to pick up the search for evidence while Tommy was gone.

chapter
six

Monday, June 4, 11:45 a.m.

Winckowski Farm, Blanchard, Minnesota

*H*ilde was walking back to join Roger and Doris while monitoring the team around the farm when she saw Belinda talking to someone who had pulled up in an old gray Cutlass. Belinda seemed exasperated and then accepted a paper bag. The driver drove off as Belinda looked at the bag, shook her head, and then ran toward Howard, who was coming back from searching behind the white single car garage. Belinda walked up to Deputy Howard and shoved the bag at him and put her hands on her hips, and seemed to be giving him a tongue lashing. Belinda turned and huffed away while Howard peeked inside the large paper sack and smiled.

Looking around, he saw Hilde and waved. Howard then walked to a stump, sat down, and proceeded to unwrap and eat his lunch. Hilde ran ahead and met Belinda on her way back to the road. "What was that all about, Belinda?"

The new officer pulled a full breath after running and said, "Apparently, Howard called his mother to come here to the crime scene and bring him his lunch."

Hilde's eyes went wide. "Oh. Well, that's weird. Huh, okay, thanks." They parted, and Hilde walked back to the picnic table where Doris and Roger were sitting.

"Doris, did you see Wayne outside or see him leave this morning?" Hilde asked.

"Yes, when I was outside pinning up the wet clothes, he was loading the bed of the truck, making several trips in and out of the house. Finally, he got in, and just like every time he gets into that horrid thing, he rapped those pipes and tore out of the driveway. Horrible man."

Hilde asked, "What time was that?"

"Um, I heard him leave about maybe eight-fifteen."

Turning her head to a sound, Doris leaped up, trying to stand, but was trapped between the bench and tabletop. Doris's eyes went wild as she pointed to the house. Hilde quickly looked and saw the coroner leaving the Winckowski house.

Doris turned back to the officers. Leaning heavily on her palms, she asked in a shaky voice, "Wha… what is he doing here? Where are the kids? And Letty?" Doris's chin wobbled, eyes wild as tears ran down her face, leaving spots on the cross-stitches of her plaid shirt. Her knees gave way, and she sat wearily back onto the bench. Staring at Roger and Hilde, she waited for an answer that she already knew. Doris held onto the edge of the table, her knuckles growing white.

Chief Jorgenson had to tell her the truth now. Just then, Tommy came running out of a field with the farmer right on his heels. They ran straight to the picnic table, both heaving for breath.

Reaching for her husband, Doris whispered, "Jim." He wrapped Doris's hand into his and sat down, pulling her into his chest, looking to the police for answers.

"What's going on?" He twisted and shot a look toward the house, then back at the chief.

The chief introduced himself to Jim and paused, allowing time to frame his words. Doris closed her eyes, fending off the words that surely would hurt her.

Roger began, "Letty and four of her children have been killed." The chief let the words pierce the couple, knowing the truth was as terrible as it could possibly be.

Doris's keening pitched to a level of utter loss. Leaning hard into Jim, she screamed into his chest, muffling her despair. Jim held Doris firmly, shaking his head, hoping what he had just heard was untrue.

Looking up, the farmer asked in a low, emotional voice, "Killed? You mean... you mean... someone actually killed them? On purpose?"

The chief nodded ever so slightly.

The look in Jim's eyes said he didn't seem to understand. "Who could do that?" Jim looked down, then his head popped back up. "Wait, you know there are five children, right?"

The chief answered, "We have one child missing. We're still searching throughout the property, and we're also looking for Wayne Winckowski."

Jim jerked upon hearing his neighbor's name.

Looking to Jim, the Chief said regretfully, "I'm sorry to have to ask you this, Jim, but I need you to come with me into the house and identify the family members. Maybe you can help us figure out which child is missing."

Jim's pupils expanded with the fear with what he was being asked to do. His shoulders pulled back, and he acquiesced with a slight nod. Kissing the top of his wife's head, he stood. The new deputy, Caroline, took Jim's place sitting next to Doris and rubbed her back. Doris sobbed, laying her head down onto her arms.

The chief and Hilde led the way into the house. Jim followed but hesitated at the front door. He cautiously tried to sidestep the shattered glass, but it was impossible.

Roger walked across the living room to the bathroom, walking in first, as Jim followed him in. The chief nodded toward the tub. Jim looked down, unprepared for the sight, and an anguished cry dropped out of his open mouth.

Jim almost could not bear to look, but slowly as his knees crackled, squatted down, and held onto the edge of the tub. Then ever so slightly, Jim leaned forward, touching Mattson's soft, light brown hair.

"Hey, big boy." Jim's gentle voice broke.

Looking up to the chief, Jim continued, "This is Mattson, thirteen, the kindest soul you'll ever meet." He stopped, then went on with a raspy voice, "He's covering Candy, twelve. She was unusually shy and very fearful of me; actually, I think Candy was afraid of all men. Mattson was her bodyguard." Jim looked back to Candy, knowing she had nothing to fear any longer.

Standing, Jim walked out of the bathroom. His insides curdled as he followed the chief to the kitchen.

Jim spotted Letty, lying unmoving under the table. Taking a breath, Jim said, "That's Letty." Something drew his attention, and he leaned to see behind the dead woman, only to jerk back, falling into the wall. He was unprepared for the sight of little Gail, her eyes open, looking straight at him. Letty's arm was still draped back, senselessly trying to protect her daughter.

A sob escaped Jim as he clasped a hand to his mouth. He opened his mouth to speak, but nothing came out. Clearing his throat, he tried again. "Gail, eleven. She was the hand holder of the family and..." Jim stood, staring down at Gail, forgetting what he was going to say.

The mild-mannered farmer lost his cool. Angrily, he said, "I'd run into Wayne every now and again at the Break it Open Bar. He'd be drunk, telling me or anyone that would listen that Letty was cheating on him. Wayne thought the four oldest kids weren't his because they had Letty's hair coloring! So, he felt no compunction to provide for them. What a stupid jerk! Stupid son of a bitch, every one of those kids has... *had* his eyes!"

Jim's fists clenched, and he said, "May I go?"

"Sorry, but we have one more," Roger said.

Jim nodded as he filled his lungs with air. His eyes darted around, searching for the next one, hoping to ease the shock of the discovery. He dragged his calloused hands over his face, then stopped the motion and said, more harshly than he meant, "Okay, where?"

Roger walked toward a door in the kitchen. Jim's face was stoic as he followed the chief into the parents' bedroom, stopping inside the doorway to study the dingy room. Among the mess in the room Jim spotted Harley curled in a fetal position on the ruined carpet. Not removing his eyes from the boy, Jim moved slowly, unaware of the trash beneath his feet. Slipping on a liquor bottle, Jim stumbled, catching himself on the bed with his right hand. He stood, quickly removing his tainted hand from the filthy bedclothes. Looking down, Jim eyed his calloused palm, searching for the invisible stains. He wiped it off on his jeans and continued the slow walk to the youngest Winckowski son.

Squatting down next to the little boy, Jim picked up the boy's pinky and started to say something to the dead child, but he couldn't. He cried.

Embarrassed in front of the chief, Jim pulled a red bandana from his back pocket and wiped his nose. Standing, Jim rubbed his face and walked back to the chief, his voice quaking as he tried to overcome the quiver. "That's Harley, ten. He's mute. Anything else?"

Averting Roger's eyes, Jim looked away, fearing fresh tears would fall again.

The chief said, "Like you said, one child is missing. My squad is still checking the outbuildings."

Jim snuck a look at the chief and offered, "Then... that would be Annabelle, nine. Wayne favored her." Jim walked straight through the house and out the front door, jumping over the front steps with Roger running after him.

Roger hustled alongside and said, "Jim, Jim, really, I'm sorry, really, but I need you to give me a description of Annabelle."

Jim stopped at the picnic table, sat down next to Doris, and wrapped his arms around his wife. Again, struggling for control, he added, "I pray that Annabelle's alive, but with all, she has gone through, what would that life be like for her without her family? Those kids had a special bond, and they were very close to Letty. Doris, can you please tell the chief what Annabelle looks like? You're better at that than I am."

Doris stiffened and looked at Jim for courage, shuddering at the implication that they might be identifying a body. Her face puffy and red, she spoke clearly and precisely. "Annabelle is almost skeletally thin but so beautiful. Her skin is a soft creamy color, and hazel eyes surrounded by a double layer of black lashes." Doris touched the corner of her eye and said, "Her lids sweep up at the outside. I would tell her that she could be a model one day." Doris took a moment. "Annabelle has very long dark brown hair, past her waist. It is thick and usually tangled. She has a little nose and freckles—"

Jim interrupted then. "Her face is always pale, but her nose has five freckles. I would always count them whenever she came over." His voice hitched. "It's a little game we played, counting her freckles." He pressed his hand to his mouth, trying to stifle a sob. Throwing his shoulders back, Jim cleared his throat and said, barely above a whisper, "Done?"

"Yes, thank you," the chief said. Jim and his wife sat rigid at the picnic table, not knowing what they should do next.

Roger signaled Tommy, then murmured that the deputy needed to drive Mr. and Mrs. Dickens back to their farm. Tommy nodded and took one of Doris's arms as Jim wrapped his arm around her back. Together, they helped her to the patrol car.

Roger kept his eyes on the car and saw the couple through the back window, clinging to one another. The chief stood with his hands on his hips, rolling his shoulders to ease the tension. His emotions collided: horror, anger, fury, sadness, and the greatest feeling of helplessness he had ever felt.

He pulled himself together when the fear hit a chord. A *child out there has either been kidnapped or worse.*

He called his people around him, jabbed his pointer finger in the air, and said, "Nine-year-old Annabelle Winckowski is still missing. We need to recheck all of those buildings; she might be hiding in one of them. We don't know if she is a victim or if her father has kidnapped her. Annabelle is small for her age, with long brown hair and hazel eyes. Be thorough and find her!"

chapter
seven

Monday, June 4, 3:00 p.m.

Winckowski Farm, Blanchard, Minnesota

*T*he voices outside the white garage startled Annabelle awake. Unmoving, straining to hear, she realized she was hearing radios and shouting commands, all good cop sounds. Feeling stiff, Annabelle slowly backed out from underneath the workbench and sucked air through her teeth as the pain slid up her back.

Standing on her tingling legs, her fragile bones felt like they needed oiling and would break if she moved too quickly. Yawning wide, Annabelle stretched carefully, holding onto the edge of the workbench. Now she would have to talk to the police, causing new fears and jittery nerves. Her stingy eyes welled, and her nose dripped. Wiping her face,

Annabelle took a couple of stuttering breaths, knowing she would have to leave the garage.

Wearing only axle grease, Annabelle felt cold. Releasing her tight grip on the workbench, she felt her heart pound against her chest wall. Yawning again, she shivered and dragged herself to the side of the open doorway, peeking out into the bright sunlight. Shading her eyes and letting them adjust, Annabelle saw a big policeman standing just outside the garage door. The cop had his back to her but was within touching distance. His arm flailed as he shouted orders to the group before him.

Taking a deep breath, Annabelle stepped forward, raising her cold, greasy hand and softly touched the policeman's fingers. Chief Jorgenson jerked back so quickly he collided with another deputy, who awkwardly caught him. The chief looked down at the shiny black little body with wild sticks of hair standing out from its head and put a palm to his heart. "Jesus H. Christ!" he swore.

Annabelle's toothy smile appeared. "I'm sorry to scare you. I live here. My name is Annabelle Winckowski."

The farm went quiet. Annabelle felt as if she was standing in a movie that had been paused. She leaned over to peek around the policeman and saw a group of people gawking at her. She stepped closer to the swearing policeman and looked up at him, hoping he'd know what to do. When he didn't say anything, Annabelle dropped her head to study the many pockets in his brown trousers.

The chief touched his mike on his shoulder and said, "Send Kathy Cleveland to the white garage, ASAP!"

Annabelle was suddenly timid with all those eyes upon her as she inched closer to her policeman, taking his hand. A flutter of pain moved within from some odd depth. Gently, Annabelle rubbed circles around her chest, smearing rings of blackness.

The chief squatted down and looked her straight in the eye. "I'm Roger, the Chief of Police. I'm glad to meet you, Annabelle. We've been looking for you. Are you okay?"

Shrinking, Annabelle was silent, which wasn't like her. She was the motormouth, the chatterbox, the one anxious to talk, but could only take the quiet in small doses—in her family, it always meant bad things were coming. So, she livened up the scary quiet with entertainment.

Annabelle swallowed, looked up at him, and quickly gave him the pat answer that she always gave to anyone with authority. Talking fast, she said, "Oh, I'm fine. I'll be in the fourth grade this September. They've put me into an advanced math class with all boys except for Amelia, my best friend, and being the only girls in the class is kinda weird. The boys pick on us a little, but it's not mean. I'm not a fast runner but, but I'm a good hider. My momma said... I...," Annabelle dropped her head, trying to swallow the lump of coal that had lodged in her throat.

The chief asked, "Annabelle, why are you all painted with grease?"

She had forgotten and flicked her eyes over to her raised, black arm. Annabelle watched as a soft, bosomy woman ran out of the house, and made her way through the crowd. The woman had hair the color of butterscotch, matching her untucked blouse, and plaid skirt. *That must be Kathy,* Annabelle thought.

Kathy stopped next to the chief and, like everyone else, stood and stared down at the greased naked girl who smelled of dead dinosaurs.

Feeling self-conscious, Annabelle tucked in closer to Roger, hoping no one could see her. His uniform pockets were really cool. She wanted to put her hands into all the different-sized pockets because some looked like they held treasures.

The chief tried again. "You must have been hiding really good. Where were you hiding?"

Looking to him, Annabelle explained, "I had to find a good spot to hide from Dad. He's a good finder. So, I greased myself to blend in with the cans and laid underneath the workbench." Annabelle pointed behind her into the garage. She looked up with pride and smiled broadly, which again touched a nerve, making her feel sick, and her smile fall.

A memory of hiding under the front steps slithered through her, making her shiver. Annabelle's face crumbled. "I think Dad shot my family."

Hearing her own words, the realization jerked her body as a guttural sound of sorrow followed. Annabelle's knees wobbled as cries stole the remaining energy from the trembling child.

Kathy stepped around Roger and gently lifted the collapsing child, cradling her firmly to her ample bosom, completely ignoring the child's nakedness. Walking with purpose toward the lone chair in the yard, Kathy cooed to the sole survivor.

Stepping carefully through the tall prairie grass to the neglected overstuffed chair, the social worker sat into the saggy seat, wrapping her arms tightly around the child. Annabelle clung to the stranger and sobbed out of control.

Deputy Paul, having been relieved from his post inside the house, rummaged in the trunk of his squad car and pulled out a plastic, zippered bag containing a homemade quilt his wife, Daneen, had made to be given away whenever it was needed.

The quilt, a vibrant red with black-and-white dancing penguins with scarves fluttering around their necks, hung from his arm as he marched toward Annabelle and tucked the colorful cotton across her sticky body, just like he did with his own grandkids.

Concern covered Kathy's face, but she met Paul's eyes and blinked a thank you. He tipped his hat and stayed close by.

Annabelle felt the heavy quilt fold around her, warming her chilled body. Kathy rocked her and softly sang "Rain, Rain Go Away."

The chief stood by Kathy's chair as she paused in her murmurs and quietly explained her instincts: something was wrong with Annabelle.

Kathy tightened her hold on Annabelle as Roger helped her rise from the deep-seated chair. Jogging ahead, Roger opened the back passenger door of Kathy's St. Louis County car as Kathy placed Annabelle inside and secured her seatbelt. Kathy scooted around the back to the driver's side.

Roger signaled to Deputy Paul, who ran back to his cruiser, ready to lead Kathy to the hospital in Two Streams.

Turning to her passenger, who was snuggled deep inside the oversized penguin quilt, Kathy said, "I'm driving you to the hospital for a check-up."

Annabelle's eyes grew round, but then Kathy reached back, touching the little girl, and said, "I'm staying with you."

Annabelle's head felt so heavy. She couldn't nod, so she tried to speak. The word was barely above a whisper: "K."

Kathy signaled to Paul, who had turned on all of his flashing turrets, and with full sirens blaring, he tore out of the yard with Kathy right on his bumper.

Annabelle shuddered with leftover hiccups, and turning, she caught a quick glimpse of her lifeless home.

She remembered the day Momma painted the door and window trim aqua on their ugly house. They had stood in awe of how pretty it was. Her momma didn't smile much, but she did that day.

Feeling sick, Annabelle tried to ignore it by thinking of memories of the house. A long time ago, the kids used to sleep upstairs in the sunny bedroom until the stairs collapsed into a heap. Nobody could get upstairs anymore, except Kitty. The only sleeping solution was to use cardboard appliance boxes in the living room. It made them all sad at the time because they lost their beds, clothing, books, and all of their toys up there. It was just too painful to remember, so they just forgot about their stuff.

Harley, where are you? I want you with me. I'm afraid, Harley.

She remembered that day in the barn when she and Harley were exploring and saw him walk backward right into a giant spiderweb. Not too long after, his neck started swelling and got really red. Then he fell down and closed his eyes. Annabelle tugged and pulled her big brother until she got him in the wagon. Screaming for her momma, Annabelle ran as fast as she could, pulling him to the house. Letty picked him up and laid him on the kitchen table and put ice on his neck.

Harley went to sleep for three days. When he finally woke up, he wasn't able to talk and never did.

Annabelle woke when Kathy screeched to a halt in front of the Dignity Christian Hospital's emergency room. The car door flew open, and hands quickly reached for Annabelle, carefully placing her on a gurney. Her head rolled, and her arms fell out of the quilt.

I feel numb.

The nurses and interns talked over each other. "Shock—" "Covered in grease?" "She's shivering—more blankets," "She needs oxygen—" "Doctor! Doctor!" "Move! Move! Faster!" "Can you hear—"

chapter eight

Monday, June 4, 9:30 a.m.

Somewhere south of Blanchard, Minnesota
Two Streams, Minnesota

*T*he plans Wayne had made for his life had been shot to hell. Well, actually, Letty screwed up his plans, starting a fight over money again. His nagging wife always needed money for her bastard kids and never considered how hard he worked for it. His original plan was simple: he would leave Letty and her kids, take Annabelle, his favorite, and they would go wherever he wanted. Annabelle could take care of the house until Wayne found a woman who could really take care of him.

Wayne was still too drunk to try and figure out what he should or shouldn't have done back there. Unfortunately, his temper had erupted, and he'd jumped the gun. Chuckling,

Wayne enjoyed his black humor, but leaving an eyewitness alive was stupid, and killing Annabelle would undoubtedly have made him feel less uneasy. Unconsciously, he scratched his forearm. Looking down at the spot, nausea circled his stomach as his skin crawled with dried flecks of blood.

Wayne hit a pothole that almost bounced him out of his seat. He damned himself for having to take his old Ford beast, which rode like a tractor. The straight pipes grated on his nerves, but he hadn't wanted to change the flat tire on Letty's car, not wanting her to have a running vehicle. That decision bit him in the ass. The little red car would certainly have been more comfortable to drive.

Having lived all of his life in and around Blanchard was a gift. His knowledge of the back roads helped to avoid the cops. Although he didn't know exactly where he was going, Wayne wanted to head south, and so far, so good. He was tired, but there was no time for sleeping.

Wayne shot past an overgrown road where a "Public Water Access" sign caught his eye. That was Beatty Lake, where he had gone fishing many times with his buddies from Break it Open Bar. Reversing and swinging hard onto the deep-rutted road, Wayne drove down to the little-known lake.

Seeing the sparkling water, Wayne let his foot off the gas, quietly rolling into the boat launch area. It was empty of cars and boat trailers. Parking on the grass, Wayne almost bumped the picnic table. He opened his door. Stepping out of the back-breaking truck Wayne's legs gave out, but catching himself, he slowly made his way. Shaking his head, Wayne leaned over the sides of the truck and searched the bed. Reaching down, he peeled back the soggy cardboard of a beer case and pulled out a warm can of cheap beer.

The can spewed foam when he popped it open, but Wayne quickly finished it and belched. The rush felt good. Scanning the diamond-studded lake, he crushed the can and dropped it back into the heaping bed, filled with rusted tools, empty whiskey bottles, and more discarded rubble.

The day was perfect for fishing, and Wayne was surprised there weren't any boaters but pleased that he was alone. Stepping down to the shore, Wayne removed his jeans and his blood-speckled white shirt and threw them into a pile. Shucking off his black cowboy boots, Wayne peeled off his socks. Gingerly walking into the water on the sharp rocks, he surface dove. Rolling over with a backstroke, he scrubbed the blood from his arms. The cold water was barely tolerable, but then again, it was only June in Minnesota.

As Wayne tiptoed back to shore, water dripped down his firm, hard chest before trickling down his legs. Rooting around in the back of his truck, Wayne finally found a partial bottle of store-brand dish soap and a crusty, dried-out bath towel. He threw the stiff gray towel onto the picnic table where it stood upright like a pyramid.

Wayne walked back into the water until he was chest deep and began to pour the soap onto his head and arms. He scrubbed until it hurt, wanting all of that bloody gore washed off thoroughly. Dunking several times, he rinsed the soap from his thick, dark hair. Wayne did not leave the water until the stained pink suds that had circled him disappeared.

Back on shore, Wayne pulled his discarded clothing into the water and dribbled them with dish soap. Squatting naked, he scrubbed his bloody garments on the rocks, Wayne felt an overwhelming sense of empowerment. He raised his face to the brilliant sun, puffed out his chest, and felt the sheer, raw savagery of power. Standing, he shivered. Holding his water-soaked clothes he paused while a new plan developed.

Rushing to the picnic table, Wayne snatched the stiff towel off the table and threw it into the back of the truck along with the wet clothes. He pulled out the bags he had packed from the farmhouse and set them on the grass next to the Ford from the cab. He placed his shotgun and his .45 Colt handgun on the ground and searched through a couple of bags for dry clothes and shaving gear. Finding his stuff, Wayne slipped on his everyday clean attire: white shirt, black pants, and a stolen silver rodeo buckle.

Wayne opened a loaf of white bread from the truck's floor, pulled out two pieces of soft bread, stuffed them into his mouth, and grabbed another beer, and drained it while walking to the picnic table. Sitting down, he turned once again to the sun, as ideas began to appear, not in the organized order that he wished, but they were coming nonetheless.

Wayne stood up and walked over to the pile of his trappings, pulling out his battery charged shaver. He floated a black bag to the ground next to the driver's side mirror and stepped into the center after removing his shirt and pants. It was difficult to see his face in the small mirror, but he began shaving, needing to find rough patches by touch. The dark whiskers fell into the bag beneath him. He took a deep breath and looked more closely into the mirror, admiring his luxurious head of thick hair, dark brown with hints of red, hanging just above his shoulders. Wayne touched it fondly. He then slowly moved the shaver back and forth over his head and watched as the clumps fell in a circle around his feet.

Wayne Winckowski was now a skinhead with a dark shadow covering his big bald head. He had considered shaving his bushy black eyebrows, but he had a large mole just under the right brow—no need to draw any more attention to his face than necessary. Looking nothing like the murderer who just hours ago killed his family, he smiled at his new reflection, pleased.

Brushing the hair from his body onto the bag beneath him, he carefully stepped out of its center and lifted up the bag's sides throwing it into the back end of the truck. He searched for his cologne, Patchouli, throughout his gear. Finding it, Wayne splashed a significant amount on his face. The pleasant smell distracted his mind from losing his hair, and he dressed.

Wayne walked a couple of feet and tripped, falling onto the cement boat ramp. Sitting with his head in his hands, he felt the pounding headache along with dizziness and the shakes from the booze still saturating his system. Feeling better than earlier but not even close to normal. One thought came to mind; he had to get rid of that damn truck.

Begrudgingly, Wayne got up to find his boots, which were sitting in the water. He slipped his feet in as his toes recoiled, rejecting the wet soles. Walking over to the pile of his things, he picked up his Colt, sucked in his stomach, and pushed the gun down behind his belt.

Tucking his shotgun under his arm, he grabbed the other bags that held his clothing and lifted his cash bag. Stepping deep into the woods so as not to be seen from the lake or launch, Wayne tucked everything under a low-hanging pine bough on a dry bed of needles.

Cautiously checking the launch before walking back to his truck, he started to leave his position behind a big pine tree when he heard a car driving in. Ducking back and squatting in the shadows, Wayne observed a nineties-vintage black Dodge minivan backing down the boat ramp, lowering a boat trailer into Beatty Lake. An old, gray-haired man was at the wheel.

The small Alumacraft was outfitted with a fifteen-horse power kicker. Fishing rods tipped and turned in the boat as its trailer bounced into the lake. Stopping the car, the guy got out and walked around to the partially submerged trailer. His wispy gray hair stuck out above his ears under a very well-worn Army-green hat. Releasing the strap from the front of the boat, he grabbed the attached line and pushed the fishing boat off the trailer to bob in the lake. Holding the rope taut, he stepped over the tongue of the trailer, pulling the fishing boat to the nearest steel cleat on the deck. Using a simple naval knot, he secured the boat.

Wayne was surprised by how agile the old guy moved as he watched him jump off the dock to the sand. Walking confidently toward his car, the white-haired man was now ready to pull the empty trailer out and park.

As the driver was about to open the door, Wayne jumped him from behind, spun him around, and slammed the soft face with several hammer-like punches. The sound of cracking bones and one small cry ruptured the serenity of the lake. The attack dropped the man to the cement, his head bouncing hard. Unconscious, the victim laid spread-eagle, his eyes closed, a trickle of blood rolling down the ramp.

Pleased with his efficiency, Wayne smiled as he quickly dragged the lifeless body into the woods, just to the side of the porta-potty. Wayne figured he was either dead or close-to. He had done the old man a favor, rushed him a bit to the eventual ending of his life. Wayne chuckled at his illogical logic.

Searching the man's clothing, Wayne found a wallet. Carl Larson was the name on his Minnesota driver's license, and he too lived in Blanchard, and not far away. Removing the small amount of cash from Carl's pocket plus the van keys, Wayne dropped the items into his own pocket.

The exertion had furthered the intensity of his headache. Wayne decided to forego burying the man. Finding a couple of large pine boughs, he threw over the man and a few handfuls of leaves. Exhausted, Wayne leaned against a tree and heaved for air. Finally, he stood, stretched his back, and walked out of the woods.

Carl's ragged Korean War Veteran Army hat lay next to the minivan. Wayne slipped the soft cloth onto his smooth pate. It felt weird touching his bare scalp, but it did add to his disguise. He fingered several of the decorative fishing and Army pins fastened throughout the well-worn cotton cap.

Wayne untied Carl's boat from the dock, stepped into the lake with his soggy boots, and dragged the small boat back onto the trailer. Standing on the trailer tongue, Wayne pulled out the winch strap, hooking it into the eyebolt on the bow. He winched the light boat up until it felt snug, then attached the safety chain to the hitch.

Getting into the minivan, Wayne adjusted the seat to fit his long legs and tall torso. He started the engine, pulled the boat trailer forward and out of the lake, and parked it off to the side near the porta-potty. Anyone snooping around would think the driver was taking a leak.

He shut off the engine, pocketed the key, and then hopped into his own truck, started it up, and tapped the accelerator twice. Wayne drove out of the boat launch, heading down the shady lane.

chapter
nine

Monday, June 4, 7:00 p.m.

Two Streams Police Department
Two Streams, Minnesota

*A*t the end of the long day, the exhausted deputies schlepped into the station, splitting off into their own cubicles. Immediately, Stan stood up and said, "Do I smell pizza?"

Liza walked through the room, carrying a stack of boxed pizzas, and shouted loud enough for everyone to hear, "Nope, plural, pizz*as*! And salads, cookies, and one can of beer each, period!"

Stan clutched his heart, did a pratfall into his chair, pretending to faint, and began quoting the poem from The Odyssey by Homer. "Be still, my heart, thou hast known worse than this. On that day when the cyclops, unrestrained in fury, devoured the mighty men—"

Tommy ran by Stan and said, "Oh, shut up, Stan. I'm having your beer."

Stan scrambled out of his chair, trying to push past the muscle-bound Norske as everyone stampeded to the meeting room. No one had eaten since breakfast, other than Howard, who was shuffled to the end of the line. The group was entirely indebted to Liza, who stood smiling in the back of the room with her hands on her ample hips. She was their den mother, and grateful she could do something nice for them to take their minds off the day.

Once the deputies were seated, the only noises heard were the sounds of munching or humming. After a few minutes, the chief stood and said, "As long as I have your rapt attention, I'm calling this a meeting, which means no seven o'clock meeting tomorrow morning. You can sleep in, but be here by eight o'clock, okay?" Heads bobbed in agreement.

"I appreciate all of your hard work today. It was the worst day of my life, and I am sure it was for you, as well." He turned to his chief deputy. "Hilde, I hate to ask, but after you're done eating, will you please go over to the hospital to make sure Annabelle is all settled in and secure?"

Chewing while holding a large piece of pizza close to her mouth, Hilde nodded.

Roger decided to tell a joke. He didn't want to be dismissive of the horror they had gone through today, but he knew it would allow them to release some stress.

"Did I ever tell you the story of Officer Lyle Larson from Pickett's Landing, and what happened to him? Well, he was staking out a particularly rowdy bar waiting to catch drunk drivers. At closing time, he saw a fellow stumble out of the bar, trip on the curb, and try his keys on five different cars before he found his. Then, the man sat in the front seat without starting the car. Everyone else left the bar and drove off. Finally, the man in the car started his engine and began to pull away. Lyle was waiting for him and roared off after the culprit. He stopped the driver, read him his rights, and administered a Breathalyzer. The results showed a reading of 0.0. Puzzled, Lyle demanded to know how that could be. The driver replied, 'Tonight, I'm the designated decoy.'"

Roger's audience burst out with overly exuberant laughter, grateful for the release of all those pent-up emotions from the murder scene.

Once the room calmed down, the chief continued. "We have good news. Wilbur, the blind dog, has been found. The stupid dog had been shut in Mattie's sewing room closet and sleeping on one of her quilts. Wilbur apparently didn't think to bark for help. Anyway, the bad news is that the free meal offer has been taken off the plate, literally."

The disappointed groaning began, with Tommy being the most disappointed. The chief continued, "We are all exhausted, and it was one tough day. This murder is the first for some of you, and I can't stress enough to seek counseling. Stress creates some strange symptoms: night terrors, sleeplessness, overeating, overdrinking, or health problems. Please consider seeing Dr. Joe Dill. We keep him on retainer, and I've gone to him myself. His number is listed on our website under the health tab." He turned to watch Liza write the doctor's name and his telephone number on the whiteboard in bold letters. Pointing to the board, Roger said, "Okay, then, no excuses. Here is Dr. Dill's number, and I want you to use his services. We need all of you in good physical and mental health.

"Down to business. Wayne Winckowski is six foot five inches with a barrel chest and massive upper arms. He always wears an ironed long-sleeved white shirt with black jeans and black cowboy boots.

"The mug shot doesn't show it, but Wayne has a black mole under his right eyebrow. His eyes are hazel, and he has shoulder-length dark brown hair.

"His silver rodeo buckle is a constant on his belt. Winckowski has bragged that he used to ride the rodeo circuit, and it's all bullshit. He's a con man, declaring that he was also a Marine, another line of bull. We'll be checking all the liquor stores across the five-state area because Winckowski's a heavy drinker and will need to feed the beast.

"It's rumored that Winckowski has recently gotten tats on his forearms, but so far, we don't know what they are or if the rumor is true. So, if anyone hears what they look like, we must get that information ASAP."

Pointing to the next board, the chief said, "Here's a description of his Ford pickup and his license plate number. It does have straight pipes."

Roger wrapped it up. "I'm done; any questions?"

Paul asked, "Any sightings of him yet?"

Roger half-smiled, feeling the flush of embarrassment reddening the tips of his ears. His exhaustion was showing. "Oh, yeah, I guess that would be helpful to discuss. Sorry 'bout that; I'm a little brain dead.

"Currently, all we know is that he headed south from the farm. Since this morning, we have not had one sighting. We all hunt, we all track, so think like a hunter. Call your friends in the surrounding states' police departments and ask them to pay close attention to the information that Liza has sent out. Your neighbors, friends, and families will be next on your list. Try to get leads on where Winckowski might be heading by checking with his bar mates, fishing buddies, and vending machine clients.

"Hilde is doing the organizing, and we'll be passing out some suggested leads for your follow-up hopefully before noon tomorrow." Roger looked over at Hilde and got her nod, but before Roger turned back, she held up three fingers to him. He nodded, pointed, and tapped his nose, understanding that she was referring to Pinpoint, Inc., a local business with three very qualified former police officers who offer their technology services to catch criminals nationwide. Of the three Pinpoint businessmen, two had disabilities but were quite capable of sitting behind multiple computer screens solving crimes.

Hilde got up and walked out of the lunchroom. She leaned into Liza's cubicle. "Call the guys at Pinpoint and set them up in the lunchroom for tonight, full spread, secure lines, and email." Hilde got a thumbs-up from Liza, who was on the phone and jotting down notes. Hilde turned away, thought a moment, and turned back. "Donuts." Liza's thumb went up again.

chapter
ten

Monday, June 4, 7:30 p.m.

Two Streams, Minnesota

Years before, Pinpoint's President, Ron Moore, a former beat cop from Chicago, originated the idea for the crime-stopping business, and it quickly was a success. Ron gave full credit to his partners: Rik Zamora, a retired police detective, and Roy Klinkheimer, a police computer technician, a wizard.

The combination of their individual memory strengths, experience, brilliance, common sense, and intuitiveness had made them famous for solving current and cold case crimes nationwide. The city of Two Streams was honored to call them locals.

The night of the murders, Monday night, Ron Moore was watching NCIS when he picked up his ringing phone, knowing it was Liza. "Ron, it's Liza. I'm sure you heard about the murders; we could use your help. Can you? We're at the station."

Ron had heard the news, so Liza's cryptic speech was understood. "Absolutely, and thank you for thinking of us. Let me call Klink. He doesn't answer his phone for just anyone." It was well-known Klink had Asperger's Syndrome and was brilliant at his job. "Sorry, Liza didn't mean it to sound that way."

Liza replied, "Understood, saves time, thanks, bye," as she disconnected. Liza was efficient.

Ron called Klink, who answered without a greeting, and was quickly informed of the case and where they would set up. Klink hung up without speaking. Ron placed the next call to Rik and repeated the same message. They hung up and got started. The team was all business, and time was much more important than courtesy.

The three men walked into the police station fifteen minutes later, with Klink pushing his stolen grocery cart. It was overflowing with all of his computer paraphernalia, cords trailing onto the floor, a pillow, office supplies, and his toothbrush sticking out of a pencil cup. Years earlier, Rik, wanting to surprise Klink, had painted the grocery cart gold, declaring it was Klink's "gold cart." Klink was over the moon when he received his shiny new toy and periodically washed and polished it.

Liza had already turned the lunchroom into their work pen: five whiteboards beside two bulletin boards with the Midwest county and state maps, and several desks for the volunteers that would eventually be assigned to Pinpoint.

Klink emptied his cart and hauled out his Army cot, which he set up next to the back wall. He tossed his soft white pillow onto the cot. Klink had the energy of two men, but when he hit the wall, he needed to be able to sleep immediately until his brain was restored. Ron and Rik preferred to sleep at home in their own beds.

The men unpacked their gear and started organizing the little information they had on the murders at the Winckowski farm.

Meanwhile, the chief was wrapping up his meeting next door. "Okay, it will be a long week, and you all need to get a good night's sleep. So do your reports, and cc your emails to Pinpoint, Hilde, and myself. They will compile a report for us. Hopefully, we'll have someplace to start in the morning."

The room of tired officers knew better than to move before the chief's period landed because he always had more to say. He spoke in a low, conversational tone, counting on his fingers. "So, we have us, two other police departments from nearby, Pinpoint, and the state patrol. It's not enough, but after Liza contacts every police department within North and South Dakota, Wisconsin, Iowa, and Minnesota, we'll have their virtual support." The chief's mind was in overdrive, and this was how he methodically solved crimes and organized his thoughts.

"Hilde, get one of the retirees or volunteers to get a list of the liquor store authorities throughout the Midwest and send Winckowski's picture out to every one of them and ask them to forward it to their local liquor stores. He's a drunk, and needs his booze."

Roger snapped his fingers and shouted at Deputy Pickens, "Stan, call Glen, the mailman, and see if he saw anything."

Roger continued, "Anything else? If anyone comes up with a good idea, a stupid idea, or one you want to talk out, contact either Hilde or me. We have five dead family members that should not have been killed, and we certainly don't want that to happen again to any other family.

"Okay, I'll be in my office if anything comes up. Get a good night's rest, because tomorrow is coming. Thank you for your help today. I really appreciate it." The chief tapped his heart and stepped away, but stopped and said, "No one, and I mean no one talks to the press, understood?"

The officers in the room mumbled, "Yes, sir." But Roger noticed Deputy Belinda Jackson had looked away. Strange. They cleared the room, making their way to their cubicles to finish their reports and get home.

chapter
eleven

Monday, June 4, 8:30 p.m.

Two Streams Police Department
Two Streams, Minnesota

*T*he chief strolled into his office, set down his Styrofoam coffee cup, and removed his holster, slinging it over the hook on the wall behind him. Liza had placed the evening edition of the *Blanchard News* on top of his desk. He looked at the headlines and slammed his fist down so hard it spilled his coffee, but a knee-jerk reaction saved the newspaper before it was totally soaked.

"That damn Friechs!" Roger swore.

Hilde rushed into his office. "What?"

With both hands, he carried the newspaper over to the meeting table, spreading it out for Hilde to see the screaming headlines, "Winckowski Family Murdered!" Underneath were six huge colored pictures of the farm. They included one of the chief, the coroner in his hazmat suit, and the ambulances without their lights. The story was without much detail, but it added all five children's school pictures, and one of Letty, smiling, probably taken from her high school yearbook.

Roger's office door was open, so he whispered, "We have to find out who the snitch is. They are taking pictures and leaking information to that freakin' Friechs."

Hilde found a roll of paper towels, and they both wiped up the coffee. Hilde closed Roger's door before she sat in the chair in front of his desk. "It's Belinda Jackson."

Roger sat slowly in his chair, holding his tired head up with his right palm. "Crap. You're right. She stood right on the road and took the pictures."

Hilde thought about the time she had invested in Belinda, feeling profoundly disappointed that she would do something like this. The deputy had started the same week as Tommy, but Belinda seemed to circle the team rather than being part of them. Hilde was surprised by the rookie's attitude because Belinda had already had a stellar career as a high school teacher and, after seven years, switched to law enforcement.

Roger said, "I'll handle this, and we'll talk again tomorrow. I'll let you go so you can get to the hospital, okay?"

"Okay. Night."

"Thanks for everything today, Hilde." Turning to his computer, Roger spoke up once again. "Did you notify kin?"

She stopped, leaned onto the doorknob, and, looking disappointed, said, "No, Liza and I have been working on that, but nothing so far. A couple of leads but no return calls."

He said, "Huh, that's surprising. I'd hate to see Annabelle getting tossed into foster care with strangers."

Hilde's soft blue eyes looked concerned. "Hope that doesn't happen." She turned and shook her head but turned back. "Chief, I have a concern. It's Howard. He was the one that checked the white garage where Annabelle was hiding, and he didn't find her."

"I was wondering about that. The whole thing with Howard's mother barging into a crime scene to bring her baby boy his lunch is beyond ridiculous. Let's see this case through and monitor how Howard does, okay?

"Yes, sir." Hilde walked out the door.

Roger waited until he heard the din from the cube to go silent. The chief nonchalantly strolled through the station, double-checking each cubicle making sure everyone had left. Once he was satisfied, Roger methodically checked each of his officers' desks, purposely saving Belinda's for last. He sat down in Belinda's chair and quickly opened the side drawers, finding nothing. Sticking his hand under the center drawer, he felt something taped to the underside and pulled out a business card:

Blanchard News
Ms. Muriel Friechs, Senior Reporter
Cell Phone: 218-555-4545

Turning it over, he saw a handwritten note: "6 pics + story".

Roger groaned; he really hoped he wouldn't find anything implicating Belinda. He had been so impressed with her initial interview, so it was hard to understand this new development. When she started, Belinda seemed open and friendly and then almost immediately changed, becoming quiet and sullen. Belinda looked younger than she was, thirty-ish, with green eyes and mellow amber skin. When he had interviewed her, he was most impressed with her past experience as a teacher and expertise with computers. The chief hated the thought of having to fire her, but leaking inside information was very serious. Roger went back to his office and tapped a text to Belinda.

Meet me in my office now!

Belinda was home, freshly showered, and just settling in to catch up with the home improvement shows before her on-call shift began at 10:00 p.m. She was surprised to hear a text alert come in at such a late hour. Quickly reading it, she knew the chief had discovered her secret.

Belinda was at the station within minutes, dressed in a fresh uniform, dreading the upcoming meeting. All the things she could lose spun inside her head: her job, her new friends, and this lovely town she adored. Feeling a trickle run down her freshly deodorized armpit, Belinda swore.

She met Roger as he was coming back from the lunch-room with a cup of coffee. All he said was, "Come back." He offered no smile.

Roger closed his office door and walked around his desk, setting his ceramic cup next to the *Blanchard News*.

Belinda sat in front of his desk, leaning slightly forward, twisting her hands. The chief looked at her quickly with a disapproving look, turning the newspaper around for her to see. He sat down and pointed at the picture of himself. Roger said, "You did a great job making me look good in this picture. Are you a professional photographer?"

She had never seen that snide smile of his before and did not like it. Her eyes grew larger, showing concern with the weight of his stare, which made her nervous, but she looked him square in the eye. "I took the pictures and gave them to Friechs."

In his calmest voice, Roger asked, "Why in the hell would you do that?"

Shrugging, child-like, taking a deep interest in her cuti-cles, she scraped them into slivered hangnails while waiting for him to fire her.

Roger continued, "I also noticed there is no mention of Annabelle being alive, or that she was in the hospital, or that the suspect is Winckowski. Although the pictures you took were good, they really offered nothing. For that, I am very grateful. So, tell me what is going on here."

Remaining silent, Belinda turned her attention to the lint on her brown pants.

Slamming his fist onto the desk, Roger shouted, making her jump. "Snitching to reporters for cash is a gross ethics violation! I will fire your ass right here and now if you don't start telling me what is really going on!'

Her deep-seated shame dampened Belinda's eyes. Snapping at him, she said, "Okay, okay!" The rookie looked him straight in the eye. "You'll probably fire me anyway, but I never took any cash. Never. Friechs approached me during my first week as a deputy. She had a friend who knew that I was charged with a drive-by shooting at age thirteen. If that had come out, I would never have this job or any other job!"

Quietly, he said, "Tell me."

"I was born and raised in Chicago, and a little shit when I reached puberty. One night I snuck out with my best friend Sue, to ride around with a couple of sixteen-year-old guys, friends of hers, Mick and Ronald.

"We passed a house where a group of people was partying. Mick told Ronald to make a U-turn. As we passed the house again, Mick pulled out a gun, pointing it at the group. They all screamed and dove for cover. Mick fired in the air several times, then Ronald hit the gas, and we flew off down the street.

Both Sue and I were so scared; I started crying. I had no idea the boys had a gun. They finally dropped me off at some gas station. I didn't know where I was but had the cashier call my folks. Mom and Dad had to drive over an hour to get me. I had never been so terrified, and when my folks asked me what happened, I told them the absolute truth.

"The next morning, the police came and arrested me, charging me with the drive-by shooting. Apparently, a bullet had ricocheted, striking a man who was not on the porch. The shot to his leg was superficial, not a severe wound but a serious crime. Mick and Ronald lied, saying that it was me who had shot the gun. Sue backed me up, and I finally got the charges expunged.

"That bitch Friechs used that information to black-mail me, getting me to take pictures and provide inside information."

The chief just sat and stared at her. Finally, Roger said, "I'm not sure I believe you, nor do I trust you. But what I do know is Muriel Friechs is a cold and calculating bitch."

Belinda nodded. The chief went silent for several minutes while Belinda sat with her anxiety.

"You'll need to be exemplary to gain my trust. If you're interested in doing something for me, and it would be a private matter."

Belinda's anxiety had saturated her pits as the underlying pink of her cheeks blossomed red. "Yes, sir, I would be interested."

"Good." Belinda looked to the chief, who was shuffling paper, when she noticed the hollow of his neck. Belinda had to look elsewhere, feeling that old familiar flutter way down deep. Crossing her legs tight, she wiped the sweat off her palms on the side of her pant legs, waiting to hear what favor the chief would ask of her.

Leaning back Roger in his chair, he tee-peed his fingertips and looked into her eyes. "I need you to continue to work with Friechs, get closer, and gain her trust. I have always felt that Mayor Conrad Taylor and Friechs are conniving bed partners." The chief rubbed his eyes, trying to clear the image of the mayor and Friechs in bed, naked.

"But they both seem to be living way beyond their means," he continued. "A Blanchard city council member confided in me that someone was fudging the town's books. Tens of thousands of dollars are missing."

Belinda cleared her throat in acknowledgment. "I wouldn't be surprised," she said. "I had to meet Muriel over at the mayor's office once while he was out. I walked in and found Muriel going through one of the file drawers in his office." Belinda shook her head. "But how will I ever figure out how they are stealing funds?"

"Am I asking you to do something that is beyond your capabilities?"

"No, no, I'm just looking for a little direction." Belinda paused to brush her pant leg of the invisible lint again. Popping her head up, she started talking very fast. "As long as I'm honest, I did join a gang when I was fifteen, and they had me do all sorts of illegal shit for my initiation. So, I know how to pick a lock, scope a house, burglarize, hot wire, pickpocket, and ambush someone's computer. I developed a very sneaky nature, and fortunately, I was never caught. But the layers of fear as a gang member brought me to my knees. I was terrified all the time. I left the gang, and we, my family, left for Minnesota."

Belinda slouched down into the chair, throwing an arm behind her, and sat gangsta style. Holding up a gang sign with her fingers, she added a pout to her already full red lips.

Roger blew out a zerbert into his hand, chuckling. "And you were a teacher before you became a cop?"

"Yeah. I got bored."

The chief dry-washed his face and said, "Apparently, I asked all the wrong questions during your interview. I now realize I know nothing about you! I think you might have more fun doing this than you should. Are you in?"

Her white teeth showing, she agreed. "I'm in, sir."

Roger leaned forward on both elbows and said, "Good. Your little traitor relationship with Friechs is over. You are on our side, a good guy. Got it?"

"Yes, sir."

"No one will know what we have just discussed, other than Hilde."

"Understood. Thank you for another chance, Chief. I'm sorry I didn't trust you. I should have come to you earlier. I love this job, really."

"No problem. Tonight, you're on call, right?

"Yes, sir."

Roger stood up, signaling the end of the meeting. "Hey, be a better teammate too. You're missing a great opportunity to know these people. They are awesome."

"Yes, sir, will do. Thank you, Rog… sir. Sorry." Standing up, she caught her toe in the leg of the chair and stumbled but caught herself, turning quickly and regaining her balance. Giving a little wave, she immediately regretted it and walked out the door. Once out of sight, she groaned, casting her eyes to the ceiling.

Roger tapped his pen on his blotter with a crooked smile playing on his lips as he watched her go. He sat down and leaned back, looking at the closed door, and thought he had really misjudged that gorgeous woman.

chapter
twelve

Monday, June 4, 9:00 p.m.

Two Streams, Minnesota

H ilde's car idled, sitting in line at the drive-thru at McDonald's. Pulling forward without looking, she used a Kleenex to dab at her eyes, catching the trailing eyedrops that were supposed to soothe tired red eyes. Blinking, Hilde reached through her car window to collect the four coffees snuggled into the cardboard cup holder that was being held mid-air by a young waiter with his tongue out, probably thinking that would help to balance the precarious tray. Carefully placing them onto the passenger seat, Hilde paid, waved good-bye, and slowly made her way out of the parking lot, anxious to get to Dignity Christian Hospital to check on Annabelle.

Stopping at the nurses' station, she saw Evelyn Nowicki, the night supervisor. They had known each other since high school. Leaving the coffees on the counter, Hilde followed Evelyn into a family conference room. They settled at the small table, and Evelyn opened Annabelle's patient file. The senior nurse spoke professionally. "Annabelle came in this morning and was in really tough shape."

Surprised, Hilde said, "Really? How come?" Anxiety scrunched her forehead.

Evelyn lightly touched Hilde's forearm. "We think she'll be okay, really, but she had several things wrong with her, and her grease-painted body wasn't helping us getting that diagnosis any faster. We began thinking that the grease was causing her symptoms, but it was just axle grease and doing no harm. Anyway, we finally found the cause, an atrial septal defect which is hole in her heart. It was a birth defect. It was a straightforward procedure, and it should have been corrected years ago."

"I had no idea."

"Her surgery was around suppertime and she had no issues in the recovery room. We got her settled into her own room, and she's been sleeping ever since. After what she's gone through today, I expect her to sleep for quite a while. I hope she's a tough kid because this will be a lot for Annabelle to get over."

Evelyn turned to the next item on her sheet. "She had a severe cut on her back, so we have her on high doses of antibiotics just in case it gets infected. She was also dehydrated, undernourished, and had several serious bruises." Evelyn shook her head. "For a nine-year-old, she's gone through a lot. I'm sure she'll be in the hospital for several days."

Neither woman spoke, but both women could hear Hilde's foot tapping under the table. Trying to calm her nerves, she placed her hand on the offending knee. "I'm so glad Kathy was intuitive enough to bring her in."

"Kathy's a peach," Evelyn agreed. "She's staying with Annabelle in her room. We're short-handed, so having her stay is a godsend. I understand the little girl was the only survivor?"

Hilde thought she should try to be less surprised by how much hospital employees knew of what went on around them. Hilde retrieved her notebook and began to take notes. Looking up to Evelyn, she said, "Yes. Annabelle hid in an old garage, and the killer wasn't able to find her. You said you hoped Annabelle was a tough kid; I'd say she is, and pretty damned smart too. Has Annabelle said anything to anyone about what happened at her house?"

"She's barely been awake, so no."

"Has anyone called inquiring or tried to visit Annabelle?"

Concern played across Evelyn's face, but she shook her head.

"The guard is still outside her room, correct?" Hilde continued.

"Yes, but there was a switch, and Deputy Tommy Johnson is out there now."

"Oh, really? I didn't get that message. What happened to the security guard that was originally there, Earl?"

"His wife went into labor tonight, two weeks early. They had a baby boy."

The two women smiled at each other, feeling the familiar hormonal tug of baby love. Hilde had been in the hospital enough times to experience the playing of a sweet lullaby over the hospital's speaker system each time a baby was born. Hilde was still smiling when she said, "Beautiful way to end this horrendous day."

With a deep sigh, Evelyn said, "Yes. I can't imagine what you all have gone through today."

"It's been really tough on everyone, but we'll get through it. Speaking of which, do you know if the psychologist, Dr. Dill, will be visiting Annabelle?"

Evelyn stood up, as did Hilde, and said, "Yes, he has her scheduled for tomorrow morning. It seems so early, but Dr. Dill is adamant about talking with the child as early as possible after an event." Evelyn glanced at her watch. "I should get back. Here's my card with my cell number. You call me anytime. Oh, I almost forgot, we have her listed as under Aryls M. Ward. We're trying to steer any reporters or inquiring strangers away from Annabelle."

"Good, that was going to be my next question. Thank you, Evelyn. I'll stop and see Annabelle and Kathy." Hilde made a note to advise Liza of the name change for Annabelle's room.

Evelyn nodded, and they continued through the door and back to the nurses' station.

The chief deputy picked up two cups of coffee from the counter and proceeded down the hall to the room of Aryls M. Ward. She spotted Tommy sitting outside Annabelle's room, fiddling with his phone. Hilde passed a cup of coffee to Tommy as he stood up to greet her.

"Hey, any problems?" she inquired.

Raising his hand to Hilde, Tommy said, "Thanks for the coffee. No, no problems. Annabelle is still sleeping. Kathy, the social worker is with her now, and will be spending the night."

"I'm going to go in and check on them. I don't think I would recognize Annabelle without the greasepaint."

"She's a cute kid," Tommy said through his wide smile and took a sip of coffee.

Hilde opened the door and waggled her fingers at Kathy, who was curled up with a book. The social worker stood and walked over to Hilde and accepted the cup of coffee from her. They stood for a few seconds and watched Annabelle sleep.

Hilde looked down at Kathy's clothes and whispered, "Darling outfit. "

Kathy looked down and nodded. "Yes, green scrubs with alligators all over them wasn't exactly what I would have picked out for pajamas, but it's better than the black grease that covered my clothes when I arrived. How are you doing, Hilde? We have to quit meeting under these terrible circumstances."

Kathy had worked for years for the social services department providing her expertise in Blanchard. The town covered over four hundred square miles and was populated with a small number of residents. Over the past decade, dirty politics, over-crowded school classrooms, domestic violence, and ongoing petty crimes inundated the ancient town. The small group of social workers working for the town has been over-worked and under-appreciated. Kathy's sweet demeanor was always at odds with the heavy and sad workload.

Hilde said, "I agree. You know, maybe we should have coffee next week. I'll come to Blanchard."

Kathy said, "That works for me." She turned the topic back to the girl. "Annabelle's been sleeping for several hours. Did you recognize her without all the greasepaint?"

Shaking her head, Hilde studied the beautiful little girl: long black feathered lashes laid below her eyes, the soft pale face almost hid the petite nose which had a dusting of freckles while the yard of dark brown hair had been sun-drenched with auburn highlights. Hilde noticed even while sleeping, Annabelle's mouth turned up at the corners. Said, "She's a darling little girl. I heard she had several bruises on her?"

"Yes. I wasn't surprised. We had reports from several of the kids' schoolteachers reporting cuts and bruising. I never once got those kids to confide in me. They seemed afraid to tell the truth, and as a family unit, they kept their code of silence. Letty was no different, and Wayne, well, he was just a liar. I feel terrible not being able to do anything earlier."

Hilde tapped the forearm of the sweet woman. "We all wish that. We both know that silence is required in abusers' homes. I wish we had more legal leverage to gain access to those homes and rescue those endangered children. Tsk."

Hilde then stepped to the side of the bed, gazing down at the child whose long, freshly washed and combed hair covered her like a blanket. Annabelle's dream or nightmare was making her eyelids twitch up and down. A moan escaped her flushed face as her body shuddered.

Annabelle's dream sang. *"Cinderella, Cinderella, all I hear is Cinderella, Cinder, Cinder... rella Cinder, Cinder..."*

Candy loves this song, and we sing it all the time.

"Candy! Where are you?"

Candy sits on the hospital bed and softly palms Annabelle's chin. Annabelle looks into her big sister's twinkling eyes as Candy speaks. "I've been here all along, but you don't sleep deep enough to see me. You're getting better now, so you'll feel us more and more as time goes on."

Fresh tears glisten in Annabelle's eyes. "Candy, I don't want to be alone. Let me come with you, please? I want Momma!" Her lip came out in a pout, diverting the dribble of tears down her jaw.

Candy slides under the covers with her little sister and holds her little sister as she sobs.

"Shh, shh, shh. We are here for you. We will never leave you."

Annabelle pauses when she sees Harley waving at her from a distance. Annabelle waves vigorously, and he signs back, "I love you to the moon and back."

Hilde watched as Annabelle raised her hand and seemed to lift her fingers purposely. Annabelle's hand dropped, and her face softened into a deep sleep, the quaking gone.

The chief deputy stepped toward the door and gave a quick wave to Kathy, and left.

chapter
thirteen

Monday, June 4, 9:45 p.m.

Dignity Christian Hospital,
Two Streams, Minnesota

Kathy jumped up, dumping her book to the floor when she heard Annabelle crying out. Gently shaking the little girl, Kathy saw Annabelle's eyes flutter open.

"Hi, sweetie. How are you doing?" Kathy asked in a low voice while stroking Annabelle's small fingers, avoiding the IV bandage on her hand.

Annabelle looked around the soft yellow room and croaked, "Where am I?"

"The hospital. You got very sick today."

"Oh. Am I better? I don't feel better, but I sure am hungry."

Kathy smiled as she pressed the nurses' call button. "I bet you are. I'm calling a nurse, and we'll see what you're able to eat, okay?"

Annabelle nodded.

A minute later, a pretty nurse walked in, leading the way with her smile, which she never released. Stopping next to the bed, she picked up Annabelle's hand, checked her pulse, and looked at the monitors.

"Hey there, sugar. How are you all feelin'?"

Annabelle tried to sit up but winced in pain and gave up. "I hurt all over. My throat really hurts."

According to her name badge, the nurse, Shelly Rae, replied, "Can you tell me exactly where you hurt?"

Annabelle bent her arm over her back, searching for what was pulling on the back of her gown. Shelly gently pulled the little girl's arm down and said, "You had a big ol' hole in your back, and it looked like it could turn into one nasty infection, so we had a lot of fixin' to do, then we put a huge bandage over it."

Shelly moved back a little as she checked Annabelle's vitals, continuing to talk in a run of octaves, her fingers expressing herself when they weren't fiddling with the machines. Annabelle could smell antiseptic cleaners on the nurse, but also a sweet, underlying scent of oranges.

"You had surgery today, and the doctor put a tube down your throat to make sure you got all the oxygen you needed. Then afterward, they took it out, and I'm sure those doctors scraped the sides of your throat a little." Shelly wiggled her fingers, fluffing off the seriousness of the surgery. She smiled, disclosing the most enchanting, slightly crooked eyetooth. "It'll be fine in a couple of days. But the good news is, you can have all the soft foods you want. You can have soup, juice, milk, ice cream, poached eggs, milquetoast, or Jell-O. How's that sound, sweetie?"

"All of it, please," Annabelle croaked with a shy smile.

Kathy and Shelly both laughed, pleased by her response. "Well, okay, then. I'll be back with a large dinner tray, just as fast as I can." Wiggling her fingers again, she left, leaving the impression of the pretty nurse who had been blessed with a soft curvaceous shape, unable to walk, only sashay. The long, blonde, wavy ponytail swayed one last time as the door closed behind her.

Kathy told Annabelle, "Shelly is from South Carolina."

Annabelle looked longingly at the departing nurse. "Really? I wish I could be from South Carolina and be happy and pretty like her. Are some states happier than others?"

Slow to respond, Kathy said, "I don't believe states are any happier than your home state."

Annabelle whispered a small, "Oh, shoot."

Annabelle noticed Kathy was wearing scrubs and asked why. Kathy explained that the nurses invited her to stay overnight with Annabelle and had offered nursing scrubs to wear as jammies. The discussion got back around to what other soft foods that Annabelle might be able to eat. They discussed her back injury and how she got it, but Annabelle offered no additional information about hiding from her father.

The little girl paused during their conversation, interrupting Kathy with a hitch in her throat, and said, "My family, are they okay?" Annabelle dropped her eyes but immediately raised them, anxious to hear what Kathy would say.

Kathy took Annabelle's hand, leaned forward, stroked her face, and looked the little girl in the eye. "No, dear."

Slowly, Annabelle felt the words inch into her brain, and suddenly the reality hit. Fat tears rolled down Annabelle's face as she held onto Kathy, who rocked the orphan while she stroked her hair.

Deep, shuddering breaths were all that was left when Annabelle had cried herself out. Suddenly Annabelle's head popped up, her eyes wild with fear, "What about Dad? Is he coming for me?" Annabelle looked around in panic.

Kathy held Annabelle's elbows and said softly, "You're safe. The police are looking for him, but you don't need to worry because you have a policeman outside your door. His name is Tommy Johnson, a big, strong guy. No one gets past Tommy."

Kathy did her best to divert the little girl from the terror that no child should feel. "Also, a little while ago, Chief Deputy Hilde Crosby stopped by to see you. She wanted to see what you looked like without all that grease." Kathy smiled. "That was pretty darn smart of you to hide like you did."

Annabelle lowered her head to the compliment, not used to them, and stuttered, "Thank you."

"Remember Chief Jorgenson? Roger?" Annabelle nodded as Kathy continued. "Roger or Hilde will come by tomorrow to question you on what happened this morning."

Annabelle looked Kathy in the eye and said in a hushed voice, "I didn't see anything." Dropping her gaze, she added, "I just heard it."

Blinking at the news, Kathy realized how terrifying it must have been for this tiny child. She felt helpless as Annabelle seemed to shrink back into her pillows.

Patting Annabelle's hand, Kathy said, "Would you like to meet Tommy?" Just then, Shelly opened the door, and behind her a blond man in a uniform swept in carrying a tray of food. He smiled at Annabelle and said, "Hey, Annabelle. I'm Tommy."

Shyness overcame Annabelle, but she waved at the man, keeping her eyes on the tray he carried. She liked his smile, but it was too much effort to be friendly right now. Her stomach growled almost painfully with the smell of the food. Shelly shimmied the bed table in front of Annabelle as Tommy set the tray down. Shelly raised the bed as the famished girl began to drink and eat all at the same time. The nurse and the deputy left while Kathy helped Annabelle with her dinner.

The lone survivor was soon asleep with a spoon in her hand and a milk ring around her mouth.

chapter
fourteen

Monday, June 4, 10:50 p.m.

Beatty Lake, Blanchard, Minnesota

*C*arl Larson sat on the end of the dock, clicking his tactical flashlight on and off. He was pointing it at a cabin across the lake owned by his best friend, Miles Lundgren. Carl could see Miles's windows flash each time a beam of light hit them but saw no response from the darkened house. He was beginning to feel Miles wasn't ever going to see his Morse code signal. Carl didn't know what else he could do.

The night sky was deepening around him, and without the aid of the moon or stars, Carl was clueless as to the time it was. The white-haired man had been sitting on the dock for quite a while and was growing weary.

Miles, please wake up and come help me.

Getting up from his sitting position, Carl suddenly felt woozy and slowly lowered himself back down to the dock. Not wanting to risk a fall into the cold lake, he crawled until he reached the end and held onto a dock post. Carl swung his legs over to the rocky shore, held onto a post, and stooped to scoop handfuls of ice-cold water into his mouth. He slurped until his thirst was quenched, then raised handfuls to his face, hoping to ease the throbbing nerve endings on the left side where he had been struck. It smarted like a son of a gun, as did the back of his head. Exhausted, he sat back down onto the dock and rested.

Hearing an old car with a large motor, Carl felt a flutter in his gut. Miles and his green 1966 Oldsmobile Toronado were rumbling down the lane to his rescue. His best friend had served with Carl during the Korean War and was once again coming to save him.

Carl pulled himself up using the dock post and walked up the cement launch over to the picnic table as he shielded his eyes against the bright headlights as Miles parked his car. The lights went off, but the running lights remained on.

Miles, a tall, hefty man, struggled to get his old body out of the car. He tottered his sore knees over to Carl, sliding across the bench, bouncing it up and down. The ex-Army soldier finally sat still, clasped his hands on the tabletop, and smiled across at his old friend. "Hey."

Carl noticed Miles had come to his rescue in well-worn green plaid pajamas and barefooted. Miles hated wearing shoes, preferring to walk on his calloused feet. Carl's smile was quick, but the pain that followed ricocheted throughout his face. His eyes watered not only from the injury but also for the gratitude at seeing his dear friend.

Miles looked over Carl's face and stated the obvious. "Oh, boy, it looks like your face got tapped pretty good."

Carl tested his jaw, moving it carefully, and said in a low voice, "Yeah, I was sucker-punched by a giant son of a bitch. I just woke up a while ago, lying in the woods. By the way, what took you so long? I didn't think you would ever see me flashing out 'SOS' at your windows."

"You're just lucky I get up to pee every two hours. I always check the lake when I get up and saw the strobe light bouncing off the lake. It was just beautiful. Then I realized it was Morse code. I just stood staring, and finally, it clicked. It's been decades since I had to read the 'dot.dot.dot, dash-dash-dash, dot.dot.dot,' but I did it! So here I am. "Miles spread his arms wide, cocking his head proudly.

Leaning across the table and looking more closely at Carl, Miles said, "Wow, who hit you anyway, Scott LeDoux?" Miles smirked sideways, showing his small old teeth. Both men enjoyed Miles's little funny, knowing the most famous Minnesota boxer died in 2011.

"It felt like it. Later I'll have you take me to the hospital, but not now. I need to talk to the cops about this guy. I just think there is more to the story than what I know. The guy buried me and left me for dead. Did you bring your phone?"

"Where's yours?"

"Well, I think the guy stole it, along with my wallet, mini-van, boat, and trailer. Dirty son of a bitch!" Carl quieted his voice, gently touching his face. The pain was rioting under the purple skin, inside his jaw, and even his ear. The intensity made Carl close his eyes momentarily.

Miles patted his thigh. "I got my phone right here."

Though he teased Miles regularly about his outdated phone, Carl was pleased he always carried it with him. He watched as Miles leaned to the side, overstretching his fingers deep into the depths of the flannel pocket, and pulled out the phone, bringing along screws that fell to the cement pad, clinking and rolling away.

Miles paid no attention to what had dropped but began to untangle his phone, which was tied up in the thread of the pocket seam.

Blowing off the lint, Miles said, "I'll dial and pass it to you." He dramatically flipped it open and punched in three digits.

The police dispatcher immediately picked up. "911, please state your emergency."

"Hi, this is Miles Lundgren. I'm passing the phone to Carl Larson. Here, Carl."

Carl fumbled, almost dropping it. It was hard to see with one eye. "Hello? Hello?"

A female operator responded again, "I'm here. What is your emergency?"

"I came here to fish today, and just as I had launched my boat, a huge man slugged me and knocked me out cold. He stole my boat, trailer, and my black minivan."

"Do you need an ambulance, sir?"

"No, no, I'll be okay. But I would like an officer to come out so I can show him a couple of things. I believe this guy is dangerous. I'm at Beatty Lake, the public launch in St. Louis County, just outside Blanchard."

Pausing, she said, "All right, I'll have someone there within thirty minutes."

"Thank you, ma'am."

Carefully, Carl handed the phone back to Miles and said, "Did you bring any food?"

Miles smiled, smacking his lips. "I did. I pulled a pan of leftover meatloaf out of the fridge right before I came. You want a beer too?"

Carl slowly shook his head. "Don't feel so good. I'll wait. Water?"

Miles got up, bouncing the table as he went, and Carl grabbed the side of it. Miles slowly made his way back to the Toronado, opened the massive door, and leaned across the seat, reaching for the rectangular pan of cold meatloaf. Backing out, he picked up the tablespoon from the dirty floor mat.

Limping back to the picnic table, he gave the pan to Carl. Miles wiped the spoon on his plaid pajama top, which was stretched tight over his enormous beer gut, showing pale moons of skin through the buttonholes. He handed the utensil to Carl. Once again, Miles reached deep down into the overtaxed pants pocket, stretching the limits of the elastic waistband that barely kept his deep belly button hidden, and finally pulled out a bottle of water and handed it to Carl.

Marta's meatloaf was the best Carl had ever eaten, and he quickly overstuffed his mouth. Almost immediately, Carl started choking. With his mouth open, he raised his arms over his head, signaling that he needed help. Carl almost fell off the bench, when the big man jumped up. Miles rounded the table, and managed to pull the little guy up, and giving him the Heimlich maneuver. A piece of barely chewed meatloaf flew out of Carl's mouth, landing with a wet plop onto the picnic table. Miles patted Carl's back and handed him the open bottle of water. Carl heaved a couple of deep breaths and cautiously took a sip of water. Sitting back down, he softly touched his painful throat, allowing the unpleasant experience to subside.

Carl nodded his thanks and, in a croaky voice, said, "That would have been something. I live through an assault and then almost choke to death on Marta's meatloaf. I'm afraid she'd kill me again in my own coffin if I died choking on food she made."

Miles giggled, his eyes twinkling when he thought of his wife, and said, "Yes, she would. Yes, she would."

Carl swiped the undigested piece of meatloaf off the table and took a smaller bite, chewing carefully and watching as Miles took a long pull of his favorite Minnesota beer,

Grain Belt Nordeast. It must have been riding in the other pajama pocket. Carl was grateful to be alive and looked forward to fishing and having beers with Miles. His smile sneaked out again as pain stabbed like an ice pick. He let his face fall as his eyes filled with tears. Carl felt like hell.

Carl stepped out of the picnic bench, picked up the pan of food, and said to Miles, "Let's sit in the car. I'm getting cold."

When they got settled in the car, Carl said, "Remind me to call Pete. He's probably still putzing around at the restaurant, but I want to tell him what happened."

"Will do. Cookie sure made a killing fishing when he came down for the opener. Is he coming again this summer?"

"Dunno. It's an all-day drive from Sawyer, and it's always a struggle to find someone to run the café. Someone offered to buy the place, and he's considering it. Probably retire, which I hope will be in Blanchard, great fishing around here. All of our family in North Dakota is gone now. My brother is all the family I have left."

Twenty minutes later, a City of Two Streams police squad car pulled in, with a black female deputy driving. Squelching the flashing lights, Belinda left her headlights to shine across the lake, making it dance with twinkling diamonds.

The temperature had dropped, so the deputy put on her jacket as she got out. Stepping over to the cool green Oldsmobile, she flicked her flashlight over the two white-haired men sitting inside with their windows down. The one in the driver's seat seemed to be wearing pajamas, and the other man sported a very swollen black-and-blue face.

Belinda peeked in. "Evening, gentlemen," she said. "I'm Deputy Belinda Jackson. Did you call dispatch tonight?"

Peering around the enormous front of Miles, Carl said, "Yes, ma'am, I did. I'm going to get out of the car, so I can talk to you more easily." He struggled to get out and stumbled but made it around the car's bodacious rear end.

Carl lowered himself onto the bumper, gently leaning back against the trunk.

"Sorry, not feeling up to par. The dispatcher probably told you I was sucker punched. I woke just a little while ago over there in the woods." Carl pointed. "The guy must have thought I had died because he buried me with leaves and pine boughs. I believe it kept me from not dying from hypothermia. The jerk took my phone, wallet, boat, trailer, and minivan.

"I had my Mach light attached to my belt, so I used that to signal Miles," Carl pointed across the lake, "who lives directly across the lake. He finally read my SOS Morse code and drove over here."

Belinda reached for Carl's elbow and gently pulled him up. "Let's sit at the picnic table. I don't want you sliding off that bumper."

Belinda got the feeble man seated on the picnic bench as Miles took a seat next to Carl. The deputy took out her notebook and began asking questions.

"What are your names and contact info, and what is your relationship with each other?"

The old boys took turns giving the information to her, periodically looking at each other, corroborating the details.

"Carl, what time were you attacked, and are you able to give me a description of the person who did it?"

"Well, I guess it was getting close to noon today. It's still today, right?" Carl asked, looking to Miles, who nodded. "I just got a passing glance, but he was huge and much taller than me, with bushy black eyebrows."

"Were you able to see what he was wearing?"

"No, but I remember getting a whiff of a really obnoxious odor of cologne when he spun me around. Phew, it was strong."

Belinda noticed the old man had started to shake. Excusing herself, she opened the trunk of her patrol car, reached in, and opened the zippered square that held a homemade quilt. Shaking the pink rosebud quilt loose, Belinda walked back to the table and draped it over the cold old man.

She thought *we haven't used these quilts in months, and now we've used two in one day.*

Carl nodded and said, "Thank you, miss; this really feels good."

"We need to get you over to the hospital, but I need just a couple more minutes, please. Describe what was in your wallet, van, et cetera."

"My wallet had just a couple of bucks, but my license was in there."

"Credit cards?"

"No, don't use them. My Alumacraft fishing boat, a Mercury fifteen-horse kicker, a very well-used boat trailer, and a 1989 black Dodge minivan, license number MDR 643."

"A Minnesota license plate, right?"

"Yes."

"Excellent. Miles, will you run Carl over to the Dignity Christian Hospital in Two Streams, please?"

"Yes, ma'am," Miles replied, standing up.

Lifting Carl's elbow, Miles caught the quilt and said, "Come on, old boy, let's get you to the hospital."

Carl stood, and they walked to the Toronado. Carl got in, buckled his seat belt, and Miles dropped the blanket onto his lap and shut the door. Stooping down to the open window, Belinda gave him her business card, passing another one over to Miles. "Call me if you think of anything else. Take care."

Carl nodded and gave a weak smile to Belinda. He lifted his right hand, and she shook his cold fingers. Standing back, she watched as the enormous V8 engine shot the car down the lane like a rocket.

Belinda sat in her squad car, reached in for the radio, and called dispatch. "This is Deputy Belinda Jackson, calling from the boat launch at Beatty Lake, Blanchard. Mr. Carl Larson was assaulted, and, by the description, I believe Wayne Winckowski was the attacker. She reiterated the details Carl had given her, and emphasized the Minnesota license plate number, MDR643. She said, "Wayne's truck is not here. The victim is on his way to Dignity Christian. Over and out."

Digging once more in the trunk, Officer Belinda brought out evidence markers and stuffed some plastic bags in her pocket. She put on latex gloves and started searching for clues with her flashlight.

Hearing sirens approaching just twenty minutes into her search, she continued until the squad car roared into the lot, raising dust.

Paul got out of his car and leaned on the door. "Hey, you got the duty?"

"Yup, how'd you get here so fast?"

Slamming his door, he said, "After I left the station, I met my cousin at The Damn Bar to have a beer but ended up having more coffee. I had just left when I got the call, and I don't live too far from here."

"I think I know your cousin. Is it Micah?"

"Yeah, good guy." Grabbing his flashlight, he turned it on and said, "I'll sure be glad when midnight strikes, so I can see today slip into history." He waved his hand in the air as if to indicate magic.

"I hear ya." She explained the assault on Carl Larson, the attacker's description, and her suspicion that the attacker was Wayne.

"Also, I found big tire tracks off to the side over there," she continued, pointing. "I think it could have been Wayne's truck. Kind of a coincidence that a truck with oversized tires just happened to drive into a deserted boat launch and an old man was attacked by a guy with bushy black eyebrows who steals his van."

Paul stood, brushed his arm, and said, "Yeah. I just got the willies thinking about it. I'm surprised the old man wasn't killed."

That made Belinda stand straight up, and she said, "Yeah, me too. Carl thought the man had left him for dead. That was his gut instinct, but it's amazing how true that could have been."

"You got that right. I'll help 'ya finish up."

chapter
fifteen

Monday, June 4, 10:50 p.m.

Sawyer, North Dakota

Once again, Wayne caught himself nodding off and shook his head, re-directing the van into his lane. He had already stopped several times to nap inconspicuously on the minimum maintenance roads, used mainly for logging trucks and four-wheelers. Wayne wouldn't drive too far in, afraid of getting stuck with the van. He was trying to make the border of Montana, but he needed to get some food. The booze had drained from his system, and driving all day had exhausted him.

Luckily, he spotted a sign for a twenty-four-hour restaurant just up ahead in Sawyer. Following the billboard directions for Cookie's Café, Wayne pulled in and parked. He felt a great relief in being able to get out of a moving car for a while.

He opened the car door and dropped his left foot to the pavement, feeling exhaustion roll through his body. The dashboard clock read 10:50, and it was overcast, and no moonlight. He wondered if he should continue to the Montana border or get a good night's rest at a motel.

Wayne pulled his other leg out and hung his head. He thought back to Beatty Lake. Wiping his hands over his face, he regretted not making sure the old man was dead. His boozy thoughts hadn't been reliable all day.

Leaving the old man in the woods, Wayne had walked back to his truck, wanting to hide it, but he was afraid of attracting attention by starting it up with those noisy straight pipes. He took the chance and drove his truck out of the boat launch. It would be the last time Wayne would ever see his Ford. He had always been sentimental about his vehicles and caressed the steering wheel several times.

A mile down, he maneuvered the pickup into the ditch and lumbered his way over an unused government program field, hoping not to get stuck. Up ahead, an ancient wooden barn was half-collapsed, standing on sheer will alone.

One large door yawned open on the right side of the barn. Pulling through as far as possible, Wayne was careful not to bump any supporting timbers. He turned the key off, and the loud truck was silenced forever. Wayne slowly got out, silently closed the door, and walked behind, patting her back end, thanking the old broad for her services.

Stumbling his way across the moldy fields, he returned to the boat launch. It didn't seem anyone had entered the area since he had left. He collected his gear from the woods and loaded through the rear door of Carl's black van.

Wayne left the boat launch around 2:00 p.m., towing Carl's boat and trailer. Wayne pulled out the old man's license and memorized the address. The small red house was only ten minutes away, and Wayne pulled into the dirt driveway and parked. He crossed his fingers, walked up to the front door, knocked once, and then a second time, but no one answered. Opening the unlocked front door Wayne stepped into the neat house. He quickly looked around and left, closing the door behind him.

Reversing the van, he backed the trailer into the side yard and unhitched the boat trailer, leaving it parked next to the garage. Now that Carl's trailer was back at his house, no one would think of searching Beatty Lake, where Carl's body lay.

Then, Wayne turned west out of Carl's driveway, heading for Montana. Miles down the road, Wayne slammed his palm against the steering wheel. He had forgotten to search the house for food and booze. His booze-laden absent-mindedness was pissing him off. There were many things he should have done. "Damn it."

Still sitting half in and half out of the van, Wayne looked up at the red blinking sign that repeated again and again, Cookie's Cafe. Wayne stood up, stretched, and walked up the steps and into the restaurant.

chapter
sixteen

Monday, June 4, 11:00 p.m.

Sawyer, North Dakota

*T*aking a stool at the red Formica counter, Wayne removed Carl's green hat and set it on the seat next to him. He pulled a sticky plastic menu from the slotted chrome holder.

A seventy-something waiter with a white crew cut came out from the back and said, "Evenin'. Coffee?"

"Yup. I'd take a beer, too, if you have any?"

"Just bottles."

"How about a Foster's?"

"Mister, this is North Dakota, not Australia. I got 1.21 Gigahops beer from Fargo, Grain Belt Nordeast from New Ulm, or a Miller made in Milwaukee. Which?"

Not wanting a pissing match with the crabby old coot, he said, "Gimme a Gigahops."

"Hope you're up for it. It's strong. Food?"

Wayne smiled to himself. The old guy saved a lot of time using so few words. "I'll take black coffee, a ham steak, three fried eggs, pancakes, and real maple syrup."

"You'll get Aunt Jemima's sweetened brown liquid and like it." The codger turned without a word, and Wayne called to his back, "Hey!"

"The name's Cookie. What?"

"I need orange juice too."

Without a word, Cookie made his way to the kitchen, watching the stranger through the kitchen's pass-thru window while he worked the griddle.

Wayne reached down the counter for the local evening newspaper. He was stunned when he read the headline: "Family of Six Murdered in Blanchard, Minnesota." Turning away. He tried to hide his surprise that the news of the killings had already gotten into the newspapers. And what was this about six being killed? Wayne hadn't killed everyone, had he? Annabelle should be alive, but when Wayne was drunk, he suffered from blackouts. How could he have forgotten that?

Cookie came out from the kitchen, set a beer and a coffee cup on the counter, and walked back to the kitchen.

Reading rapidly through the article, Wayne noticed there wasn't much detail about the murders or about him. It said assailant *unknown*. That was good news, but his nerves tingled when he saw all five school pictures of his kids and Letty's photo from her sophomore year. He felt nervous being out in public. Wayne picked up Carl's hat and put it back on his head, adjusting the rim low.

Ten minutes later, Cookie came out with two food plates, walking carefully with his eyes trained on the food piled high. Setting the plates down in front of the stranger, he turned and poured a glass of orange juice from the dispenser, turned, and put it onto the counter.

"Anything else?" Looking up, Cookie's eyes strayed to Wayne's hat, and he suddenly starting coughing. Wayne looked up at him with surprise.

Cookie started tapping his chest. "Sorry, damn asthma does surprise attacks on me every now and again."

Wayne emptied the bottle of beer and started filling his mouth to overcapacity with the hot food. He nodded at the man and went back to eating.

Cookie picked up the empty beer bottle by sticking a finger in it and walked back to the kitchen and threw a question over his shoulder, "You want another beer?"

Wayne nodded with his face just two inches above the dinner plate, nearly nosing the pile of pancakes.

Cookie carefully set the empty bottle down by the kitchen sink, covered it with a dishtowel, and stood out of sight, trying to settle his racing heart.

The stranger was wearing his brother's hat! *Carl never takes it off*, he thought. *What the hell?*

Walking with purpose, he went into his office, pulled a switchblade from his desk drawer, and slipped it into his pants pocket. He nonchalantly walked out with a cold beer and plunked it down. Cookie smiled as Wayne looked him straight in the eyes.

Wayne nervously asked, "Say, do you know where there is a cheap motel around here?"

Cookie leaned heavily on the back counter, placing a fresh toothpick into his mouth, and looked up to the ceiling for an answer.

"Nothin' round here 'til Minot. Then they're all clustered alongside Highway Fifty-two. Lots of choices for ya."

Cookie's eyes didn't leave Wayne, and he wondered if the old man had read the headlines about the killings in Blanchard. Slowly Wayne pulled his right hand off the counter and tapped the front of his jeans, checking that his gun was there and ready.

Just then, Cookie pointed his toothpick at the customer and asked, "Are you related to the Bovines, here in Sawyer?"

"No, why?"

"Well, one of their kids has a similar tattoo to yours that one there one on your forearm, the two smoking skulls. Yours is more customized, though, beautiful in a terrifying way. Did you get your tats around here?"

Wayne's shoulders softened "'Fraid not. I was stationed in Afghanistan and had leave time in Japan. I got both my forearms done there. I was released on a medical two years ago after being shot up."

Cookie stood up and presented his hand. "Thank you for your service." Cookie shook Wayne's hand, then turned to grab another beer for the stranger.

Walking back from the kitchen a minute later, Cookie slapped the beer down on the counter and said, "You are not paying me a dime for this meal, including the beer. It's on the house. I don't charge our military folks." Cookie felt chilled thinking of what this creep may have done to his brother, but he needed to befriend him.

Wayne's mind jumped to the great idea of getting more free meals using the military ploy. He offered Cookie his best smile and graciously said, "Thank you."

Cookie chuckled and pointed to Wayne's hat. He said, "I know you're too young for the Korean War, so where'd you get the cool hat?"

"It was my Dad's," Wayne lied easily. "I'm from Montana, and I'm just driving back from his funeral in Minnesota. Wearing it makes me feel closer to him."

Unconsciously Cookie shuddered at the underlying implication that his brother might be dead.

"Gosh, I'm sorry 'bout that." Cookie returned to the kitchen, silenced his phone, turned on the phone's camera, and took several pictures of the tatted customer, who sat unaware. Upon checking the images, Cookie realized how poor they were, showing only the top of Wayne's head as the customer gorged himself.

Cookie returned with yet another beer, along with a slice of apple pie topped with ice cream, setting it in front of the stranger. He picked up the conversation where they had left off.

"Anyway, the Bovine kid, Levi, is a senior this year, and he's really good at drawing. He wants to be a tattoo artist. Would you mind if I drew a picture of the geisha tattoo on your other arm? He'll never have the first-hand experience of those foreign tattoo artists like you had."

Wayne pulled his sleeve higher so Cookie could get a good picture of his geisha. "Here you go." Wayne dug into his apple pie with his left arm upright toward Cookie.

Cookie looked around and found a receipt tablet and a pencil. Leaning on the counter and with an intentionally shaky hand, Cookie started to draw the geisha onto the white backside of the receipt, looking over at Wayne's arm periodically.

Wayne chewed his food, watching the old cook as he attempted to draw, which looked more like scribbling.

Wayne stood up and said, "Hey, hey, let's do this. Why don't you take a picture?"

"Oh, I don't keep my camera here at the café."

"Don't you have a cell phone?"

"Yeah, so?" Cookie looked puzzled.

Wayne said, "You probably have a camera on your cell phone."

"Oh, right, right, I forgot they put those things in there." Stroking his chin, mumbling to himself, Cookie walked back into the kitchen to search for his phone. "Where did I put that thing?" Finally, he said, "Oh, here it is."

Wayne was ready for Cookie, standing before him at the counter. The four strong beers were taking their toll on Wayne. He swayed as he held onto the counter.

The geisha tattoo was fully displayed, and she indeed was a remarkable piece of work. A long red gown clung provocatively to her sensual body. The geisha's eyes were dusted with a searing red eyeshadow and lined with kohl. She held a skull by its black ponytail, the empty eye sockets devoid of life. A gray tongue protruded from the open mouth, making the skull look fiendish. In her other hand, the geisha proudly held a Samurai sword. Wayne allowed Cookie to take several pictures.

Wayne's arm gave way, and he almost fell over but recovered quickly, sitting back on his stool. Slurring his words, he asked, "Did you get enough pictures there, Mr. Cookie?"

"I sure did. Thanks!" Cookie ambled toward the back, checking the new pictures on his phone. Loudly, he said, "You are one lucky son of a bitch to get a tat like that. I'm feeling a little horny!"

Wayne burst out laughing, spraying spittle over his empty plate. He hadn't expected that kind of a reaction from the old geezer.

Cookie hid the phone in the kitchen and walked back out. "Hey, Levi will definitely appreciate this. What else can I get ya?" Cookie leaned forward onto the counter with his arms extended on either side but pulled back when he smelled the man's strong cologne. Cookie nonchalantly pinched his nose, rubbing it.

Wayne stood up from his stool and said, "Nothin'. Full." Sweeping his arm wide, he tipped just a little, but he was able to say, "You make a mean breakfast."

Cookie stuck out his hand and said, "Thank you, my friend. Be safe and have a good trip."

Wayne shook Cookie's hand and made a feeble attempt to reach for his wallet. "Here, let me get this."

"Nope, I told you, I do not charge our military boys or girls." Cookie crossed his arms firmly, taking a stand.

Wayne swayed and said, "Thanks." A huge burp rolled out of Wayne as he waved good-bye. Stumbling on the threshold, he proceeded down the steps, missing the last one but quickly recovering. Cookie watched Wayne get into a black minivan, which looked like Carl's. He noticed the one white-side wall tire on the rear passenger side. He trembled. It most definitely was his brother's.

Trying not to be obvious, Cookie cleaned up the counter and stacked the dishes, as he kept an eye on the van. Slowly making his way to the front with a wet dishcloth, he began wiping down a table near the window, sneaking a peek at the vehicle as the stranger bumped over the curb, missing the driveway completely. Cookie waved good-bye with his wet rag, memorizing the license plate, MDR 643, noting the van had turned east, not west, toward the motels in Minot.

Cookie casually began to mosey around the café, picking up garbage. Passing the front door, he locked it, not wanting the stranger to double back and surprise him. Cookie ambled back toward the kitchen.

Once inside the kitchen, he ducked below the pass-through, turned to the back door, and locked it too. He slipped into his windowless office and locked himself in. He let out a breath he didn't realize he'd been holding. He pulled out his gun from the top desk drawer, checked it, and laid it close by on his desk.

His hands shook as he tried to dial the black desk phone calling Carl's home number, but it just rang and rang. He didn't dare dial his brother's cell phone number, fearing that the stranger might have that too.

How was he going to get a hold of Carl? He thought, Miles. Cookie dialed Miles's cell phone, and someone picked up the call but disconnected it just as quickly.

Hanging up the phone, he swore, "Damn!" Suddenly, the deafening ring of the black telephone scared the crap out of him. He grabbed the receiver and said, "Hello?"

With his irritating sing-song voice, Miles said, "Hey, sorry I hung up on you. They don't want us to use cell phones here. I'm outside now. How are you?"

"Me? How am I? Miles, I'm calling to find out how Carl is!"

Miles went silent for a sec and asked, "How'd you know about Carl? We just got here."

"Where?"

"The hospital."

"Why?"

Miles sounded exasperated. "Cookie, I thought that's why you were calling. Then why are you calling?"

Pete, Cookie's given name, was getting more agitated. Miles was the only one, besides customers, who called him Cookie. "I'm at the café, and a guy walked in here wearing Carl's Korean War hat. The one Carl never takes off."

"What kind of crazy son of a bitch is he?"

"Who, Miles, who, and is Carl okay? Tell me what's going on!"

Finally, Miles began explaining. "Some big guy cold-cocked Carl while he was launching his boat at Beatty Lake this morning. Carl just woke up a few hours ago and found himself in the dark, lying in the woods, kinda buried. He was smart enough to flash my windows at the cabin with a flashlight, you know, the Mach one that I bought him 'cause he always used that silly pink penlight that was his wife's?"

Pete made a fist and wished he could punch something. Between clenched teeth, he said overly sweet, "Go on."

Miles seemingly had turned away from his call with Pete and was carrying on a conversation with someone else. He came back and said, "What? Oh, yeah. So, he was flash-ing 'SOS' at my cabin windows. I found him at the boat launch, and his face is a mess. Whoever attacked him broke his eye socket. They're keeping him overnight in case he has a concussion, which wouldn't surprise me at all. The back of his head was split wide open. Can you believe they used glue instead of sewing it up? I guess they've been doing that a long time now. When Carl fell, he apparently hit his head on the cement launch. Did you know they finally got it cemented it just this spring? It should have been done years... Wait a minute, this means that dumbass is in Sawyer? I gotta go and tell the cops."

Pete had been holding his head with his free hand while the ex-soldier blabbered. Popping up, Pete said, "Miles, wait, wait! Give me a minute to process here. Is there a cop with Carl now?"

"No, oh cripes, do you think there should be? Hey, but I have a card from a pretty deputy who was out at Beatty Lake. You want her number?"

Pete grabbed a pen and wrote Deputy Belinda Jackson's info on a well-used blotter, a giant 1988 desk calendar. Once he got rid of Miles, he dialed her up.

chapter
seventeen

Monday, June 4, 11:00 p.m.

Two Streams, Minnesota

Hilde was hustling through Dignity Christian's emergency room, taking a shortcut to the parking lot to retrieve her car for her short drive home. Someone called out just before Hilde hit the door. From across the room, a big man in green plaid pajamas and bare feet lumbered toward her. The old guy had his hand stuck out halfway across the room, ready to shake hers.

She paused, trying not to look perturbed, but her exhaustion had to be showing on her face—no time for groupies wanting inside information on the murder today. Hilde stood unsmiling with both hands on her thick leather belt.

Miles stepped up to Hilde, towering over her by a full head, and they shook hands. "Hi, I'm sorry to bother you, but I should talk to you. I'm Miles Lundgren."

Hilde said quickly, "Certainly, go ahead." Miles lowered his booming voice to a loud whisper. "Um, we'd better talk privately. There's a family room just across the hall here."

Hilde groaned inwardly, then followed him. Looking down at the man's dirty feet, she shuddered, wondering how many billions of microorganisms were sticking to those monkey toes.

Miles opened the door for her, and Hilde stepped in. He plopped down on a chair next to the round table, but she remained standing, hoping to keep their conversation short.

"What may I help you with?"

Now behind closed doors, Miles was able to use his loud booming voice. "My friend, Carl Larson, went to go fish at Beatty Lake this afternoon but was coldcocked by this big guy. He's here being seen now for a broken eye socket and maybe a concussion. I just hung up from his brother, Cookie, I mean, Pete, who lives in Sawyer, North Dakota, and owns Cookie's Café. A stranger came in for a meal and was wearing Carl's hat from the Korean War. Pete knew something was wrong because Carl never takes that hat off."

Hilde was not processing why this should be important to her. "So?"

"The man that slugged Carl had big black bushy eyebrows and looked like the little girl with the dark hair that was in the evening edition of the newspaper. One of 'em that was... murdered. Waiting for the doctor, Carl had been trying to read the paper with his good eye and recognized the similarities."

Hilde's eyes went wide when it all came together. The fisherman had recognized Annabelle and connected to the man who had attacked him at Beatty Lake. Good grief! Hilde sat down, and her leg started jacking up and down while she asked Miles to begin again, without leaving anything out. Miles repeated the story as Hilde took notes.

He said, "I literally just got off the phone with Pete, so Carl doesn't know anything about what Pete told me."

Hilde stood up and said they were going back to the ER and see Carl. They went back and found the patient waiting inside one of the green-curtained rooms. Carl was trying to stay awake but continually jerked as he caught himself dozing off. He was glad his buddy had returned to entertain him. The chief deputy introduced herself and stood on the other side of the bed, looking very serious.

Hilde studied the poor man's face, with his left eye blackish purple and grossly distended. The dark blood colors had spilled down past his cheekbone. The skin was taut, filling his wrinkles and the white around his blue iris was Christmas red. The last detail was a trail of blood from the back of his neck, settling in his collar bone. The total look made her want to gag.

Hilde asked Carl, "Will you tell me exactly what happened today at the lake?" Carl wiggled into a more comfortable position and repeated the story exactly as he had relayed it to Officer Belinda.

Hilde then turned to Miles and asked, "When did you step into the picture?"

Miles took a stool that was lost under him and rolled closer to the hospital bed. He explained his arrival at the boat launch was around ten-ish and called the police around that time. Turning to Carl, Miles told him that his brother had called and relayed the story, Pete had told him about the stranger who had eaten at the café.

Carl let his head fall back, showing his exhaustion. "Winckowski was wearing my hat? I thought I had left it at home. Wow, I'm so glad the son of a bitch didn't hurt Pete. He's younger than me, and his head is harder, but still..."
Suddenly Carl burst into tears, holding both hands gently

over his face. Miles awkwardly patted Carl's shoulder, wiping at his own eyes. Just then, an older woman wearing a pink embroidered sweatshirt and matching sweatpants parted the green curtain. Miles gave Marta a weepy smile.

Marta marched over to Carl's bedside, stepping in front of where Miles sat, wrapping her arms around Carl and said, "It's going to be all right, honey." She continued patting and cooing until Carl stopped crying.

Presenting him with a Kleenex box, she took two steps back to stand next to her seated husband, who pulled his wife into a hug with his giant arms around her mid-section. It was clear the recent experience had shaken both men.

After such a long day, Hilde was ready to wail with them. Straightening her spine, she tried to maintain a professional air, knowing she could release her wobbly emotions at home. She snapped at her wrist.

Marta looked at Hilde and said, "Good to see you, sweetie."

Hilde stepped in for one of Marta's infamous warm hugs. "Marta, it's been too long." Nurse Lundgren had been a hospice nurse for Hilde's mother just a couple years back.

Hilde had gotten enough information for now, and Carl was in good hands. Leaving the group, the chief deputy headed back to the station.

Carl looked fondly over to Miles and Marta and, with a watery voice, said, "You two are such great people, and I don't know how I will ever repay you. But I'm going to try. This is as close to death as I have been since the war. I'm going to book the longest cruise on the Mississippi River for all of us, including Pete. I haven't spent any money since my sweet Pearl died." She had always wanted to go on that cruise, but her aneurysm made that dream impossible. "The trip will be on me, everything included. How 'bout it?"

Miles and Marta looked at each other and turned in tandem, and Miles said, "Hell, yes!"

Marta confirmed, "We're not getting any younger; fatter, but not younger! We're in!"

Carl unintentionally started laughing and quickly held his face while pursing his lips as his good eye twinkled. The doctor entered just then to finish Carl's exam. The Lundgrens' were walking through the curtain when they overheard Carl tell the doctor, "I'm buying a crystal white Cadillac CT6 when I get out of here!" The doctor shushed him while he listened to his heart. Carl tucked his lips in.

chapter
eighteen

Tuesday, June 5, 12:10 a.m.

Blanchard, Minnesota

"This is Deputy Jackson," Belinda said into her phone.

Hilde responded, "Hey, Belinda. Are you still out at Beatty Lake? Who else is with you?"

"Just, Paul."

"Okay, why don't you wrap it up and tell him to head home. I need you to come to the station, and we'll do the report together. We need to consolidate all the information we both have."

"Yes, ma'am. I should be there in about forty-five minutes."

"See you then."

Hilde walked over to the lunchroom to see the Pinpoint guys. Tapping lightly on the door, she walked in. Ron Moore stood, rubbing his left shoulder, and walked towards her. He had taken a bullet to his shoulder when he was a young cop with the Chicago Police Department. Ron recovered with eighty-five percent mobility but was placed on desk duty. Not pleased, he quit, moved to Minneapolis, accepting a job as a beat cop, and began law school. His wife refused to move from her beloved Chicago, and, to the delight of both parties, they divorced.

"Evenin', Hilde. I thought we might see you tonight. Have something new?"

Hilde said, "I do." Nodding hello to Rik, she saw Klink, his nose buried in three lit-up computer screens. Klink said, "Hilde, hi." That was his special greeting. Hilde smiled and returned the greeting. "Klink, hi."

Most of the time, Klink used a limited number of words when he had to communicate, but other times the brilliant man would ramble, trying to get everything out of his thought bank. Hilde had learned long ago not to ask complex personal questions such as, "How are you?" or "What do you think?" She rephrased her questions so they could be answered with either "yes" or "no." "Do you feel okay today?" "Do you think we should interview him?"

Hilde continued to Ron's desk and pulled out a chair for herself. Rik pulled his wheeled oxygen tank across the room and sat down to join the meeting adjusting the nasal cannula. Hilde wondered how Rik's remission from lung cancer was doing. His humor had not wavered, but his stamina had slipped, to everyone's dismay.

Klink was intentionally left out of all conversations with more than two people, preferring to receive detailed information in a written format. Hilde watched as Klink put on a sound-reducing headset.

Ron, always the consummate host, poured Hilde a coffee and presented her with a large baker box filled with donuts.

"Oh, just coffee, thanks. Let me update you with the latest, and then you can chime in as to what you know." Ron and Rik both nodded.

"We just had a sighting of Wayne in Sawyer, North Dakota, by a man who runs a café off of Highway Fifty-two, Cookie's Café."

Ron spoke up without emotion. "Know him. Pete Larson, a fishing buddy of mine. He was the one who named my fishing boat *Reel Justice*." He smiled obnoxiously.

Hilde tried to hide her surprise, but Ron literally knew everyone. He had flown to China once for a conference and had an overnight layover in Shanghai. While entertaining a high-profile client at a very exclusive restaurant, he bumped into an old classmate from the police academy who was the maître d'. It never ceased to amaze Hilde who Ron knew.

She licked her lips, with a look that said, "show-off."

Smiling, she wiggled in her seat and said, "Anyway, a stranger stopped at Cookie's Café, and Pete recognized his brother's hat the guy was wearing___

Ron cut in, "Carl Larson's."

"I want to tell the story," Hilde whined playfully.

Ron's eyes crinkled with delight as Rik took a deep breath, trying not to laugh.

Squirming in her chair, she said, "Anyway, the stranger was Wayne. Cookie fed and served him several strong beers, and Wayne got so looped that he let Pete take pictures of his tattoos, which even included full body shots!" Hilde sat back in her chair and let her grin take over.

Ron held his mouth with both hands trying to keep his laugh from bellowing out. It was useless. He let his laughter steamroll through the room. He ended with a giggle and admiring words. "Pete is one son of a bitch. I can't wait to hear the story direct from him."

Hilde smiled. She loved hearing Ron's donkey laugh. "Are you done now?"

Nodding, Ron grinned, locking his lips with an imaginary key.

Rik turned up his oxygen, trying to offset his own laughing, which had tapped his lungs.

"So, at this moment, we have Pete Larson being interviewed by the police in North Dakota, and tomorrow Pete will be driving here to see Carl in the hospital." Hilde looked at her watch. "Yikes, he'll be here in just a few hours. Cripes, that can't be all I was going to tell you. Damn you, Ron, you get me so flustered I forget what I was going to say!"

Ron mumbled, "Sorry," through a tiny crack in his locked lips. Hilde slapped him on his knee.

The chief deputy dropped her head, unable to concentrate while looking at Ron. "Okay, now, let me think. You know I should be in bed by now." She looked down at her hand, releasing a finger with each detail. "One: we're pretty sure Wayne is still driving Carl's black van. Two: he might be going west to a motel in Minot for some shut-eye, but Pete saw him heading east. We need to contact just the cheap hotels since Wayne hates parting with his money. Three: Wayne offered to pay cash for his meal at the diner, but Cookie wouldn't accept it, saying that no serviceman will ever pay a penny in his place. Cookie did see the huge roll of money that Wayne flashed. Four: Wayne has shaved off his hair and is now bald. To summarize: He is now bald, using only cash, no credit cards, heading east, and he's lying about being in the service. Again."

Hilde dropped the hand she had been counting on, looking up at the stained dropped ceiling, and continued, "Carl has a broken eye socket with a possible concussion, and I think that's all I have for you. You did receive the information about Carl's attack at Beatty Lake, right?"

Rik spoke up. "Yes, and we'll have the tire prints and fingerprints from that location in a few hours, but just from

Carl's description, we're pretty certain that it was Winckowski who assaulted him."

Just then, a text beeped on Hilde's phone. "One sec." She scrolled and found a text from Deputy Paul Nelson and read it out loud. "Carl Larson's boat and trailer are at Carl's house, tucked behind the garage." Silence followed.

Hilde looked at the boys with a quizzical look on her face and said, "Does that make any sense?"

She texted back to Paul, "Rec'd thx."

She looked from Ron to Rik, who were also clueless when Klink spoke up from across the room.

"Diverting attention."

All three said, "Who?"

Klink said, "Dah, Winckowski."

"Oh." All three shifted uncomfortably in their chairs, feeling foolish for their "dah" moment. Klink spoke to the threesome without turning around, "Wayne thought he had killed Carl, and buried him in the woods. Wayne didn't want Carl to be found too soon, so he put the boat and trailer back at Carl's house. No one would think to look for Carl at Beatty Lake. Winckowski doesn't know that Carl is alive. He hid his truck *near* Beatty Lake." Klink returned his attention to the screens before him.

Hilde made a note in her notebook to get someone searching the area around Beatty Lake for Wayne's truck.

Ron spoke up and said, "That reminds me. I have a realtor/friend, Captain Adams, who is fascinated with abandoned homes, buying and selling them. Captain purchases them for a dollar from the banks, which is fine with the banks because the houses are finally off their books. Captain does fix some of them, but mostly he sells them as is. The Captain's unique thing is that he uses them for photoshoots, writers' camps, séances, and haunted house adventures. Quite a forward thinker."

Hilde sat impressed with what people do as a business, but she felt stumped, not knowing Ron's point. "So?" Hilde said for the second time that night. Her exhaustion was rearing its tired head.

"Yeah, I guess I did just let that lie there. You know Highway Fifty-Two, the one that goes east 'n west in North Dakota? Well, Captain knows the locations of those abandoned houses better than anyone." Ron got up, motioning Hilde to follow him to a bulletin board with a colorful real estate map, a North Dakota cross-section.

"Captain sent over a map of all of the abandoned houses in that area. Of course, it comes with sales prices and such, but it's a great map. So, what I thought, what if Winckowski decides to travel west, he may be resting in one of these abandoned houses."

"Holy mackerel! This is great, but do you think Captain might have this kind of map for South Dakota and Minnesota, in case we need it?"

"He doesn't know if this type of map exists for any other state. I don't know if we need a Minnesota map, but before I get off track, look at the pins from Blanchard to Sawyer." Ron ran his finger west to Sawyer and said, "He was heading toward Montana, but Pete saw him turn east. This makes no sense. "

Hilde studied the map and said, "Unless Wayne was so drunk after Cookie's place that he turned the wrong way. And tagging on to what you just said, Ron, we need an expert in abandoned places in Minnesota. If Wayne finds out Annabelle is alive, he might come back for her. Do you have a source locally that knows where those abandoned homes are?"

Ron and Rik shook their heads. A resounding "Yes," came from Klink, who added, "Pinterest!"

Looking confused, they walked over to Klink's desk and looked at his screens. Photographs of the most beautiful and disgusting abandoned houses were displayed over all three monitors.

"Where were these taken?" Hilde asked.

"Minnesota. Patrice Whitehand, a professional photographer, wrote a coffee table book about abandoned houses." Never taking his eyes off the screens, he waved a pink 3M sticky note. Rik reached over and took it and said, "I'm on it."

Klink was highly educated but a strange duck. Roy Klinkheimer was single and a night owl, which explained his pasty features. Ron Moore and Klink both worked at the same Minneapolis police station, but the noisy caustic environment seemed to depress Klink. When Ron offered Klink a job at Pinpoint, Klink stood and began packing up his desk, as Klink gave Ron a momentary grin that had not been seen in a long time.

The back door slammed shut.

"Shoot," Hilde said as she heard Belinda come into the station. She hated to leave this discussion, but she'd have to catch up with them later. Hilde excused herself and headed back into her office to meet with Belinda.

Meanwhile, Rik checked his watch—almost one a.m.—and dialed the number for Patrice Whitehand, knowing full well he would be waking her up.

"Hello?" a sleepy woman croaked.

"Hello, this is Rik Zamora, retired detective, calling from Two Streams Police Station in Minnesota. Our private company, Pinpoint, is currently working with the police to track down a murder suspect who killed his family yesterday morning in Blanchard."

Rik heard her trying to cover the sound of her clearing her throat. She said, "I heard about it on the news. What could I possibly help you with?"

"We think the suspect may be hiding out in abandoned houses or barns, whatever is available. You have written a book on abandoned houses in Minnesota. Is there any chance that you have a map with the locations of those houses?"

Patrice threw off the bedclothes, wiped her face, and sat up. "I do. It's hanging on my wall in my office. Wait, are you asking to use it? "

"Yes, Ma'am, I am."

"Well, you are welcome to it, but I do need it back, detective."

"Where are you located?"

"I live in Superior, Wisconsin, maybe about an hour and a half southeast of Two Streams. Would you like me to deliver it? I know where you are. My cousin lives there." Rik pulled the phone off his ear and looked at it. He never expected someone to offer that kind of assistance.

"Ma'am, I can't tell you how grateful I would be if you would bring it here."

"Okay, no problem. I should be there in about one hour and thirty-five minutes. See you then."

Rik's eyes grew large, realizing she was coming *now*, and he shouted into the phone, "Watch out for deer!" but Patrice had already hung up.

Ron looked over at Rik and said, "What was that all about?"

"Patrice Whitehand is driving an hour and a half to deliver her Minnesota abandoned house locator map right now."

"Here?" Ron glanced at his watch.

"You bet!" Rik answered.

"No way!"

"Way."

"Way!" gleefully shouted Klink. Ron and Rik looked at Klink's back, assuming a smile was shining somewhere in that man.

chapter
nineteen

Tuesday, June 5, 12:10 a.m.

Two Streams, Minnesota

*H*ilde flipped on lights in the darkened police station and walked into her office with Belinda following her. Standing behind her desk, Hilde pulled a giant bag of burgers from a fast food restaurant and passed half the food and a drink to Belinda.

The young deputy accepted the lukewarm burger and a box of fries from Hilde while managing to open a paper napkin over her lap. Shuffling the paper off the burger, Belinda took a bite. "It seems like days since we had pizza," she mumbled. "I'm starving." Belinda slurped her pop. "Oh my gosh, this tastes so good. Thank you."

Hilde held off eating and began speaking. "Before we get started, I want you to know the chief called me and caught me up on the conversation that you had with him about Friechs. I'm really disappointed, but I trust Roger's instincts, and..." as Hilde pointed her finger at Belinda, "I'll be watching you like a hawk. Do not disappoint us."

Belinda crossed her heart with the burger and said, "I won't, Hilde. I will do my best to gain your trust again, and I'm terribly sorry." Belinda sighed and said, "In fact, it was time for it to come out. I haven't felt this relieved in months."

"Okay, let's get to work," Hilde said as she bit a huge chunk of her burger and continued. "I have a warm bed waiting for me. "You talked with Carl. Do you think we need to have him guarded?"

"Well, if we can keep the whole Beatty Lake thing from Muriel Friechs, the news won't be mentioning finding Carl, and Wayne will continue to assume that he killed him."

"Keeping it out of the paper, that's your job," Hilde directed. "Anytime there is any news, it will be your job to divert it away from Muriel or pass her untruths. They are keeping Carl in the hospital, and he's listed anonymously as Stewart Granger."

"Okay, but you do know that I have to give Friechs something. Otherwise, she'll get suspicious."

"Yes, but let me know what you'll be feeding her, okay? If Friechs happens to call me, I can back up your story. Now tell me everything you know about the attack on Carl Larson, and I'll do the same, and then we'll do the report together."

Belinda checked her phone and said, "This Pete Larson is amazing. He recognized his brother's hat and convinced Wayne that he knew a kid studying tattooing as a career. Wayne was too drunk to see anything wrong with having pictures taken of his tats so Pete could pass them on to the kid. Here, take a look at this."

Belinda turned her phone over to Hilde, who twittered, sat back, and said, "Wow, unbelievable." Her mind wandered. How stupid can one person be?

"Send them also to Pinpoint and Liza. They will send it out to their contacts in the five-state area."

Belinda fiddled with her phone, sending the photos to the additional recipients. She continued, "I'm sure Wayne was too drunk to drive, and hopefully, there was no one else on the road."

Shaking her head, Hilde said, "Nah, not many would be out on the roads at this hour, especially mid-week. Can you imagine having someone like Pete working for us would cut our job in half?"

"No shit, ma'am."

Finishing their meal and the report, they parted company in under thirty minutes. Hilde emailed Roger's information and told him she wouldn't be in until nine o'clock, knowing he would be at the station by seven o'clock. Tag teaming with Roger definitely had its advantages.

Shelly jutted out her chin as she popped out her hip, with a slim hand on top, and said, "Born in the US of A, and Southern by the grace of God."

The two old fogies twittered and flushed.

Carl started moving his tray, working his legs free from the covers, and said, "Why am I being wheeled up to another floor?"

"Well, I'm not supposed to tell you, but I'm gonna anyway. That man that attacked you is probably the same man that killed his family in Blanchard today. "

Carl stopped what he was doing and mumbled, "So it's true that the man who punched me is the father of the dead girl with the dark hair in the paper?"

Nodding, Shelly said, "Actually, sir, that little girl is alive and the only survivor. Please don't tell anyone. She's on another floor, being guarded. The police chief called and wants Tommy— sorry, Deputy Johnson—to ask you a few more questions. Would you do that for them, pretty please, with sugar on top?"

Carl began freeing his legs. "Yes, ma'am." Shelly rolled the chair over, easing it to the side of the bed.

Miles and Shelly both helped Carl into the chair and covered him with a blanket. Shelly turned back to a shelf where a generic box stood, lifted something blue out, and handed Miles a large pair of socks with grippers on the bottom. "You all shouldn't really be walking around this hospital in your bare tootsies," she reprimanded the man. "You'll catch yourself a death of a cold." Miles sat down, smiled up at her as he struggled to get the socks on.

Shelly started pushing the wheelchair out of the room when Miles popped up, still trying to get his sock on, and piped in, "I'd better tag along with y'all and help Carl, here. He's kinda poorly." Miles stood, and his face flushed when he realized he had suddenly picked up some version of a Southern accent.

Carl turned around fully, looked up at the blushing war vet, and said quietly, "Don't let Marta catch you—" But before Carl was able to finish, Miles waving off his friend's shaming with a "tut, tut, tut."

The two continued their bantering and rode the elevator with Shelly on their way to see Deputy Tommy.

Unloading off the elevator, Shelly wheeled Carl the short distance to Annabelle's room, where she stopped in front of Tommy. Rising, the deputy tipped his head and said to the pretty nurse, "Hey, Shelly."

Her brilliant smile delighted him. "Hey, back at ya." Shelly made introductions.

Displaying her palm to each, the nurse said, "This is Mr. Carl Larson and Mr. Miles Lundgren. I will be over at the nurses' station so you boys can talk." She wiggled her fingers at the smiling group as they all stared after her. Carl finally snapped his fingers at the other two, and the gaping stopped as the boys moved with intention.

Tommy said, "Miles, I'm going to ask you to sit right here and guard this door. I'm only wheeling Carl down to the window at the end of the hall so we can talk privately, okay?"

"Absolutely. You know, I am a war veteran."

Carl said, "Well, Miles, if things go bad, you can always sit on them."

"Oh, shut up, you blue-faced old fart."

"Gee whiz, Miles, is that the best you can do?"

Pointing to Annabelle's door, Tommy butted in and said, "Hey, hey, you two. There is a sleeping child in that room." The bickering men closed their traps.

Miles stuck his tongue out at the retreating wheelchair.

Tommy and Carl reached the end of the hallway, and the deputy secured the brakes on the wheelchair. Moving to face Carl, Tommy leaned back onto the marble windowsill with his ankles crossed and pulled out his phone.

Tommy flicked at the face of the phone for a moment, then raised his head. "I want to see if you recognize this picture." He turned the phone to Carl, which displayed a picture of a man standing and showing off his tattoos.

Carl leaned forward, turning his face to look closely at the picture with his good eye. He rubbed his eye and took another look at the image on the phone. Carl lurched forward and gasped, "Yes, that's him! He's the one that hit me!"

Tommy stood up and put a steady hand on the old guy's shoulder. He was growing agitated. In a calm voice, Tommy said, "Easy now."

Carl sat back into his chair, breathing heavily. "I'm okay; I just didn't think you would catch him this soon."

"Don't I wish? He's still on the run. Your brother took these pictures of him while he was in his café."

"*What?* How in the hell did he get those pictures?"

Tommy relayed a shortened version of the story about the drunken Winckowski and the picture-taking session.

"My gosh! Pete has balls as big as melons. He worked secretly for some USA covert organization years back. I still am not sure what he did," Carl admitted.

"Do you remember anything else, other than what you told the Chief Deputy Crosby or Deputy Jackson?"

Carl sat back and stared out at the darkened city through the window. "Yes. When I drove into the boat launch, there was a huge cream-colored Ford truck with straight pipes. It was gone when I came to."

"Do you remember the license number?"

"No, but it was Minnesota."

"Is there anything else you could recall?"

"I caught a whiff of strong cologne off of him, but other than that, nothing else."

Tommy stood and said, "This was excellent information, and I will pass it on immediately. Time to get you back."

Carl stared at Tommy, cleared his throat, and said, "I've been walking here on this beautiful earth, a hollowed-out man since my wife, Pearl died. That sucker-punch was a wake-up call from God. I need to start living again. It is, after all, the fourth quarter of my life."

Tommy snickered and said, "Not many people have a positive outlook after nearly being killed. Best of luck to you, Mr. Larson."

"Thank you, young man. You have a brilliant career."

Tommy wheeled him back down the hall. Miles stood up and saluted him. "No problems, sir."

Tommy chuckled, thinking he could have some fun times with these guys while also finding ways to improve his own life. "Goodnight, you two."

Tommy watched them leave. The old guys stopped at the nurses' station to chat with Shelly. Carl and Miles left smiling and jabbering away. Tommy was pleased when he saw Shelly scoot around the station and head his way.

Shelly never took her eyes off him. Stepping into his space she presented him with a cup of coffee and a massive slice of buttered banana bread. Tommy took it gratefully, smiling as he whispered, "Thank you."

She curtsied and sashayed her way back to the nurses' station. Tommy really liked watching her walk, coming or going.

chapter
twenty-one

Tuesday, June 5, 12:10 a.m.

Sawyer, North Dakota

*L*eaving Sawyer, Wayne was feeling good and sang at the top of his lungs to Garth Brooks' *Thunder Road*. His stomach was full; along with several strong beers were his just desserts. He was driving crazy, but who cared. Wayne caught the edge of a ditch and bumped over something, losing control momentarily. He accelerated his way through it and was back in the lane again.

When he left Cookie's, Wayne headed southeast, deciding against a motel. Instead, he drove to his favorite abandoned house north of Highway 200, just outside Lincoln Valley. He had discovered hundreds of deserted places during his travels across the Midwest while collecting from vending machines. You never knew what you would get when you walked into one of the decomposing homes: squatters, rats, or if the house had collapsed upon itself. It always was titillating walking in the first time.

Wayne had to backtrack quite a way to get to his familiar house, but time was on his side. Spending his hard-earned cash on motels just to clean up and sleep was something he hated to do. He saved a ton of money sleeping free.

He turned up onto the long, dark drive that wound up into the familiar farmyard. Wayne was just too smart, and the cops would never figure out where he was.

The memory of his vending machine business brought his mind up short. Some son of a bitch would eventually take over his deserted business and collect the money left in the machines. He swore, hitting the steering wheel several times. One moment of bad judgment, kills his family, and it cost him his business. It was the best job he ever had, giving the steering wheel another whack.

Reaching the farmhouse, Wayne pulled the van around the back of the barn and snugged it close to the side. The minivan was pretty well hidden among the tall weeds. Grabbing his flashlight and sleeping bag, he walked the familiar path to the house.

The back door had settled, keeping the critters out, but it was a pain to open. He forced it and heard the scurrying of small animal feet. Wayne stomped his way into the house, warning other animals or vagrants to vacate.

It was pitch black inside other than the beam from his flashlight, for which Wayne was grateful. This way, he couldn't see the water damage that bowed the ceilings. The litter the juvenile delinquents had left from their partying was disgusting. The old, stained wallpaper reminded him of his childhood homes, not good memories. Unfortunately, the dark did not keep out the stench of rot and mold.

He walked to the living room, dropped his sleeping bag on the floor, and reached to pull the couch over, pounding its back, hoping to dislodge the mice and their babies. Wayne couldn't see the dust, but he smelled it and sneezed several times in a row. He returned the old couch back onto its feet and fluffed the back cushions. Wayne untied his sleeping bag, draped it onto the sofa, and then squirreled his way inside and fell asleep instantly.

chapter
twenty-two

Tuesday, June 5, 12:10 a.m.

Sawyer, North Dakota

*F*ifteen-year-old Brendan laid in the ditch, moaning. His wrist hurt like hell. Afraid to release his grip on it, he looked down, trying to see the damage, but it was so frickin' dark he couldn't see anything. The kid stood, but immediately bent over, trying to catch his breath. Standing tall once more, he took an assessment and realized it was only his wrist that hurt, nothing else. But the ditch was deep, and he would have to crawl back up to the road with one hand. Trying again, Brendan fell back, re-injuring his wrist and intensifying the pain.

Laying on his back, he whimpered while uncontrolled tears rolled down the side of his face. Now mad at himself for crying, he was determined to try it again. Brendan stood until he had enough power and demanded his legs and feet to climb the slippery hill. Nearing the top, he dug his elbows into the wet grass and plopped to the pavement.

Heaving for breath, Brendan sat cross-legged, holding his aching wrist as his emotions wrestled for attention. He felt proud for getting himself out of that ditch but ashamed of what a mess he had made of a simple overnight at his friend's house. His best friend, Kevin, had invited Brendan to stay overnight. Then they would go to their baseball practice together first thing in the morning.

They had a great time playing their favorite video games. Kevin fell asleep on the basement couch around eleven, but Brendan was fully awake. He felt like such a wimp, having never stayed overnight with anyone before, something Kevin didn't know. Hopefully, Kevin would *never* find out.

Brendan sat alone in the Johnsons' basement with all the lights on. His mom texted him at 10:45 and told him she was going to bed. He almost asked her to come and get him, but he didn't want to wuss out in front of Kevin.

Brendan tried going to sleep on the cot that Mrs. Johnson had made up for him, but that didn't work. He played with his phone for a while, but sleep would not come. Brendan finally wrote Kevin a note:

"11:45 p.m. K— heading home on my bike, couldn't sleep, c you @ practice at 9. B"

Brendan carried his shoes up the stairs and crept out the front door. The door locked behind, not allowing a chance for him to change his mind. He stomped his feet into his unlaced black tennis shoes tucking the laces inside, ran to his bike, stood it upright, and hopped on his bike and headed home to his family's farm, just two miles over the dark country roads.

Minutes from his house, some crazy driver suddenly appeared, steering right for him. Brendan tried to swerve his bike out of the way but lost control as the car clipped his back tire, sending Brendan tumbling down into the ditch. He heard the distinct crunch of his bike being run over as the driver continued on his way.

Still sitting cross-legged on the side of the road, he expressed his pain. "Shit, shit, shit!!" Drawing air through his clenched teeth, he rocked back and forth. He was so mad and so hurt Brendan didn't know which emotion he should attend to.

Pulling in a deep breath, and with his legs still crossed, he hoisted himself into a standing position. Then the baseball player walked home.

Waking his mom meant waking the whole house, and it escalated into an uproar. Brendan's dad was screaming at him about how he almost got killed, and why didn't he just call them on the goddamn phone and get a ride home? His mother was shaking with the thoughts of "what ifs" while pulling him to the kitchen sink and running cold water over his expanding wrist as Brendan winced. His three younger siblings were up as well, adding tension to the already volatile mix of emotions.

His only thought was, *why didn't I just shut my eyes at Kevin's and go to sleep?* He made a promise to himself that he would sleep over at Kevin's again until he got used to it. *What a pain. Literally.*

Brendan's mom took him to the emergency room, leaving her husband to wrangle the other three back into bed. After the paperwork was finished, they sat and waited in the empty waiting room. The cops had been called, and they were coming to the hospital to interview Brendan.

A police officer from Sawyer walked in while Brendan was having his cast put on and asked several questions. The interview was short, to the point, and the cop left. Shortly after, Brendan waited outside the hospital with a navy-blue cast on his arm, feeling bad that he would miss baseball for several weeks. Exhaustion wove through him, and he let the worry go for another day. His mother drove up, and they went home.

At the same time, Deputy Stan Pickens received a text from a cop friend of his over in Sawyer. Stan immediately sent a group text to everyone that needed to know, and Ron read it aloud to his co-workers at Pinpoint: "msg fr Sawyer cop: so. of town after midnt boy knocked off his bike on Simmons Rd. by blk minivan, license plate xxx x43. boy okay, broken wrist, no baseball 6 wks +. could van be WW?"

Klink stood looking at the North Dakota map and said, "Killer heading south now."

chapter
twenty-three

Tuesday, June 5, 6:00 a.m.

Lincoln Valley, North Dakota

Winckowski awoke, yawning as he rolled onto his back with his tongue swollen and dried out. His meal from the night before wasn't sustaining, and he needed more but was unsure as to how to do that without exposing himself to the public again. One hundred thousand dollars sat in his cash bag, but he hated to use it. So far, he'd been smart avoiding the cops and needed his good luck to continue.

There was an old, torn newspaper lying on the floor. Wayne shimmied out of the sleeping bag and saw a quarter page advertisement for new camper trailers. Rolling his bag, he stopped to think, *a camper?* That certainly would solve a lot of problems. Finding a camper that was being sold privately meant Winckowski wouldn't need to use his driver's license, but if he went to a regular trailer lot, he would need to show his ID to make the purchase. He was unsure if the daily papers were carrying his photo as the family killer in their early morning editions, and he wasn't planning on taking any chances flashing his driver's license around. The picture on Carl Larson's license certainly didn't look like him. Gathering up his things, he walked outside, leaving the door open, and headed for the minivan.

When he had abandoned his truck in the crumbling barn, he forgot to take the beers from the back of his truck. He didn't like starting a day without a taste of yeasty foam.

Taking a leak before he hit the road, he figured the gas in the van would take him another two hundred miles. He had to disable the GPS on the old man's phone, but then Winckowski was left with no idea of where the closest gas station might be. North Dakota tended to get a little desolate, with vast distances between cafés and gas stations. The next time he got gas, he would, for sure, buy several gas cans and fill them up. That would stretch his need having to stop, which would decrease his chance for exposure.

Thinking back to the camper ad, he wondered if he should buy a used camper trailer or an RV. He had heard an RV averaged as low as four miles to a gallon, and that wouldn't do. He just couldn't see any advantages of buying a motorhome or a travel trailer, which could cost him around $4,000. Nope, not happening.

Snapping his fingers, he realized a cheaper and simpler solution: camping gear! This would allow him a respite at a campground or on the road. Sitting in the van, he tried to pull the plan together. Before he could buy camping gear, Wayne needed to eat, get something to drink, and find a new license plate for the minivan. He also would need a forged driver's license and passport, but he didn't know how to do that. Winckowski had heard that you could get anything in a sanctuary city, including brand new license plates and a passport. Wayne decided that Montana was out, and instead, he would head to the closest sanctuary city, anywhere in Colorado. He was uncomfortable traveling to a state he had never been to before, but it was so far the best idea. Shifting into gear, Wayne drove down the driveway, his destination south.

A dispatcher, just coming home from his shift at the police station, noticed a black van pulling away from his neighbor's abandoned house. He continued and drove up his driveway but turned his truck around to face down to the road. As soon as the black van drove past, the dispatcher followed him, keeping a reasonable distance between them.

Heading for the state highway, the van could have headed west, but instead, it continued south. The dispatcher got stuck between two semi-trailers, lost the tail, and took the next exit, and headed back home. Turning into his neighbor's yard, he checked the property finding the back door open and decided a call to the station chief was warranted.

chapter
twenty-four

Tuesday, June 5, 6:00 a.m.

Dignity Christian Hospital,
Two Streams, Minnesota

Annabelle woke with a gasp, the nightmare freshly wound around her. Swiveling her head, she found nothing to fear in the soft yellow hospital room. Kathy was asleep on her cot, facing the wall. Annabelle couldn't remember the latest nightmare, but her goosebumps didn't know that.

The little patient carefully leaned back onto her pillows, trying not to cause any undue pain to the cut on her back. The nurses had monkeyed with it the day before, but it was very sensitive. Annabelle didn't feel like her head was going to drop off her neck any longer, so that was good, but she still felt exhausted. The nightmares continued to be horrendous, and afterward, she struggled to fall back to sleep, feeling alone and afraid.

Rubbing the inside of her elbow, Annabelle rubbed the last of the stinky axle grease out of the folds. Looking over at Kathy, Annabelle wished she'd wake up but felt selfish. Last night Kathy had gotten up with Annabelle at all hours, calming her down from the night terrors.

Today the nurses were planning on taking her off soft food, which made Annabelle wonder if she would get hard food? That didn't sound right. Maybe they called it whole foods or non-soft foods? She'd have to ask Nurse Shelly.

Glancing at the stack of books someone had brought, she selected one that was the third in a series of nine about magic and warlocks. She started to read, only to have her mind drift off, thinking of the talk with Dr. Phalen last night. Annabelle was surprised to learn that there was a hole in her heart, but it made sense. The doctor had asked about her limitations as a child with such a severe condition.

She explained, "If I ran or got really excited, I would faint. But I learned how to control it."

Dr. Phalen said, "What did the doctors say when your parents brought you in because you were fainting during physical activity?"

"I never saw a doctor. This week is the first time I've ever seen a nurse. I would have come sooner if I had known they were so nice." Dr. Phalen returned her smile, but his eyes looked sad.

The doctor stood then, explaining to Annabelle that she would remain in the hospital for a long time due to the wound on her back. Dr. Phalen was pleased with the repair of her heart but concerned with the seriousness of the injury and worried about infection, which could delay her heart's healing. Secretly, he had decided not to allow that sweet little orphan to be released until he was assured, she would be going to a good home. Until the doctor ran out of excuses, his patient would remain in the hospital.

Continuing to hope that Kathy would wake up soon, Annabelle heard the nurses talking outside her room. "You know the psychologist, Dr. Dill? Well, he'll be counseling the little girl from the murders; you know the one? From the Winckowski killings? He specializes in dealing with children or adults that have experienced trauma."

Then the other one said, "Glad to hear that. I feel so sorry for the little thing, being all alone now. Hey, speaking of, I think something is going on with Dr. Dill and Kathy Cleveland, the social worker. I think they have a thing going on." The nurses' voices faded as they walked down the hall.

Annabelle wasn't sure what a psychologist was, but he must help people with problems if he was a doctor. Just then, Kathy rolled over and smiled at Annabelle. Without a greeting, Annabelle said quickly, "Can you help me to the bathroom, please, pretty please, Kathy?" Kathy ungracefully hopped off the low cot, and dropped to one knee while her other leg splayed away behind her. Busting out laughing, the ordinarily quiet social worker tried futilely to get up, making her laugh even harder.

Annabelle would have laughed out loud if she didn't fear wetting the bed. Finally, Kathy got untangled and helped the little girl to the bathroom.

Annabelle was seated on the toilet, enjoying the flood of relief when she finally started giggling at the funny sight of Kathy falling out of bed. Standing outside the closed door, the social worker listened to the giggling, and started laughing along with her.

Once Annabelle was situated back in bed waiting for breakfast, Kathy left the room for a few minutes to make some phone calls. Annabelle thought about how comfortable being with Kathy was and how quickly she had learned to trust her.

chapter
twenty-five

Tuesday, June 5, after breakfast

Dignity Christian Hospital,
Two Streams, Minnesota

Kathy and Annabelle were playing cards when Dr. Joseph Dill entered the room. Annabelle noticed Kathy look up to the tall man, as her face flushed and her smile went wide.

Dr. Dill's own smile widened, meeting her eyes. He then turned his attention to Annabelle, who seemed a little fearful, as the doctor was just as big as her dad. Annabelle studied the tall man, thinking he must have been a football player, with his broad, sloping shoulders and huge chest. His cheek held a slice of a scar that dimpled when he smiled. A warmth exuded about him that his size could not hide.

"Good morning," he said in greeting. "I'm Dr. Joe Dill or Dr. Joe." He took Annabelle's hand softly into both of his giant hands and lightly shook it. Annabelle still did not smile.

Kathy excused herself. Annabelle looked up to the tall man, seeing his eyes crinkle whenever he smiled. Annabelle decided he was safe. Feeling her shoulders relax, she wiggled to loosen them further.

"How are you feeling this morning? I heard you have a wound on your back that is causing you some pain?"

Annabelle shrugged and said, "I've had worse."

Annabelle's answer did not surprise Dr. Joe. Researching Annabelle's past, he had found that one or both of the girl's parents had abused their children.

"I'm a doctor of psychology, and my job is to help kids talk out their feelings and try to help them understand their lives a little bit better," Dr. Joe said.

"What's that mean?"

Dr. Dill pulled over a chair, realizing he was towering over the small nine-year-old girl.

"The children I work with have had, maybe, a difficult time in school," he explained, "or with their brothers and sisters or with their parents. Or possibly they saw something terrible and were having nightmares."

Annabelle quickly looked to her lap, smoothing the wrinkles out of her blanket.

He continued, "I help to identify what is causing the nightmares and work with the children to try and help them get a good night's sleep."

Annabelle didn't look at him but nodded her head.

"Would you mind if I got you a wheelchair so we could go down to the sunroom? It's a beautiful day, and it will feel like we're outside."

"Sure." She nodded.

"Would you like me to take your orange juice and toast along? Then you can finish it in there."

"Yes, please."

Dr. Dill stepped outside the room and rolled in a kid's sized wheelchair. Shelly was right behind him, dancing around the big man to help Annabelle get out of bed and settle her into the wheelchair. She attached an IV pole to the wheelchair, and Dr. Dill placed a tray onto Annabelle's lap with her leftover breakfast and started for the sunroom.

Annabelle waved at Shelly and said, "Bye!"

Shelly stood with a big smile, and her arms crossed and said, "See ya later, alligator."

Dr. Joe pushed the wheelchair, slumping to reach the short handles and allowing Annabelle to hear him. Walking down the hall, Dr. Joe said, "My dad was no cook, but when our family would go to our little cabin on Lake Waboose, he would always make us breakfast. It was orange juice, bananas, and his specialty, cabin toast."

"What's that?"

"Well, it's the *best* damn toast I have ever had! Sorry. The best *darn* toast. My dad would toast almost a whole loaf of white bread slathered with real butter, then spread each piece thick with peanut butter and spoonfuls of Mom's homemade jelly or jam. It was a towering pyramid of toast, and all for us, me, my two brothers and Janet, my sister. Dad always sliced off the crust for our persnickety Janet.

"He would set it down on the picnic table out on the deck so we could see the lake. I remember how beautiful it was with the variety of colored jams and jellies covering the thick gobs of peanut butter. It is still the best PB&J I have ever had."

"Gosh, it sounds so good." Annabelle was salivating. What a cool dad to have.

Dr. Joe found a quiet, bright corner in the solarium, and he positioned her chair facing the large window, which was outlined in floral stained glass. The stippling colors of the sun danced around the room. Dr. Joe closed the door, and they were alone.

Dr. Dill sat down in a big comfortable chair facing her and pulled out a notebook with an attached pen.

"I'm terribly sorry for the loss of your family yesterday." His eyes softened as his brows dropped, causing the single crease on his forehead to appear. He looked directly into Annabelle's eyes.

Her exhaustion showing, she turned and looked away. Her prickly emotions were colliding. Annabelle couldn't identify which emotions were bothering her, but she knew she was mad. She then realized when Dr. Joe said, "loss of your family," she immediately felt his callousness in referring to the brutal murder of her entire family.

Gripping the armrest, she leaned forward, close enough to smell the clean scent of his soap. Looking up to the doctor with her eyes livid, her voice shallow, the little girl said, "My family was murdered. They did not die of old age, were not lost and it's mean for you to act as if they did."

Taken aback by her bluntness, Dr. Joe realized he had been fooled by her small stature. Annabelle Winckowski was much more mature than he had given her credit. Looking down at the floor, the doctor refreshed his style of speaking. When his head came up, his eyes told her the truth.

"I am deeply sorry for offending you. It was unintentional, but you were right, I was careless with minimizing the manner of your family's death. Never, ever will I be reckless in that way again with you or anyone else."

She was surprised that a man would apologize to a kid, since no man had ever apologized to her, especially not her father. Dr. Joe's apology felt good and she accepted it with grace. Swiping at her tears, she said, "That's okay. I'm kinda touchy today. I didn't sleep very well last night.

Nightmares." Giving a small shrug, she took a sip of juice and sat back.

He responded, "I believe those nightmares are in response to what you went through yesterday. But first, you and I need to figure out how we can respectfully discuss the murder of your family."

Immediately, upon hearing the word *murder* her eyes teared up again. Looking into Dr. Joe's, she thought about what he had said. Would she ever be able to talk about how Wayne killed her family without the sensation of her body parts dropping off one by one? Nausea swam through her stomach.

Loneliness for her family was tangled up with all of those other emotions. It scared Annabelle to think of a future. Would her home be an orphanage, like in the movie *Annie*? Annabelle had had a home. Not a good home, but when Wayne was gone, her family had loved her unconditionally, as she did them. It made up for a lot. Could she ever expect that kind of love again? Or safety? Lips trembling, she took a bite of cold toast, giving them something else to do.

Dr. Joe and Annabelle cautiously discussed the question of how to approach the subject of the murder. An idea came to him. Looking off toward a window before turning back to Annabelle, he said, "The dawn each morning is also called aurora." He took his phone from his hip pocket and tapped it with his wiener-sized fingers, bringing up a dictionary app and said, "Aurora is described this way: 'an atmospheric phenomenon consisting of bands, curtains, or streamers of light, usually green, red, or yellow, that move across the sky in polar regions. It is caused by collisions between air molecules and charged sun particles that are trapped in the earth's magnetic field.'"

He continued, "In other words, dawn is described as a charged collision that had been trapped but burst into beautiful colors? You and your family were trapped in your home by a mad man who sent your family to Heaven, and they became vibrant angels. How would you feel about referring to the murders or the day of the murders as an aurora?"

Her dewy eyes softened as she sat silently, processing, then she nodded. Last year she and Harley had snuck out of the house very late one summer night to get away from the sounds of their parents fighting. They laid on their backs, breathing hard from the run, and saw the sky lit up with beautiful floating colors of neon green, purple and blue. It was their first time seeing the Aurora Borealis.

Testing the word, Dr. Joe said, "Your father ran away after the Aurora. Each day begins with the dawn, an Aurora, a time to remember your family.

Annabelle loved the word. It might just work.

As the counseling session continued, Annabelle recalled so many memories of the killings but had not seen anything. Maybe she had been lucky. But it didn't stop her mind from creating the most horrific nightmares. Her nose held onto the stench of the burnt gunpowder and the odd, rusty tang of something else that she just couldn't place.

Annabelle's memories suddenly slipped into their conversation, interrupting Dr. Joe. He stopped talking, noticing her white knuckles gripping the arms of the wheelchair.

Staring off at the stained-glass window Annabelle stuttered, "I could hear them screaming... begging, and. . . and could smell the gunpowder. But I didn't. . . see them... shot." Annabelle looked away, allowing a moment to calm herself.

"I don't dream about what I didn't see. My nightmares are the sounds, with flashing lights that I don't recognize. I hear those noises as they move through my head. It scares me so bad. Is that why you're here, to help me stop hearing the sounds? Please?" Her tears tumbled down, dropping small wet drops onto her hospital gown, leaving ice cold spots.

Dr. Joe lightly touched her hand. "I will do whatever it takes to try to help you put all of that away," he promised. Sniffling, Annabelle used the tips of her fingertips to try to stem the flow of tears.

The doctor gave her a small square box of Kleenex. She tried to laugh, but it came out as a bark. Reading the side of the small box, she said, "You really think seventy-five Kleenexes are enough?"

Cocking his head, he patted his pants pocket, and in a conspiratorial way, said, "I have friends in high places. We'll find more." Then he winked.

Her face softened once more as she relaxed with her Dr. Joe.

Annabelle began feeling safe and liked having the sun streaming through the long windows warming her through and through.

Studying the big doctor, Annabelle realized he was one who never seemed to sit in one position for long as she observed his long legs crossed with his hands folded hanging off to other side of his lap. She appreciated his direct-ness, "What started the aurora?"

Her eyes twitched as her right shoulder, jerked back and forth. Annabelle's taut face showed anger as she recalled that day. Her momma knew that Wayne was full-on crazy after he had been drinking and sneaking pills all night, and he hadn't gone to sleep. No one had slept. They were awake and on guard, waiting.

Annabelle began, "I was the familys 'court jester' because I was dad's favorite. When he would get into one of his foul moods, I was there to make him laugh or distract him."

Dr. Dill asked, "How old were you when you took on this new role?"

"Six. I remember the day. Dad almost beat Momma to death. Then he packed his suitcase and went to work. It could have been a week or more before she could get out of bed. Not sure how long. Mattson was in charge, he was only ten, but he really took good care of Momma. Candy took care of us and did like everything else that needed to be done. Gail would run to the neighbors for food, and Harley went with her. I was the littlest and not sure what I could do.

"Us kids were scared that Momma might not get better. So, I started acting up, making everyone laugh, including momma. It helped us get through the hard times. When dad finally got home, I tried my new act on him, and he would laugh, and give me big hugs.

"Yesterday, dad's mood was worse than ever. It silenced everyone. Even our cat hid all day. Dad kept picking on Momma and starting fights. We were terrified for her, so we stayed close just in case she needed us.

"Before breakfast, I was standing in the kitchen with her. She was hoarse from Dad choking her during the night. We were all screaming seeing him squeezing Momma's neck, as she kicked and kicked. But Mattson stopped him. Out of nowhere, he held out a bottle of booze. Grabbing it, he knocked Mattson down, and rolled off of momma.

"It didn't help. Dad's mood just got worse as he kept on drinking. I don't know what time it was, but the sun had been up for a while. I was so tired. I couldn't believe dad was staying up so long.

"Momma whispered for me to go and see if I couldn't get him to agree to go to bed. I thought she was thinking crazy. How could I get him out of that mood he was in? I didn't want to let her down, but I couldn't take my eyes off of Momma as she rubbed her poor neck. It was red and purple. Her eyes were all watery and bloodshot. I felt so sorry for her, but I was so afraid of him.

"I told her no, but she pinched my arm and pushed me into the living room. I looked back, but she was shooing me away."

Wiggling in her chair, Annabelle slid a finger under her nose, rubbing it.

"In case things went bad, I checked out the room, and found the fastest escape route. I was also trying to think of something that would cheer dad up. I was at the back of the living room, watching him sit in his chair watching *The Ren & Stimpy Show*, laughing hysterically. The other kids were stationed around the room, keeping their eyes on him too.

"My mistake was walking between him and his TV. Dad screamed terrible words at me and kicked my tailbone with his boot. That really hurt. I ran to the back of the room when I saw Gail run to Momma, hiding behind her. Gail wasn't brave around dad, and she was always shaking or crying. Gail could never hide her fear, like the rest of us. Dad was especially mean around Gail, scaring her, and laughing at her.

"I looked over at Momma, and she tilted her head putting her hands on her hips, but she wasn't looking mad, more like afraid, and I knew she was counting on me."

Annabelle sat as tears rained onto her lap and said with a watery voice, "That was the last time I saw my Mother."

Annabelle paused and earnestly said, "I really did try. I went back again, but he jumped up after me so fast I didn't have time to get out of his way. Dad punched me in the stomach so hard, I flew across the room and hit my back against the windowsill. I was on my butt trying to catch my breath when I saw Dad standing over me. His eyes looked like swirl holes. He turned away from me, and walked toward the back of the house but he slipped and fell down but he got up again.

"I didn't even think. I blasted out the front door so fast and crawled under the front step to hide. Dad had gone to get the shotgun, but I didn't know that. Honest." Annabelle's face had paled, her gold freckles peeked out, as her eyes pleaded for Dr. Joe to believe her.

The doctor spoke, but his lips barely moved. "Why did you hide under the stoop?"

"He's never found me there before. This time I had trouble crawling under there because I had grown since I hid there the last time. The space was too small for me, and that's probably why I got stabbed by the nail."

Shuddering, Annabelle pawed at her watery eyes, annoyed that they were interfering with what she wanted to say.

"Dad had gone crazy, and I didn't know what he was going to do. I wanted to help, but my stomach hurt so bad, I had trouble breathing." The octaves in her voice rose significantly. Annabelle hung her head and said, "I should have done better to try to get him to go to bed. I couldn't save my family." Annabelle was now choking on tears, her face bright red. She grabbed a handful of tissues, covered her face, and sobbed.

After several moments Annabelle lifted her head, wiped her face, and blew her nose, throwing the wad into the trashcan near her wheelchair. Her face was blotchy and puffy, and she shuddered with each breath. She raised her glistening eyes to Dr. Joe, and they silently looked at each other. Slowly, Annabelle's shuddering evaporated.

Dr. Joe looked out the window and then turned back to the lost child. "You're right," he said. "There was no way a nine-year-old little girl could have saved her family. It was unfair of your momma to expect you to try to make her crazy, drunk husband un-drunk. It was an impossible task.

"Your momma was also terrified of Wayne. Her fear was so great that she asked her youngest daughter to save the family. Something she couldn't do herself. She knew you were courageous. You tried *twice*." Dr. Joe raised two fingers. "But your dad was violently drunk and doped up on pills. You saw the danger in his eyes. Because of your great instincts, you took that extra nanosecond to hide. Your family did not see his satanic eyes, so they were surprised by his actions. I repeat, you saw his eyes as dangerous swirl holes, giving you that one nanosecond of time, allowing you to save your life. You had already done all you could do."

Dr. Joe's words seeped into Annabelle's head, and understanding processed slowly. Sorrow showed on Annabelle's face as she slumped further down in the wheelchair. Silence overcame her as his words slowly made sense. She did try, did show courage, and now felt sad for her mother, knowing she, too, had tried to save them. She never expected things to go the way they did. None of them did.

Annabelle felt relief as the anger at her momma dissolved, wishing she could have seen her one more time. A quick touch of memory of all those wonderful hugs her mother had given her, warm and tight, always warm and tight.

Exhaustion was deeply etched on the little girl's face. The first session had gone long, and Dr. Joe called it a day, wheeling Annabelle back to her room in silence. When they reached the side of the hospital bed, Annabelle climbed in, facing the opposite wall. Dr. Joe untangled the IV pole tubes, reattached it to the stand and gently covered her. Annabelle pulled the blankets up over her head. He touched her shoulder lightly and left the room. Dr. Joseph Dill stopped by the nurses' station and instructed them that Annabelle was not to be disturbed. She was sleeping.

chapter
twenty-six

Tuesday, June 5, late afternoon

Dignity Christian Hospital,
Two Streams, Minnesota

Annabelle had slept through lunch without nightmares. The session with Dr. Joe seemed to have changed her in some way. Having had a late lunch, she felt her stomach growling again when the aroma of dinner wafted down the corridor. The bed felt comfortable, and she wiggled further down into her pillows.

Checking the wall clock, she sighed seeing that it was nearly dinnertime. Shelly popped in and said, "Hey, honeybunch, you up for a visitor?"

"Sure, who is it?"

"Oh, you don't know her. She's a local gal. I'll bring her in."

Annabelle sat stumped but anxious for visitors.

Shelly opened the door and kept looking down. Annabelle stretched her neck but couldn't see who was coming in.

"Up," Shelly commanded, and a pure white West Highland terrier jumped up onto Annabelle's bed and sat down. The little dog cocked her head, and her black eyes drilled straight into Annabelle's soul. Her silky fur was curly, and her ears pointed straight up so Annabelle could see the pink inside. Always at attention, the dog's tail stood straight up. The small dog seemed to be smiling, showing her teeth.

Shelly introduced the dog to Annabelle. "This is Sally. She's our hospital pet and has been sniffing at your door since you came in yesterday."

Annabelle's face lit up with sheer joy. "Ohhhh, how cute." Softly she coached, "Come here, Sally, come on." Sally laid down, stretching her body to its full length, and crawled into Annabelle's arms.

"Careful." Shelly wagged her finger at the little dog.

Sally looked back at Shelly then dropped her head into Annabelle's lap.

The nurse continued, "Sally has been trained to be careful with patients. She is very loving and loves to be petted. So, you two do your thing, and I'll go check on your dinner, hon." Shelly, smiled, and walked out the door.

Annabelle curled into Sally and loved the feel and sweet scent of her fur. The dog licked her hand with enthusiasm and when the door clicked closed, Sally sat up, looked over her shoulder, and quickly stood up putting her paws on Annabelle's shoulders, licking her face all over. Erupting into giggles Annabelle pulled Sally into her chest, and hugged.

Still smiling, Annabelle reached for a tissue and wiped off the unexpected tears. She had been feeling so sad, never realizing that she could feel happy again. But here it was, just a tickle.

Leaning back into her pillows, Annabelle held Sally like an infant and talked baby talk to the dog, who seemed to enjoy the conversation, as her tongue lolled out of her mouth. Sally stuck her cold black nose into Annabelle's armpit making the little girl squeal.

Sally seemed to have a plan as she jumped down to the floor, flew back up to the bed, and turned in circles three times in front of Annabelle. Just then, Shelly walked in and said, "No walk." Grinning, Shelly looked over to Annabelle and said, "Sally circles three times when she wants a walk, and that's tomorrow when we get you walking on down the hall, and Sally, you are invited.

"I'll bring in your dinner, Miss Annabelle," Shelly passed over a pan of soapy water and said, "Please wash your hands, and here's a towel too. I'll take Sally back to her owner and have this little princess back here tomorrow morning around seven o'clock.

"Down!" Shelly commanded, and the Westie did as she was told.

Prancing towards the door the white dog stopped when Annabelle called, "Bye, Sally."

Sally looked back at Annabelle, twitched her tail, and walked out to the corridor.

Annabelle ate her dinner, pausing from chewing and thinking of that friendly police chief Roger Jorgenson, who had stopped by earlier in the day. She hadn't known Dr. Dill had asked that all visitors be kept away, but of course, the chief hadn't been turned away. Roger asked her a laundry list of questions, some quite uncomfortable.

When Roger first came into the room, he acted surprised, as if he didn't know her. Annabelle quickly realized the last time he had seen her; she had been naked, covered in grease. Waving to him, she said, "Hi, Roger, it's me, Annabelle!"

The chief chuckled, looking at the little girl with the deep dark circles under her eyes, which didn't distract from her striking beauty. The sun shining through the window picked up the red in her dark hair, which seemed to be several feet long.

Walking to the side of the bed, he asked her how she was doing.

"Good, and you?"

Roger smiled and said, "Just fine, now that I see you looking clean and not smelling of dead dinosaurs."

A shy smile crept out from underneath her lashes.

The chief cautiously interviewed the lone survivor. "I spoke with Dr. Dill, and he explained how we are to use the word "aurora." You okay with that?"

Annabelle jerked a nod, knowing those questions would bring those memories from yesterday. "Does anyone else know how to use the shotgun that was used during the Aurora? Or was anyone else besides your family inside the house?"

"No."

"Why was your family inside and you outside?"

"Dad had hurt me, and his eyes got all scary looking. When he turned away, I ran outside and hid under the steps."

"Did you see anything?"

Shaking her head, her eyes began to leak. She said, "I should have gone back into the house, but I couldn't. I couldn't."

"Annabelle, you are so fortunate that you did not go back into that house. It sounds like your dad had gone crazy, and there really was nothing that you could have done. Truly. Can you tell me how many shots were fired inside the house?"

"Four. I had heard dad re-loading, and that's when I ran to the garage. I heard the fifth when I was in there." She paused, trying to breathe through the heaviness in his chest, thinking of her loss of Harley. "Then he killed a raccoon in the garage, so that is six shots."

Roger's head twitched, reacting to the fact that Winckowski had re-loaded. The chief washed his face with his hands, trying to get his face back to neutral.

"Apparently, your dad was looking for you in the garage, but he never found you. That was the perfect hiding space. Good girl. Do you have any idea as to where your dad might have gone?"

Wiping her face with a Kleenex, she shook her head and said, "He'd go drinking at the bar in town lots of time. I really don't know where he went."

"Well, thank you, Anna…"

"Oh, wait. I think Dad took his cash bag. It has lots of money in it. He walked fast past the garage when he was packing the truck and was gone for a long time. Then when he came back, he walked slower. He would always hide it somewhere in the back buildings."

Annabelle answered the questions as best she could. She shuddered, thinking he might come back to kill her. Not wanting to ask that question, she skipped to a different one: "Are you taking care of the funerals?"

Caught off-guard, Roger told her he would find out who was doing the planning.

The questioning ended, and he stood up, giving her hand a pat. "Keep getting better. Do you need anything?"

"No, thank you."

Roger felt the sadness and hated to leave. He patted Annabelle's hand again and said, "Well, I'd better get going. We haven't found your dad yet, but you won't need a security guard anymore when we do. For now, we'll have Jesús guarding during the day, and Earl will be on watch at night.

Plus, another guard will fill in those other hours." Turning to leave, Roger turned back when she spoke up.

"Can I ask you something?"

"Sure."

Annabelle paused, turning red, and finally blurted out, "What do you have in all those pockets?"

Roger chuckled and placed his hat on the seat of a chair. He started opening his shirt pocket and took out a pack of toothpicks, a pen, three business cards, and his cheaters. He continued going through his pockets, placing all of the treasures on top of the white blanket so Annabelle could pick them up for inspection. Leaving his gun in his holster, Roger held his arms out and said, "I'm empty and weigh about twenty pounds less."

Her eyes twinkled with glee, and she said, "That was really fun."

Placing portions of the bounty into the rightful pocket, he finished and picked up his hat, bent down, giving the child a kiss on her head. He said good-bye and began to turn when Annabelle said, "Thank you for helping us at the house."

The word "us" stopped him in his tracks. Roger nodded and whispered, "You're welcome, and I'm glad you're doing better. Bye."

Once Roger was clear of the room, he called Liza and asked if she knew anything about the Winckowski's funeral arrangements. Fortunately, she was well aware. Liza had put herself in charge of organizing it with the townspeople. She had been in contact with Dr. Phalen, asking if Annabelle would be able to attend or not, and that was up in the air. Plans were in place, just no date yet, all dependent upon Annabelle's slow-moving recovery. No worries.

The chief let out a huge breath. Roger needed to remember this kind gesture when it came time for a raise for Liza.

His dispatcher has an incredible sense of what needed to be done and always seemed to find the time to do it.

Roger stopped at the nurses' station to speak to Nurse Nowicki. He reiterated his request for no visitors and then handed the supervisor his list of exceptions to the rule.

chapter
twenty-seven

Tuesday, June 5, 7:00 p.m.

Dignity Christian Hospital,
Two Streams, Minnesota

After dinner, Annabelle was dozing when she heard a *tap-tap* on her door. "Come in," she called.

It was Jesús, her daytime guard, who was working overtime. He peeked in and asked, "Jim and Doris Dickens are here to visit. Are you up to it?"

With a squeaky voice, she said, "Oh, yes, please!" Annabelle felt her exhaustion peel away in her excitement to see her favorite neighbors.

Annabelle immediately began crying when the couple entered and held her arms out to them. Rushing over, Doris hugged her gently, kissing the top of Annabelle's head. Jim stepped into the hug, wrapping his arms around both.

Feeling embarrassed for crying, Annabelle pulled back, trying to straighten her face out while hiccupping. "Sorry."

Doris took her hand, sat carefully on the bed, and stroked Annabelle's tangled mass of bed hair. "And may I ask why you are apologizing to us?"

Annabelle looked up from under her long, wet lashes and said, "I shouldn't be crying all the time. Especially since you were so nice to come and visit me." Annabelle's chest rose with each new hiccup, and her eyes strained against the fresh batch of tears. She squeezed Doris' hand. "I'm really, really glad to see you."

Holding Annabelle's hand, Doris mumbled to Jim, who was pulling handfuls of Kleenex from the box on the windowsill and passing them to the girls. They all wiped their eyes, smiling through their embarrassment.

Jim was clearing his throat as he pulled up a chair. Doris said, "I could not stand not seeing you one more minute, so we decided we would just show up."

Tasting salt on her lips, Annabelle took a drink of water, trying to get her voice back. "I'm really glad you did. Thank you for all you do for our family. We'll never forget it." Annabelle blinked, realizing she had used the plural pronoun, along with the present tense.

Doris didn't acknowledge the error. "You all have always blessed our lives, and we loved having you come over." She changed the subject and asked, "How are you feeling?"

"Better. Did you know I had a hole in my heart?" The couple looked at each other, surprised, and shook their heads. "So, I had surgery to fill it," Annabelle continued, "but I'm just fine. I'm eating a lot of food! I've never tried so many different kinds of food in all my life. It's delicious. Do you want me to see if I can get you some?"

Smiling, Doris said, "No, that's okay. We just had dinner a couple of hours ago."

Jim wanted to talk, so he cut in before his wife could continue. "I didn't think you could get any prettier. Hey, now, come here and let me count those freckles."

Annabelle leaned over to him, and he began to count, "One, two, three, four, five, and six! What the heck, you grew another freckle!"

Doris said, "Holy cow!"

Annabelle embraced the old, familiar comfort she had always gotten from Mr. and Mrs. Dickens.

They had brought in several shopping bags, and now Doris stood up to retrieve them.

"We hope you don't mind, Annabelle, but we went shopping, and all of these bags are for you."

Annabelle's eyes grew wide with questions. Bending her head to get a better view of all the bags, she began reading the stores' names on them. "You mean it's new stuff?"

Doris blinked and said, "Oh, yes, everything is all-new, right from the stores. Now, if something doesn't fit or you don't like it, you have to tell me because I can just return it to the store and get a different size or color."

Annabelle felt shy, not knowing how to act in this new circumstance of being given gifts. Even being alone with Mr. and Mrs. Dickens was different; she was always with her brothers and sisters.

Redirecting her thoughts, Annabelle felt the deepest gratitude for her kind neighbors. They piled bags and bags all around her on the bed, and the gifts were all for her. Annabelle had a quizzical look on her face.

Jim said to Annabelle, "Let 'er rip!"

Annabelle looked at him and said, "Really?"

"Yup."

Annabelle carefully moved up onto her knees with Doris helping her. Excitement built into a crescendo that she had never felt before, and she tore into the bags, excited to see what was inside.

She found books, puzzles, pants, tops, leggings, socks, ballet flats, pretty underwear, camisoles, tee shirts, shorts, jeans, shoes, a purse, jewelry, and pretty-smelling soap. Annabelle's eyes grew large as she looked at the stash and softly touched each piece. Exhausted, Annabelle leaned back onto her pillows. "Thank you."

Jim pulled another package from behind his back and said, "I bought this one for you." Jim set the box in her lap and lifted the lid, and Annabelle said, her voice trilling octaves higher, "Ohhhh, how cute!" She held the gift out at arm's length and then pulled it into her chest.

Jim said, "I figured you could use a sleeping buddy." Annabelle's response was a nod as she hugged her pink stuffed owl with its enormous dark blue eyes to her chest. She pulled it back out to look at the owl and said, "Hi, Ollie, short for Oliver Hardy. You know Laurel and Hardy? We used to watch their movies whenever we could."

Jim broke out in a huge smile, tickled that Annabelle liked the owl.

Then Jim lifted yet another box to her and said sternly, "This is *now* the last present." Grinning, Doris looked at her husband, so pleased to see the relief on his face now that he was able to see Annabelle.

The little girl cocked her head and said sassily, "Really, this is it?" as she swept her free hand across her bed, overflowing with beautiful items and torn packaging.

The couple hooted at Annabelle's cuteness, appreciating her joy. Jim played into it. "Yes, well, I'm getting tough with you, young lady." He tapped her nose with his finger.

The last present was another box, but flatter than the others. Peeking inside, the little girl found a mini iPad. Her mouth fell open as she looked up to Mr. Dickens, finding no words.

Annabelle crawled onto her knees to the sweet neighbors and hugged them. She kissed them both on their cheeks and choked out, "Thank you." She was overwhelmed with her new set of thrilling emotions, appreciating the soft feeling after the dark, sagging memories from yesterday.

Doris stood and helped Annabelle back onto her pillows, giving her a wad of Kleenexes as the empty box landed on the floor. Annabelle laughed. "I told Dr. Joe that there weren't enough boxes of Kleenexes for me, and I was right!"

Doris cleared her throat, said, "Now that we know you are doing better, we will be stopping by more often. Is there anything else we can get for you?" Jim had the mini iPad in his lap, setting it up with the Wi-Fi password.

Overcome, Annabelle said quietly without looking at her, "I would like to see you tomorrow if you're not busy."

Doris took Annabelle's hand, shaking it ever so slightly, "We're not too busy." Doris's smile wobbled, her eyes glistening, and then standing, she began folding the new clothes and putting them in the closet cubies. She crumpled some of the gift wraps and started tossing the ribbon when Annabelle put out her hand and said, "I'll do that. It's so pretty, I'd like to save some."

"Absolutely, my dear." Doris smoothed out the wrapping paper and folded it neatly.

Jim looked adoringly at his wife. The last couple of days had been very hard on them, especially on Doris. In their community, they were both known for their courage and strength in times of need. But this tragedy hit them incredibly hard, and they had not been able to hold themselves strong for others.

Jim and Doris had periodic bouts of tears and guilt over what they should have done to save the Winckowski family. Their only comfort was the memories of welcoming those sweet kids into their home when they were hungry. That little bit wasn't enough to save their lives, and that regret would leave their hearts tender for the rest of their lives.

Jim and Doris had left the Winckowski Farm before Annabelle emerged from the garage, so they hadn't known Annabelle had survived her father's rampage. It was only when Doris received a call from Roger that she found out that Annabelle was alive and recovering in the hospital.

Annabelle was showing her exhaustion, and it was time for them to leave. Doris and Jim stood up and gave her gentle hugs. Jim handed her a business card, explaining, "Annabelle, here is all of our contact information, and you are welcome to call, FaceTime, text, or email us at any time, day or night, with your iPad. Tomorrow, when we come by, I will show you even more, okay? But we mean it; you can contact us anytime. You've been through a lot, with…"

Annabelle shook her head as her face crumpled. Twisting her fingers, feeling nervous about what she was about to say, but it needed to be said. Looking down at the bed covers, she said, "Don't, please don't talk. Sorry, but I can't hear or say certain words." Annabelle drew a breath, looking up. "Dr. Dill helped me find a word that seems to work: "aurora." That's what yesterday was, an aurora. It just helps me." She tapped her chest, hoping they would understand.

As Doris covered her mouth, streams of tears cooled her flushed face. Jim's face was strained but he was able to choke out, "Sure, honey, of course.". He blew his nose into a Kleenex, having discovered a new box. "We are your *go-to*… friends." Jim gave her a weak smile while Doris' shoulders continued to heave.

Annabelle stared at Doris, who had moved in a chair next to Jim. Reaching for her IV pole, Annabelle clamored out of bed and climbed onto Mrs. Dickens's lap, squeezing her. Holding Annabelle, Doris crossed her leg, pulling up her knee, so they were body to body. Hugging her, Doris kissed the little girls' sweet-smelling neck.

A nurse popped in, announcing that visiting hours were officially over. Doris gently released the little girl and kissed her softly on the lips. Annabelle rose and went to Jim and wrapped her arms around his neck. Leaning down, Jim gently picked her up, snuggling like he had with his own daughter, and then kissed her soft head. Jim swept her up in his arms and settled her back onto the bed. Doris organized some of the gifts on the windowsill as Jim tucked Ollie back into Annabelle's arms and pulled the covers over her.

With both hands, Jim wiped his face up and down, said, "Okay, Mrs. Dickens, we have to let this little girl get her rest so she can get her strength back, although that was a stronger hug than I was expecting!" Jim winked at Annabelle. A cough-laugh popped out of Annabelle's mouth.

Annabelle waved and waved good-bye, trying to hold onto all of those beautiful feelings crisscrossing over her, not wanting them to slip away. The Dickens waved back at her through the open door as they waited for the elevator. Annabelle had to support her arm with her other hand to continue waving at them.

The elevator door opened, and just as they stepped in, Mrs. Dickens said, "Oh, shoot." Doris strode back out of the elevator as Jim scrambled to hold the closing doors open, stabbing at the elevator's control panel. Watching his wife sashay to the open doorway, Doris leaned in and simply said, "We have Kitty!"

Annabelle's mouth dropped open, but no sound came out. Then one word popped out: "How?"

Doris stood looking pleased as punch and continued. "Kitty walked over to our house and yowled at the back door until I opened it. She walked in like she owned the joint, went straight to the cold woodstove, ducked under it, curled into a circle, and fell asleep."

Mrs. Dickens gave a quick air kiss and ran to join Jim as Annabelle stared at the closed elevator doors. A slow smile began, and she whispered, "Kitty."

chapter
twenty-eight

Tuesday, June 5, 8:00 p.m.

Blanchard, Minnesota

*C*hief Deputy Hilde Crosby was at the Break it Open Bar trying to talk with Fabian and Blaze, friends of Wayne Winckowski. They were both tanked. The unshaven construction workers still wore their filthy work clothes and sported puffy red faces and rheumy eyes. Broken capillaries were apparent on the side of Fabian's nose, and Blaze had his on the tip of his bulbous nose. This was evidence that both were either heavy drinkers or alcoholics.

Hilde hoped she might get some of her questions answered about their good friend, the family killer. Currently, they were both trying their best to encourage Hilde to drink with them. She politely refused their offer, as well as Fabian's suggestion for a date.

Her phone rang, and excusing herself, she walked to a quieter area. "Hey, Chief, what's up?"

The chief passed the pleasantries and plainly stated his concern. "A police dispatcher from Lincoln Valley, South Dakota, had spotted a suspicious black van. He followed the van until a semi-trailer cut him off. I want to meet with Pinpoint and you as soon as possible."

"Will do, give me twenty minutes. I'm interviewing Dopey and Dopier at the Break it Open."

"Good luck with that." With a click of his tongue, Roger hung up.

Hilde returned to her high-top stool and asked the boys about Wayne's relationship with his now-deceased wife. The boys said they hadn't seen Letty in several years, but apparently, Letty used to occasionally go to the bar with Wayne to drink and party. That ended when Wayne didn't want Letty knowing about his affair with one of the local barflies.

"When Wayne would come here, who would he hang out with?"

Fabian said, "He doesn't have any friends in Blanchard."

With a quizzical look, Hilde asked, "I thought you two were his best friends?"

Fabian, a fleck smarter of the two idiots, said, "Well, not really. I mean, we'd get together and have a beer or two once in a while. I mean, like, we're not buds or anything."

Blaze stepped in to help. "We went fishing a lot with Wayne." Fabian looked at Blaze, shaking his head ever so slightly as if trying to remind Blaze that being friends with Winckowski was not a good thing.

Fabian jumped in and said, "Yeah, but we're not friends with him now that he killed his family, right?"

Blaze said, "Oh, yeah, right. That's probably why he's not here now. Winckowski meets us here every Tuesday and Thursday night and most Fridays or Saturdays too." Fabian

turned his stool around, facing Blaze, whose blinking eyelids seemed to be backpedaling. "What?" Blaze asked
innocently.

Hilde wasn't sure if they were born stupid or if their
drinking had meticulously disseminated most of their brain
cells.

"Where did you go fishing?"

In unison, the boys answered, "Beatty Lake."

Under her breath, Hilde said, "Of course."

Fabian said, "What?"

"Nothing, thank you." Hilde rose and walked out of the
bar, pulling her ringing phone out of her pocket.

"Hey, Tillie, how's my girl?" Hilde unlocked her squad
car, got in, slammed and locked the door, protecting herself
from the worst neighborhood in downtown Blanchard.

Hilde's daughter soberly responded, "Okay, I guess. I
didn't think it through when I signed up for summer classes.
I want to graduate early, but I'll be missing the most beautiful June Minnesota has ever had! What was I thinking? And
the classes are so intense!" Tillie sniffled and said, "I miss
you, Momma."

Hilde was surprised to hear her tough daughter crying
and felt the sting of tears behind her eyes. "Do you need
chocolate?"

Tillie giggled. "Yes, and I'm out. I haven't gotten to the
grocery store this week."

"Well, I am proud of you for taking these summer
courses, and I do know how you feel. I did those two sum-
mers myself, and it was awful, but graduating early was a
huge relief."

"I know, I'm just feeling whiny and lonely." Through the
phone, Hilde heard knocking. Tillie said, "Oops, Penny is
here; we're going to go have coffee. Love you to the moon…"

Hearing the silence of the disconnected phone, Hilde
softly whispered, "… and back." She was beaming, knowing

she was a good mother to her beautiful daughter, Matilda Anna Crosby. The freshman was currently majoring in the "juggles." Tillie had begun college majoring in meteorology but had immediately lost interest. So the freshman was now juggling her courses, trying to figure out what she really wanted for a career.

Hilde shifted into gear, driving back to her home in Two Streams feeling the warm glow for her daughter.

chapter
twenty-nine

Tuesday, June 5, 5:00 p.m.

Madra, South Dakota

W ayne looked down at his gas gauge, realizing the van was nearly out of gas. He pulled into the nearest filling station and went into the office.

"Afternoon." A young girl behind the counter greeted him with a stunning smile. "Sue" was embroidered on her gray-and-red sleeveless shirt. Sue's long, light brown hair was tucked behind her ears and fell behind her to unknown depths.

Wayne was struck with how similar the cashier looked to his twelve-year-old daughter Candy, who also had lovely, soft arms and a stunning smile. It made him mad that Candy never shared a smile with him. Candy was one unhappy kid, just like Letty. They were like two peas in a pod, never appreciative of what he had done for them.

Catching himself leering at the girl, Wayne returned her smile with one of his own stunning smiles. "Hi, I'm looking for gas cans," he said. "Do you sell them here?"

"Oh, sure. Follow me. The cans are in the back of the garage."

Wayne jumped in front of Sue and opened the door to the back of the dank garage. He followed her in, which gave him the perfect vantage point to enjoy Sue's slim features. Walking into the back, Sue showed him a stack of several sizes of red plastic gas cans. After he selected two five-gallon cans, Wayne and the cashier walked side-by-side back to the office, making small talk, mostly about his rodeo days.

Wayne pushed his way out the door, then stopped and said, "I'll be back in to settle up. Oh, say, do you happen to know where I could get some camping gear? It's a gift for a young man who has cancer, a friend of the family."

Eager to please, the teen pointed out the window to the road, giving him directions. "If you continue on Main Street about two blocks, you'll see a surplus store on the left, and across the street is a hardware store. They both have camping gear."

"Great!" Wayne said, and he left to pump his gas.

Sue pulled out the latest edition of the Madra newspaper and read the headline, "Mass Murderer Still at Large!" The article did not have any picture of the suspect but described him quite clearly: hazel eyes, bald, six foot five, broad shoulders, skull tattoos on his forearms, possibly wearing a green hat. She reread the description again, realizing it had to be the customer who was just talking with her. Sue remembered seeing the lower jaw of a skull tattoo just under his sleeve.

Wayne had finished pumping and was hanging up the gas hose. The girl saw that he was heading back inside to pay, so Sue threw the newspaper to the floor, trying to hide it, but it tangled between her feet. Standing stock-still, she tried to keep the crinkling of the paper quiet.

She gave Wayne a wobbly smile as he re-entered the office, handing her the cash. Sue had to count the twenties twice before making change, and as she passed it to him, the coins spilled to the floor. Unable to move, Wayne gave her a sympathetic smile and picked up the change.

Wayne never took his eyes off Sue, which gave her the creeps. Graciously thanking Sue, Wayne gave her a lascivious wink and left the office. Trembling, Sue watched as the giant man walked away. He was dressed in a white shirt, black pants adorned with a rodeo belt buckle. Hoisting the gas cans easily into the backend, Wayne secured them with bungee cords and slammed the rear doors. The teen stood, gripping the counter edge, afraid she was going to pee her pants.

After watching the van merge into traffic, she threw herself around the counter, locked the door, and ran down the hall to the toilet. Leaving the bathroom, she peeked around the doorway, checked the office, making sure he hadn't doubled back. Then she called her boss, left a message for him about the stranger and asked him to call the police.

Wayne quickly found the surplus store and bought a tent, a large cot, a cooler, a lantern, a coffee pot, matches, kerosene, a grill, and a camp chair. The tent was enormous, as he needed to accommodate his height. The cashier gave him a free South Dakota map for buying so much stuff. After loading the van, he grumbled, not wanting to get into the stifling car.

His stomach growled, and his headache began again. Getting to a grocery store was the next order of business. Pulling on his sunglasses, he looked around the parking lot for cops. Seeing none, he decided to get himself something to eat.

One block further was a large grocery and variety store, which was a gem. Wayne found a large cooler, a twenty-pound bag of ice, a case of water, lots of food, and a considerable quantity of liquor. Sauntering down an aisle, Wayne abruptly stopped by a stack of trashy magazines and added them to his overflowing cart. A pile of swimming trunks caught his eye, and he selected a red pair. His face relaxed with the thought that he was going to have himself a regular vacation.

Closing the door to the van after piling in the goods, Wayne felt relief at having his much-needed supplies. Sitting behind the steering wheel, he finished two caramel rolls, took a large pull from his quart of Kentucky bourbon, and continued eating beef jerky along with a bag of spicy tortilla chips. Taking a sip of coffee, Wayne began to feel like himself again. He peeked continually over his shoulder, checking out his new camping gear feeling excited about his plan to camp.

chapter thirty

Tuesday, June 5, 10:00 p.m.

East Elsewhere, South Dakota

*E*xhaustion was consuming Wayne even though he had napped in the afternoon on an old fire road. He had entered the small town of East Elsewhere and pulled in behind a closed business, needing to figure out just where he was.

Opening up the massive South Dakota paper map, Wayne used his penlight to see. Immediately pissed, he realized he had made a colossal mistake—these last several hours, he had driven southeast, not southwest toward Colorado. East Elsewhere, a small burg, sat barely inside the South Dakota border, hovering on being a Minnesota town if it was hit with a strong west wind. Totally distracted by buying all of his fun supplies in Madra and downing half the bourbon bottle, he wasn't conscious of where he was, or where he should go or what his plan was. Wayne threw the map to the floor.

Drumming his fingers on the steering wheel, he looked around for cops and turned on the van. Where would he find a campground to stay overnight without a state or federal park permit? Pulling the map from the floor, he looked at it again. Heading east toward Minnesota was an excellent way to avoid the cops that were on the hunt for him. They would never guess he would be heading into Minnesota, his home state. He needed to consider picking up Annabelle as the only witness and decide later what to do with her. He had considered making a run to Canada. It was risky, but he decided he didn't want to go to Colorado, a state he knew nothing about. Wayne dropped the van into gear and headed east.

Almost immediately, Wayne passed a very lit-up bar, with cars filling the parking lot. Making a U-turn, he pulled into the packed lot of William's Wild Will Bar. He snapped his fingers to the tune he could hear blaring inside. It was one of his favorites, "Lonesome On'ry and Mean," one of Waylon Jennings's best songs. The temptation was great, but he did not go in for a quick drink that he knew would put him on his ass.

Scanning the area, Wayne cautiously stepped out of the van, putting a screwdriver into his back pocket and carrying the penlight. Holding the penlight between his teeth, he squatted first in front and then in the back of Carl's minivan, unscrewing both license plates. Cautiously, he looked around for another set of plates to replace Carl's.

Wayne swapped out a set of Minnesota plates from an older model red Ford Explorer, JJJ 458, and attached them onto Carl's car. Wayne continued swapping out plates on several vehicles.

Poking his head up, he looked around, and feeling safe, he stood and went to the van. He left the parking lot, pretty pleased with his cleverness, hoping the cops would think it was kids switching the license plates, an old prank. As he drove away, Wayne was confident his plan would go unnoticed for a long, long time.

Heading farther east, Wayne slowed the van down when he found the campground he was looking for. Twenty miles back, Wayne had noticed a faded billboard advertising Chili Con Camp as the only campground in East Elsewhere. After eleven o'clock, he pulled into the shoddy campground, which was noisy but not full.

Winckowski buttoned his white shirt's long sleeves to cover the visible tats and added his reader glasses, leaving his hat off. Stepping into the hot and stuffy office, Wayne dinged the bell. Magically a young boy appeared with his hands in the pockets of his shorts, wearing no shirt. The kid was sleepy-eyed, with a slothful demeanor. The boy responded, "Yeah?"

Wayne said, "I need a tent campsite, a quiet place. I'm recovering from cancer treatments and need to rest." Wayne stroked his bald pate, emphasizing the chemo treatments that had taken his hair.

The kid barely looked at him and turned a sign-in tablet toward him. "Put down your car license number here, and your signature there."

Wayne signed in as Carl Larson, using a sloppy, unrecognizable signature, and hoping the kid would not ask for Carl's driver's license. He added the new license plate number JJJ 458 to the registration.

The kid said, "It's ten bucks a night. You wanna pay for a few nights?"

"Yeah, here's fifty, and I'll see how I'm feeling. Say, does that gas pump work out there?" Wayne was referring to the stand-alone gas tank that had seen better years.

"Yeah."

"Great, here's fifty more to fill the tank and two five-gallon cans."

The kid's eyes widened when he saw the enormous amount of cash. He counted it and slipped it into his pocket before he turned on the tank. The boy tore off a piece of adhesive tape and taped it to the backside of the parking permit. "Take this little green thing with your campsite number on it and tape it to the inside of your windshield. It will let my dad know you paid. The spot is thirty-seven, in the northwest corner of the campground. It's next to the creek, has a water spigot, and trees." The kid looked at Wayne without smiling, turned, and left. Wayne heard the *whoosh* of an overstuffed chair and the TV volume increasing.

Wayne left the hot office as sweat poured off of him.

Relieved, Wayne had pulled off his act of being a cancer patient. Happily, he hopped into the van, taped the permit on the inside of his windshield, drove to the gas pump, and filled up.

Driving to the northwest corner, he passed several well-worn pop-up tent trailers and some old, rusty RVs that appeared permanent if their flat tires were any indication.

The campsite thirty-seven was a welcome sight. The boy had described it correctly. Leaving his headlights on, Wayne unloaded his gear, set up the tent, and laid the sleeping bag onto the cot inside the enormous shelter. The cooler was loaded with food, beer, mix, and ice. A cardboard box was filled with several large bottles of hard liquor, which he set inside the tent, then went to check his cash, where the bag was still stuffed under the spare tire. Wayne grabbed his nine-millimeter handgun from beneath the driver's seat and slipped it inside his belt, undoing his shirttail, so it covered the weapon.

Before turning off the headlights, he built his campfire with cardboard and a few dry sticks. Sitting down into his new cloth camp chair, Wayne kicked off his boots, peeled off his damp socks, and from the ice chest sitting next to him pulled out a cold roadie, a twenty-five-ounce Foster's. The red and yellow flames of the campfire warmed his face while he listened to the rushing creek. Opening two cans of Spam and a jar of banana peppers, he started munching on them alternating with barbeque chips. A smile reached his eyes.

After quickly downing three Fosters, he felt the release of the weight from the past few days and promptly fell out of his chair. He managed to crawl into his tent but passed out on the plastic sheeting, unable to pull his feet inside. They protruded out of the flap while the mosquitos had a party with his fresh blood, and the campfire put itself out.

chapter
thirty-one

Tuesday, June 5, 11:30 p.m.

East Elsewhere, South Dakota

"Hello, is this the cops? I'm Lila. Just came out from having a few drinks, and somebody has stolen my license plates right off my car! Then they put on different ones, and I don't like those!" Lila wailed, "I want mine back!"

Dorothy, the East Elsewhere police dispatcher, rolled her eyes. Another senseless call for the police to attend to. Dorothy had been a dispatcher long enough to know this woman had way too much to drink.

Snidely, Dorothy replied, "Ma'am, how do you know those aren't your license plates?"

Lila pulled her phone away from her ear, looked at it confused, and then placed it back to her ear. "Because my license plate is customized with the initials of my three kids and their birth years, JJJ 458. They're dead now, so I need my license plates back right now!" Lila screeched. The mother of three dead children started crying.

Dorothy immediately felt guilty for getting impatient with this woman. "Ma'am, I will send an officer right over. Where are you located?"

Slurring her words, Lila managed, "William's Wilt… Wild Will Bar, three W's. I'll be in the parking lot. My car is a red Ford Explorer. 1999."

Dorothy asked, "Are you near your car, and can you read me the license plate number that is on there now?"

Lila stumbled around to the front of her car and put one hand on the hood, squatting slightly to see the plate. She read, "MDR 643."

Dorothy held her headset tightly to her ear and said, "Repeat that!"

Lila shouted out. "M D R 6 4 3! Can you hear me now?"

"Hold, please." The line went dead.

Lila was screaming into the phone. "No, no, no, do not put me on hold! You bitch!" Lila whipped the phone from her ear, stabbing her finger at the blurry red ball that seemed to be circling the screen. Finally she hit it, and the line disconnected.

Lila had already drunk plenty at the triple W and decided that maybe she should go have some coffee before the cops made her take a Breathalyzer. Staggering across the parking lot, Lila pushed her way through the splintered plywood door, back into the comfort of the deafening noise. Finding no one had taken her spot, she lifted herself onto the stool, threw her giant purse on the bar top, settled her arms, and ordered an Irish coffee, double shot.

The police dispatcher came back on the line, but the caller had hung up. "Dang!" She felt bad for losing the caller, but Dorothy had needed to double-check the license plate number that Lila had given her, verifying it against an all-points-bulletin they had received. The dispatcher remembered the van's plate number; it was just too easy: murder 643.

Dispatching Deputy Bart Towsley, the newest East Elsewhere rookie, to the William's Wild Will Bar, she first explained the man who had most likely switched the license plates on Lila's car was the one who had murdered his family yesterday morning in Blanchard, Minnesota.

"Be careful, Bart; he's armed," she said in warning.

"Will do. Over and out."

Dorothy's next call was to the Two Streams Police Department to advise them that their suspect may have been or could still be in East Elsewhere, South Dakota.

Deputy Towsley sat for two seconds in his squad car, digesting what the dispatcher had just told him. Turning on his lights, he tore out from behind a billboard-like a bat out of hell. His adrenaline kicked in, and the smile left his face.

Bart loved this part of being a cop, the adrenaline rush. Since he was five years old, he had been planning his career as a cop, had taken every class, read several detective books, watched every TV cop show, and had volunteered for every job related to police work.

After settling into his new job, he only after realized there was a lot of time waiting for the radio to crackle. Bart admitted to himself that he was just plain bored and had been thinking of leaving East Elsewhere, maybe moving to a bigger city, Minneapolis or Chicago, where there would be more action. He had a low tolerance for boredom.

Deputy Bart roared into the triple W's parking and found a group of men standing around their cars. Silencing the sirens, he walked over to the group and asked what was going on.

One thin man waved and said, "We just found several of our license plates have been taken off our cars and switched.

We've untangled a few and gotten some back to the rightful owners, but there are still some people in the bar that don't know they've been switched."

The deputy asked, "Who is Lila Emmons?"

The men looked at each other, then a thin man stepped closer to the officer and said, "She found her license plates were stolen and gave you guys a call. Lila's in there now, crying her eyes out. Years ago, our kids died in a freak accident, and her vanity plate pays homage to them.

"Lila didn't recover well from their deaths and took up drinking. It would really be a big help for Lila getting her plates back. She doesn't have much else to hold onto these days."

Bart replied, "I'll do all I can, but we are also looking for a mass murderer."

A murmur went through the crowd. The man being questioned said, "What? Wait, you mean the guy from Minnesota? Wink something? What's that got to do with anything here in East Elsewhere?"

"The license plate that was switched with Lila's was off a black van, and we're fairly certain it's from the car that Wayne Winckowski stole." Bart knew he had said too much, but maybe it would draw out some useful information for the case.

Out of the dark came a faint light from the tip of a cigarette, with a man behind it. Sauntering into the group, the guy had his lips pinched tight onto a dangling Marlboro, his left eye twitching against the irritating smoke. The Marlboro man said, "Say, are you here about someone fooling around with the cars?" Bart nodded.

The man removed his cigarette and tapped the ashes to the ground. "I came out to have a smoke, so I sat on a log just on the edge of the woods over there." The man pointed in the opposite direction of the bar. "I saw a big man popping up and down amongst the cars. The guy was in the shadows, so I couldn't tell what he looked like, but he was bald. The lights from the bar were shining off of the top of his head."

chapter
thirty-two

Tuesday, June 5, 11:50 p.m.

East Elsewhere, South Dakota

Deputy Towsley saw a crying woman sitting at the bar and assumed it was the woman who had called dispatch. Another woman was patting her back and consoling her. Bart took a stool on the other side of them. The second woman looked up at Bart, nodded, and walked to a table, joining a man who seemed to be waiting for her.

The bartender came over and gave the deputy a glass of water and then went back to the other end of the bar.

"Are you Lila Emmons?" Bart asked gently.

Lila nodded while wiping her nose on a red cocktail napkin. Quietly, he asked, "Will you please tell me what happened tonight?"

Lila had calmed down, and she figured the caffeine in the Irish coffee was settling her nerves. "I left the bar to go home, and I always look at my vanity license plate on my car before I get in. It doesn't look like a vanity plate, but it means an awful lot to me. It's JJJ 458; Jill was born in 1994, John born in 1995, and Jesse was born in 1998. "

Lila's voice quivered as she began to tell Bart the story. "One night, my husband and I went out to celebrate our anniversary, twelve years. We left the kids home with our neighbor's daughter, Terry, seventeen, and a great babysitter. They were all down in our basement, watching a kids' movie and eating popcorn. Apparently, the furnace was defective, and the kids died of carbon monoxide poisoning. Terry knew something was wrong and was finally able to reach a phone and called for help. Terry lived, but..." Lila shook her head and continued. "She almost didn't make it. But she's okay now, married, kids.

"My kids have been gone for years. I see people that have experienced similar tragedies, and they just keep on going, living their lives. I can't seem to."

Sorrow filled Bart's eyes. "Why do you have a Minnesota license plate? Are you visiting?"

Lila nodded again and squeaked, "Mom, my mom, she's dying. Diabetes. I'm staying at her place."

"Are the new plates that someone put onto your car Minnesota or South Dakota?"

"Minnesota."

"Will you show me your car, please?"

Lila nodded and lifted her arm for him to help her down off the barstool. She felt very light. The deputy leaned over to the bartender and asked for a clean plastic bag. The bartender quickly retrieved a new garbage bag and handed it over.

Bart held Lila's elbow securely as they left the bar and walked over to her red Explorer. He noticed the same men were still milling around the parking lot, watching as the deputy helped the drunken woman. Carefully leaning the inebriated Lila against the side of her SUV, the deputy took out his Leatherman, clicked open a screwdriver, and put on a plastic glove. Squatting down, he unscrewed the license plate, carefully placing it into the plastic bag without getting his fingerprints on it.

Standing up, Bart checked Lila to make sure she was still stable and went to the back of the car, removed the license plate, and dropped it into the evidence bag as well.

"Lila, did you touch the license plate?" he asked, coming to stand next to the woman again.

"No."

"Good."

He crooked a finger at the group, looking for a volunteer.

"I'm going to have one of these nice gentlemen take you home. No driving tonight, Lila."

Lila nodded, but the effort made her tip sideways. Bart caught Lila and corrected her lean.

The thin man stepped up and said, "Come on, Lila. I'll take you home."

Lila looked up to the thin man, "Thanks, Hank." Lila then began to blubber into the thin man's shoulder.

"I know, I know. Let's get you home." Hank held her tight, and they walked to his car.

One of the men leaned toward Bart and said, "Hank is Lila's ex-husband."

Bart sat back in his squad car and radioed the information back to Dorothy at the station. Staring up at the flashing bar sign, he tried to think like Wayne Winckowski. Where would Winckowski hide? He must be finding food, water, and rest somewhere, but where?

South Dakota had many abandoned houses, so that was a possibility, but Winckowski still needed food and water. Where else? Motels, but most of them required a driver's license to rent a room. He had heard Winckowski was carrying lots of cash, so that was a significant benefit, except for those trying to track him down. Most of the time, cashiers would not log in a cash sale, which meant no receipt either. Unreported cash sales equaled untaxed income.

Bart popped straight up in the driver's seat. Winckowski could have gone to Chili Con Camp, and it wasn't a typical family campground. It was a dump, and Bart had responded to several calls to handle fights, thefts, domestics, and lewd behavior. The campground attracted the worst kind of people.

Chili Con Camp might be a perfect spot for Winckowski to use as a hideout. It was a good hunch, but Bart didn't want to risk calling his chief this late and setting him off. Chief Francis Furlong was a bully, a change brought on years ago when he shot a twelve-year-old boy. It had been determined it was an intentional suicide by police.

Bart assured himself, Winckowski would likely still be at the campground in the morning. Bart would wait till morning to notify the chief.

chapter
thirty-three

Wednesday, June 6, 5:30 a.m.

East Elsewhere, South Dakota

Sleep did not come to Deputy Bart Towsley; his antsy brain swirled around Winckowski. He knew he should have called in his hunch to the chief the night before, but Bart wanted to do some self-role playing making sure he didn't piss off the boss and getting himself kicked off the team that would eventually apprehend the killer.

Throwing the covers off, he got up and made a pot of coffee. While the coffee was brewing, he did a twenty-minute workout, precisely a third of the time he would typically spend. Dressed, he poured a sizeable to-go mug and drove straight to the East Elsewhere police station, arriving at 7:00 a.m.

Bart poked his head into the chief's office and asked if he could talk to him. Francis Furlong waved him in.

The pudgy-faced man sat behind his desk, allowing his rotund belly plenty of room; his doughy forearms rested on the edge of the desk blotter.

The chief had once been a powerful, accomplished man, but his strong personality had withered over the years. Afraid of being criticized again, he refused any public presence and stayed in his office. The chief's demeanor had become permanent character flaws, including periodic outbursts of anger, especially during stressful times. Often doubting his own decisions and those made by his staff, Furlong's speech pattern often included stuttering and sputtering.

Bart sat across from the chief and reviewed the events from the night before at William's Wild Will Bar. The deputy explained the reason behind Lila's custom vanity plates and how the switching of the license plates was caught so quickly, giving kudos to Dorothy for remembering the license plate's characters from the stolen van. The chief just harrumphed. Bart continued, explaining his theory that the killer, Winckowski, might be hiding at Chili Con Camp. He put it all together into a neat package for the chief, knowing the senior officer would rip it apart if it was incomplete.

The chief pondered and then responded, "Okay, um, drive over to the campground and check the guest register. If this Lila's license plate is listed, then you are to call for backup. There is to be no engagement with this, this Wink fella. Besides, he's from Minnesota. Those cops should be here looking for him. By the way..." The chief shot up from his office chair, stomped to his open door, and yelled, "Hey, girl up front!"

"Shit." Dorothy wheeled around from her desk, threw her headset off, and stood over the room full of cops to face off with her superior. Dorothy shouted right back at him, "The name is Dorothy. What do you want?"

Pointing his wiener sized finger at her, and said, "Hey, don't get smart, okay?"

Dorothy cocked her hip and jutted her chin out, "Because you won't be able to understand me?" Several of the smiling cops had to turn and laugh into their hands.

Pursing his lips, the chief's face went purple, screaming, "Shut up! Did you notify whatever that city is with um... um, the family that was uh, killer... killed that we might have the killer around here?"

"Yes, very early this morning."

"Well? What did they say, dumbass?"

Dipping her head ever so slightly, she glared at him. "Proceed with caution. It's all in the report, which I sent to you first thing this morning."

Clenching his fists, Francis shouted back at her, "I haven't had time to read it. So, we're supposed to handle this fella ourselves?"

The chief deputy, Hal Morton, stood up and said, "Chief, if he entered our jurisdiction, then it's on us to help capture him."

Turning to Hal, Furlong said, "That's my decision! Okay, right, okay?" The furious chief hated his chief deputy and rarely spoke to him.

Turning back into his office, Furlong slammed the door. Falling slowly into his chair, Chief Furlong looked up, surprised at seeing Bart still sitting there. The chief's face pulsated as he screamed, "Get out of here!"

Bart jumped out of the chair, and the junior cop left to find a killer.

chapter
thirty-four

Wednesday, June 6, 10:45 a.m.

East Elsewhere, South Dakota

Nervous about his first real murder case Deputy Bart spent far too much time studying Wayne Winckowski's file. The murder report alone was gruesome, then he checked the web and found out more about the man's business and the variety of police reports. It was hard to grasp what type of man he was dealing with, but the guy sure seemed to go off half-cocked a lot with or without the aid of alcohol. Taking a deep breath, he finally collected his courage and left the station.

The rookie arrived at the campground well past noon. He drove into the littered driveway of Chili Con Camp and parked. He took a long sip of water while checking out his surroundings. Disgusting. A couple of boys tried to play basketball, but the backcourt looked like a groundhog had been digging holes. Someone had placed a large piece of plywood under the basketball hoop in the frontcourt, apparently hoping to prevent broken ankles.

The yellow lawn was sparse with patches of dirt. One of the cabins looked deserted, while the others looked like they should be. Bart shook his head and stepped out of his car. Upon leaving the confines of his patrol car, he was immediately sorry as he smelled the putrid air of a leaking septic system. Coughing, he covered his nose as he made his way to the office.

The deputy found a sweaty little man arguing with Spice, the owner, who sat behind the counter in an overstuffed chair, cleaning his teeth with a red Swiss Army knife. Spice seemed unconcerned that the customer's campsite was flooded with sewage. Spice took the offense charging the unhappy camper for overusing the facilities, which didn't turn out to be funny. The wiry camper was just about ready to take on the owner when Deputy Bart walked into the office. The customer took one look at Bart and quickly side-stepped the officer, and fled out the door.

The unhappy camper posted himself outside the screen door and listened to Spice and the East Elsewhere deputy.

Bart felt his armpits prickle in the hot, stuffy office as he tried not to breathe in Spice's body odor.

Spice draped one leg over the arm of the chair and asked, "What, Bart?"

"Deputy Towsley, Spice."

"Okay, Deputy Towsley. You may address me as Mr. Spice."

Bart mentally shook his head at Spice, who was a pathetic excuse for a man. He had purchased the campground over ten years ago and immediately ran it into the ground. Spice gave himself his own nickname, referring to his infamous spicy chili recipe. The intolerable chili had a watery red consistency, overpowered with a low grade of catsup, and contained several secret ingredients. Per the rumors, the secret to Spice's chili was using leftover meat from the customers' plates, grinding it up, and adding it into the chili. Bart was reasonably sure it was no rumor, having found a piece of a hamburger bun with his first try of the intestine-challenging chili.

The deputy continued, "I'm looking for a man who might be staying here. He's big, bald with bushy black eyebrows. Did you see anyone fitting that description?"

"Nope."

"I'd like to check your books for license numbers."

"Fine." Spice stood up and turned the registration book around for Bart to see.

Bart rubbed underneath his nose and scanned the book. He spotted the license number, campsite, and the date: "JJJ 458, site 37, 6/5."

Winckowski did check-in yesterday.

The signature next to the license number was illegible. Heart racing, Bart casually asked, "Where is campsite thirty-seven?"

"Northwest corner."

"Is there a way to get all of your campers inside one building?"

Spice looked incredulous and snidely said, "Why?"

"Because," was Bart's only response.

Sensing the urgency from the young deputy's voice, Spice nervously said, "Ah, I could use the loudspeaker and tell 'em we need to see if all the campers will fit in the new storm shelter."

Looking Spice straight in the eye, Bart took charge. "I'm going to make a call, then let you know what we're going to do."

Spice said nothing, but he knew trouble when he saw it.

Bart pushed through the screen door and ran to his patrol car.

The unhappy camper had heard it all and ran toward the northwest corner of the campground.

Tucking his tall, muscular body back inside the patrol car Bart called the station, asking for the chief, and then spotted the camper hurrying across the dried-up lawn heading northwest. Furious with himself, Bart realized that the guy had probably overheard the entire conversation with Spice.

The chief came on the line, and Bart clipped his words. "Chief, I'm sure Winckowski is at the CCC."

"What? No shit, Sharleen! Oh, God, Okay, okay." Bart had to pull the phone away from his ear when he heard the chief screaming.

Chief Furlong ran to the squad room with the cell phone still to his ear and screamed, "Dell, Jerry, get out and assist Bart at the Chili Con Camp, and bring all of you guys!" The chief swept his arm, referring to the entire room, and almost knocked himself over with the mighty sweep. "That, that, that, okay, okay, Wink fella is… is… is at the Con, Con…the CCC! Get *moving!*"

Not moving a muscle, the deputies watched the chief as he returned to his office. Then they snapped their attention to the chief deputy, who was already on the move toward the exit, shouting instructions as they barreled out of the room.

Pacing while on the phone with Bart, the chief returned to the call, "Okay, okay, all right now. Ummm, don't engage. Okay, um… I'm sending the cavalry for you, son. The boys will be… are… okay… on their way, and they'll meet you somewhere. But for now, don't let the murdering son of a bitch leave. Post yourself so that he doesn't see you, and just watch him. Right? Okay, okay, okay?" Francis Furlong peeked through the blinds as he heard the squad cars squealing out of the parking lot. "Bart, wait, what about all those campers? The kids?"

Bart was way ahead of the chief, and ran toward the office. "I'm taking care of that," and hung up. Bart ran back inside and hollered at Spice, "Make that announcement now!" Spice jumped and scrambled for the microphone but dropped it. Ignoring it, Spice opened the cash drawer and pulled out the bills, stuffing it into his pockets.

Chief Furlong returned to the squad room, looking confused, and continued talking into the phone, which had gone silent. "Okay, okay, man, oh, gosh. I'll stay here and call the cops in B-B-B-Blanchard..sending... going ... send Jell and Derry. They'll be right there. Okay, okay, good work, Tart." The chief screamed, "Dispatcher, dispatcher! Where the hell is that dumb blonde?"

Someone ran by and shouted to the chief, "Dorothy's on the phone with a suicidal teen. Leave her alone!"

"Shit, pit, okay, okay, okay, oh, poop scoopert, skilert…" The chief turned slowly back into his office, slamming the door, and leaned back against it. His eyes wide with concern as he tried to whisper coherent words, adjusting his aching jaw. Chief Francis Furlong stumbled across to his desk and sat heavily into his chair. Placing his hands flat onto the blotter, he waited to hear from his guys at Chili Con Camp.

Dorothy knocked on the chief's door after she had gotten a couple of cops to do a welfare check at the home of the suicidal teen. Dorothy was thinking of quitting her job, not wanting to take the verbal abuse from the chief any longer. She had knocked once and then tried again. Calling his name, she slipped the door open. Dorothy found the police chief with his head on his desk and his cloudy eyes open. Rushing over, she checked his vitals and called for an ambulance. Dorothy knew it was too late, but dragging him to the floor, she performed CPR on the cold chief.

chapter
thirty-five

Wednesday, June 6, 12:45 p.m.

East Elsewhere, South Dakota

The unhappy camper ran across the grounds, heading for campsite number thirty-seven. Finding a big man in a red camp chair, the intruder accidentally tripped on an empty beer bottle, startling the sleeping man. Jumping up, Wayne pulled his gun and pointed it at the stranger. As Winckowski tried to see through his blurry eyes, he wobbled, unsteady as he tried to focus.

The camper held up his hands, stepped back quickly, and explained, "Whoa, Whoa, pal, sorry. I'm here doing you a favor. There's a cop at the front office coming to check you out. Thought you'd like to know."

Blinking repeatedly at the man, Wayne said, "Wha?"

"Cops, man! They're coming for you!" The camper studied the drunk and said, "You are drunk off your ass. Well, good luck to 'ya,'" saluted, and walked back the way he came.

All of a sudden, noises vibrated over the loudspeaker, and Spice could be heard screaming into the microphone, "Hey everybody, git to the storm shelter ASAP! Uh, um, to see if we'll all fit in case of a tornado. Hurry up! Run! Free beer! Hurry the hell up!"

Wayne covered his ears, protecting them from the screeching speaker, but it positively affected the regulars. The campers stampeded across the campground, heading for the cement bunker and the free beer. Adding to the confusion, some twenty-plus startled dogs began running and barking.

The disturbing noise prickled Wayne's head as he quickly scanned the campground with his gun out in front of him. Just then, he spotted a cop ducking low behind a pop-up tent trailer down the road not far from where he stood.

His adrenaline kicked in, reducing his drunken state, but not by much. Wayne turned quickly, trying to duck into his tent, but the toe of his cowboy boot caught and he fell flat inside. Scrambling around, he tried to find his gun, which had skidded across the slick plastic floor. Rushing on all fours, Wayne snatched it from the far corner. Holding the gun steady with both hands, he walked on his knees to peek out the tent flap.

The cop was racing to duck behind a big trailer across from number thirty-seven. Wayne spotted the deputy, shot wildly, getting off four shots, and heard a yelp.

The power of the shots knocked Wayne sideways out of the tent and onto the dirt. Kicking the flap of the tent until he was clear, he struggled to stand. He shook his head hard, trying to see straight as the campers' screams ramped up several decibels.

Wayne stumbled across the road toward the oversized trailer, then ducked in front of it; creeping around the side, he heard the deputy talking into his shoulder mike. Taking a peek around the back end, Wayne spotted the deputy, alive, but with blood pouring out from below his armpit and his foot. The back of the deputy's boot had been blown off. Wayne was pleased and surprised he had wounded him. The deputy was looking out the other side of the trailer toward the Winckowski's campsite, whispering into his mike.

Wayne screamed at him, "You are not stopping me from going home!"

Bart twisted around fast, just as Wayne jumped the wounded cop. The muscular deputy was well matched to Winkowski's size as they both wrestled for control of the gun. Deputy Bart fought hard, trying to grab the killer's gun, but when Wayne caught a break, he slammed the butt of his weapon twice into the deputy's forehead. Bart's eyes rolled back into his head, and he fell to the ground like a giant tree.

Holding onto the back of the bumper, Wayne steadied himself. The chaotic noise around him was so distracting. Standing up, he waved his gun, ready to plug anyone who was a threat. The campground had become a madhouse. He spied a screaming woman trying to untie the rope to release her dog from a tree while her wailing child clung to her legs. Children ran for cover behind a tent, not understanding the power of a bullet. Men outran the women and children.

Wayne saw one man, apparently in shock, standing facing him, presenting himself as a perfect target. Wayne took advantage of the opportunity, pointed his gun at the fool, and mouthed, "*Pow.*" The man fainted.

It was time to leave, but he was unsure of what he should do with the downed deputy. Wayne grabbed the front of the deputy's shirt and dragged him across the road, dropping him near his cold campfire. Dropping on all fours, Wayne hung his head, trying to catch his breath. Righting his camp chair, he used it for support as he moved to a standing position. Winckowski tried to think of what to pack. Looking around quickly, he got the whirlies and decided he didn't need anything because his cash was still in the van.

Scrambling around the van to the driver's side door, he threw himself in, snapped the key to "on," and blew backward in reverse, running over a birch sapling. The leafy top broke off and attached itself to the undercarriage, where it dragged behind the car as the vehicle rocketed toward the main road. The driver's door bobbed back and forth, unable to shut.

Wayne stomped the accelerator, swerving dangerously, sideswiping a tent, with kids huddling behind it. The four kids toppled over like Tinker toys.

Flying down the gravel road toward the exit, Wayne looked behind him and saw a pack of mad dogs tearing after him. He reached the exit and made a sharp left onto the road, nearly falling out of the still-open door as he clipped the teetering Chili Con Camp sign. The sign made a valiant attempt to stand but finally collapsed into kindling.

Wayne slammed his palm on the steering wheel, swearing and cursing. Jerking the car to the right, the force finally slammed his door shut. Looking in his rearview mirror, he saw that the treetop had finally dislodged itself. Winckowski rubbed his itchy eyes and immediately felt regrets start to fill his head. A case of liquor, camping gear, shotgun, water, and food had all been left behind. What was he thinking? Well, apparently, he wasn't, and driving was the last thing he wanted to be doing.

chapter
thirty-six

Wednesday, June 6, 6:00 p.m.

Jesus Hospital, East Elsewhere, South Dakota

"Deputy Bartholomew is coming around, but all he's saying is, 'Home. Home.' I guess he wants to go home." The nurse looked up to the tall, thin chief deputy, Hal Morton, who had a pained look of concern on his face.

"Bart lives alone. Why would he want to go home?" Hal questioned. "Please, call him Bart. He hates Bartholomew."

At that moment, Bart tried to pry his eyes open but quickly turned away from the bright, sunlit windows. The nurse rushed across the room, closing the blinds, and moved again to his bedside. His swollen eyes were being shoved down into his face by his black-and-blue, bulging forehead.

The chief deputy spoke up and said, "Bart, we are so glad you're awake. How are you feeling?"

Bart tried to look at the chief deputy but was unable to focus. Giving up, he relaxed his lids and allowed them to close. Bart whispered, and the chief deputy had to bend down to hear him. "What, Bart?"

"Home."

"You'll be home in a couple of days." The chief deputy patted his deputy's hand.

Bart seemed agitated, slowly shaking his head, but winced in pain and quickly stopped the motion. "Wayne going... home."

"Wayne, who? Oh, wait, you mean Wayne Winckowski? How do you know that?"

"Before... hit me... said, 'You are not going... to stop me from going... home.'" The exertion sank Bart deeper into his pillows.

Hal rushed out of the room, dialing his phone.

The nurse stepped over to Bart and said, "What do you need?"

"Pain pill, water... food."

She smiled and straightened his bedclothes. "All righty-dighty then. You're going to be just fine, good as new." She helped him sit up a little and left to fill his requests.

Chief Deputy Morton called his buddy, the Blanchard Chief of Police, Roger Jorgenson.

Roger picked up immediately and said, "News, Hal?"

"Yes. Bart just woke up in the hospital. The first thing my deputy said was Winckowski told him, 'You are not going to stop me from going home.'"

Roger flew up to his full height with his hand on his hip and shouted, "What? That is just plain stupid. That son of a bitch has dodged us continually, and he has to be the luckiest blind drunk I have ever seen. So now Winckowski's feeling confident enough that he thinks he can just walk right back into Blanchard unnoticed?"

Hal sympathized with Roger. "Apparently so. But if you think about it, your work tracking him has finally paid off. Now you have a more defined area, and he's not going to surprise you when he does show up in Blanchard. You'll be ready."

"True, true. We're all so damn tired it's amazing we can even eat. Hal, I gotta go, but before I do, were there any casualties at the campground?"

"Well, since the shooting, it seems the whole campground is ready to party, and they are drunk. I was sure I saw a few kids staggering as well. We've had to go back and stop the fights. But so far, one old biker had a mild heart attack, released himself from the hospital, and is back at the CCC drinking brandy. The campground did have one dog that was killed when Wayne ran over him. Other than that, there were a few tents with bullet holes, and the Chili Con Camp sign was destroyed. I'd say we're damn lucky, considering over thirty people were out and about.

"And my deputy will be fit as a fiddle," Hal continued. "He was shot twice, both minor wounds, thank God. But that wallop on his forehead caused a concussion, which was no worse than when he was hit playing football just a few years back. He's young and strong, and I'm not worried about him."

Roger replied, "I'm really glad to hear it. What kind of evidence did you find at Winckowski's campsite?"

"None."

"What do you mean none? Winckowski overnighted, right?"

"Correct, but you gotta see this campground to believe it. It's a garbage dump, with like-minded people camping there. By the time my team got there, Winckowski's campsite had been stripped clean. No tent, no weapons, no supplies.

Absolutely nothing. There seemed to be a gag order on all the campers because no one saw or took anything. They are all a bunch of thieving bastards."

"Jeez. Remind me never to camp there."

"Believe me, you would never consider it."

"Hey, change of subjects. Let's plan on going pheasant hunting over your way, October twentieth. That's the opener. You in?"

"Done deal, same group?"

"Yup, I'll get the trip scheduled. Okay, I really have to go. Thanks for the update."

Hal said, "Hold on, Roger, there's something else. Chief Furlong died this morning of a stroke."

Roger paused and said without emotion, "Oh... too bad." Roger spoke up and said, "Well, Hal, you will make one hellva' chief. Congratulations, you deserve it. Talk to you later."

Hal wasn't surprised by Roger's reaction. Furlong's lousy reputation and foul mouth had made enemies throughout the Midwest.

Hanging up, Roger marched into the lunchroom, where the Pinpoint men were working.

"Guys." All three gave him their attention.

"I just had word from the chief deputy of East Elsewhere, South Dakota, that Winckowski is heading home to Blanchard. Before he knocked out the deputy who he had shot—just minor injuries—Winckowski told him, "You are not going to stop me from going home."

Klink turned back to his computer while the other two stared at Roger. Then they both nodded, started talking among themselves, and walked over to the latest addition to their collection of maps. Ron looked back at Roger. "Thanks," he said. "We'll get back to you."

The chief noticed that Ron's daily humor was absent. All three looked like they hadn't slept much. Roger quietly closed the door and went back to his office to call Hilde.

The Pinpoint men stared at a Minnesota abandoned house map, the one Patrice Whitehand had so generously provided. She was conveniently close by with her cousin in case they had any questions for her. Ron was more than grateful and hoped to get to know her a little better after Winckowski was captured.

Ron thought Patrice Whitehand was a striking woman. In their short meeting, her dark eyes seemed to be always smiling. Her tumbling salt-and-pepper hair made him want to touch it. Patrice was a full head shorter than him, but they talked eye to eye.

Ron decided that maybe he should give her a call and pulled out his phone.

"Hey, Patrice. I have an update and was wondering if you could come over, and we could discuss it?"

"Absolutely. I'll walk over and see you in five."

A smile hung on Ron's face. He was hoping Patrice might identify a logical abandoned house that Winckowski might stay in overnight. His mind was set only on finding the killer, but her small distraction was appreciated.

chapter
thirty-seven

Wednesday, June 6, 6:00 p.m.

Dignity Christian Hospital,
Two Streams, Minnesota

Annabelle opened her eyes and tried to scream, but a giant hand was clamped over her face, covering her nose and mouth. Her eyes wild as she struggled to remove her dad's hands that held her down. She couldn't breathe. Her raw throat continued to try to scream as his lopsided grin grew.

"Shut up!" he rasped, shaking her. "Glad to see you're alive. I didn't think I had killed you. You know I killed the family, though, right?"

Nodding, her wide eyes glistened, her face hurt, trapped in his hairy knuckles.

"So, you know what I can do, so don't make any trouble. We're getting you out of here, and we'll be our own little family. How's that sound?"

Annabelle couldn't go with him, she wouldn't! Wayne shook her shoulders, screaming at her, "Come on! Come on!"

Wayne yanked her arm as she pulled back. They wrestled until Annabelle's arm ripped away from her body. Blood poured out over her white bed, shocked she kept her eyes trained on the thick red fluid. Looking up at Wayne, Annabelle saw him staring at the blood, and his face went white. He turned and vanished.

The stench! That's what I smelled when I was under the front step! It was my family's blood!

She roared awake, sitting straight up, heaving for air, and whirling her head around. She was alone.

Annabelle's damp, tangled hair spun around her sweaty body and plastered onto her face. It felt like she was caught in a sticky spiderweb. Her wild eyes held the fear of the nightmare from her nap. She felt the flow of warm blood pouring down her arm from her IV being ripped out when she was thrashing about. Her gown and bedclothes were soaked in blood.

Her head snapped to the sound of her door being slowly opened. A freak entered her room. Annabelle clutched the bedrails, trying to find the call button. The woman-creature was walking toward her bed. A phone was poised against her eye, and she spoke in a low, raspy voice, as if to herself, and said, "Oh, so Annabelle, your daddy didn't kill you. Those dirty bastards kept you a secret." The old lady crept closer and closer as Annabelle saw the flash of pictures being taken.

Terrified, Annabelle screamed. Flying off of the bed, scrambling to hide behind the wing chair, she bumped her back on the corner of the wall, crying out. She heard a crash from outside her room, and Nurse Shelly Rae blew through the door. The frantic nurse spun the woman around, grabbing the intruder's upper arm, and shouted into her face, "What the hell are you doing in here? You are not allowed in here!"

Muriel Friechs carefully slid her phone into her pocket and then feigned surprise, acting like a doddering old woman. She dabbed at her heavily made-up eyes and apologetically said, "I must have entered the wrong room. Oh, dear, I scared that sweet child. I better leave."

Shelly pushed her out into the hall, closing Annabelle's door. The old reporter walked straight to the elevator and pressed the down button. Muriel's smile was pressed firmly against her teeth.

Pat, a male nurse, ran into the room and found Shelly in the wing chair, holding the trembling child on her lap, rocking back and forth as she simultaneously tried to stem the flow of blood pouring out of the IV site and the sutures holding the wound together, ruptured on Annabelle's back. Pat said, "The new guard is gone!"

Shelly spoke over the top of Annabelle's head, saying, "Get Dr. Phalen first, then Dill, then the police. Then come back and bring bandages to wrap this thing up." Shelly nodded toward Annabelle's bloody forearm.

Pat flew out of the room.

Twenty minutes later, Roger strode into the room with Dr. Dill right behind him. They spotted the pale little girl curled up in a fetal position under heaps of warm blankets, hiccupping. They both spoke at once. "What happened?"

Shelly's uniform was rife with blood as she monkeyed with the monitors. Turning to the two men, she still had a look of fury on her face, and said, "The new guard left his post, and some creepy old woman came in and scared poor Annabelle nearly to death!"

Dr. Dill pulled a chair next to Annabelle and lifted her right hand. Her left arm was bandaged, and Annabelle winced as Shelly examined her sore back. She was shuddering with hiccups, but she managed a small smile for Dr. Joe and whispered, "Hi."

He smiled at her in return. "Hi," he said. "Do you want to tell me what happened?"

She didn't want to move or couldn't. Dr. Dill leaned in to hear her. "I had another nightmare, and it was terrible. Dad had come for me, and he was going to take me away. He kept yanking my arm until he pulled it off." She squeezed her eyes tight and touched her bandaged arm just to make sure it was still there.

"It hurt so bad, and my arm just kept bleeding and bleeding. Dad doesn't like the sight of blood, and then he vanished as if he was a warlock or something. When I woke up, this creepy old horrible person was taking pictures of me with her phone."

A stunned look crossed Shelly's face. "What? She was taking pictures of you? The old woman said she was lost and had entered the wrong room."

Roger's face and ears were now crimson as he said, "I think it was a reporter. We've kept the secret that Annabelle was in the hospital, and now it'll be all over the press. And I mean all over!" Roger didn't mention that Annabelle's Dad probably had seen the earlier newspapers reporting that the entire family had been killed. Now tomorrow's edition would say Annabelle was alive. His mind was tangled with the complications of this new development.

Opening and closing his hands several times, Roger said to Annabelle, "I'll handle it, honey. No worries." But he was worried about Annabelle's safety. What would Winckowski do? Take Annabelle? Kill her? Roger's brain hit overdrive.

He gave Annabelle a quick smile and rushed out the door, hurrying down the hall. His first mission was to find the security guard, the new one the hospital had hired.

Fidgeting in the elevator, it dawned on Roger that it was quite a coincidence that Muriel Friechs had found Annabelle's room, which was listed under another name, during the time the security guard had gone missing.

Dr. Dill ordered a mild sedative for Annabelle while the nurses picked up the blood-soaked gown and sheets. Another nurse came in and sat next to Annabelle while Shelly left to get herself cleaned up.

Kathy had left before the chaos in Annabelle's room. She had decided while Annabelle was sleeping, she would make a few return phone calls. Walking back into the hospital room, Pat told her what had happened. Kathy felt terrible, leaving Annabelle alone, but of course, she was blameless, because the security guard should have been there. Kathy took her post on the single bed, wiping away her tears as she watched Annabelle sleep.

Roger went down to the hospital cafeteria and looked for someone wearing a security guard's uniform. He found him with his head almost in his plate, chowing down dinner. Roger scraped a chair back and pulled it right up close to the guard, who looked pretty cocksure, considering the Chief of Police was in his space.

Roger announced the obvious, "You left your post."

"I had to eat. Are you suggesting I can't eat on the job?" He let his beef stew–filled mouth drop open as he pitched his head forward, staring incredulously at the chief.

"You were advised not to leave the child alone under any circumstances, and if you needed to eat, you were to order it up to the floor." He paused. "Wait a minute, I remember you. You're Muriel Friechs' nephew, Jeff Whalen. You've been fleecing local homeowners out of their hard-earned cash with your promises to repair their homes." Roger folded his arms and leaned back. "How did you get away with not being charged?"

"It's not a crime, according to the state's Department of Labor and Industry."

Roger scooted his chair back and stood with his arms crossed, looking down at Whalen. "So, you don't have a record since it's not a crime? Now I get it. You were hired as a security guard because you have no record."

"Correct. I have every right to work here."

"Not after today. I will make sure you never work in Minnesota as a security guard, crossing guard, or a contractor ever again. And by the way, you are fired!"

"You're not the boss of me!"

Behind Jeff, Roger saw the hospital administrator, Mr. Albert Torgelson, marching straight for them. Two beefy security guards were right on Torgelson's heels, trying to keep up with the fast little man.

The administrator was dressed impeccably and had an air of authority surrounding him. Mr. Torgelson got in Whalen's face and shouted down at him, "But I am! You are fired, you dirty son of a bitch!" Whalen wiped the spittle from his face, unfazed. Kind-hearted Mr. Albert Torgelson was on fire, and Whalen wisely decided not to say a word.

It was dinner time, and the bustling cafeteria had been noisy until the shouting silenced the room. The diners watched the scene play out. The administrator's final words were, "Get out of my hospital, *now!*" The short man stood to his full height and pointed to the exit.

The two beefy guards roughly pulled Whalen up as his silverware clattered to the floor. They marched him out of the cafeteria door and threw him to the curb just as viciously as any bar bouncer would do.

Stepping back inside, the duo brushed their hands and wiped them on their creased pants, trying to rid themselves of Whalen's filth. They looked up to the sound of applause.

Surprisingly, they were being given a thunderous standing ovation from the grateful patrons of the hospital. They did what any good security guards would do in that situation. The two bullish men curtsied.

chapter
thirty-eight
Wednesday, June 6, 9:00 p.m.
North of Clinton, Minnesota

W ayne was sick and tired of driving. He couldn't seem to sober up enough to go in the right direction, frequently getting lost. It was so hot in the van he thought he might be melting. His life sure blew up just when things were going so well.

The run-in with the deputy had caught him off guard, unnerving him. He had allowed himself to relax too much at that damn campground. The smell of vomit from the front of his shirt wafted up, making him gag. Stretching his neck, he tried to distance himself from the stench, unable to recall when he puked. His temper increased, smelling his ripe body odor, realizing he should have taken a shower back at the campsite. Being hungry, hungover, and having his brain banging off in different directions didn't raise his confidence about deciding what he should do next to keep the law off his back.

His original plan for the evening had been shot down, literally. The hot dogs that he would cook over his campfire were in the cooler back at the campsite. Thinking about it made his mouth water, and Wayne was royally pissed that he was forced to run again. He hadn't eaten since the night before. The idea of staying in another abandoned house turned him off. Wayne needed food, booze, a shower, and clean clothes. Where was he going to get all that?

How the hell did the deputy find him?

He shouted to the windshield, "I hope that son of a bitch is dead!"

His brain flitted, and a new thought made him smile. "I guess I'm coming to get you, AnnieBelly!"

The life I knew is gone: my cash business, my freedom, and my home. Being on the road gave me so much independence. Leaving Letty and her brats should have been my plan long ago. Then Annabelle and I would have moved to Mexico. And killing my family, well, I didn't know what I was doing. Also, those pills? They could've been bad. Not my fault.

Letty really got what she deserved, though. She made me feel bad about myself. Always needing something, begging for my money. Pointing that shotgun got those kids screaming like I had never heard before. The racket! I nearly stopped shooting, seeing all of the blood, but I had already gone too far.

I don't miss them at all, except for AnnieBelly. She is really my only child, and she loved me. I wouldn't have killed her. I don't think?

Once again, dust was flying behind him, and Wayne found himself driving aimlessly, backtracking over the gravel roads and hoping he was heading home to Blanchard. It seemed to be the smartest thing to do, outsmarting the cops. Chuckling, Wayne invisibly patted himself on the back. Not such a bad plan for a pickled brain.

Once he rolled into his hometown, he would love to stop at the Break it Open Bar to see his buddies. What would they think of him for killing his family? Unconcerned, Wayne had always been pretty good at convincing them to his way of thinking, whether it was right or wrong. Fabian and Blaze were both dumb, but although he hated to admit it they were his only friends.

Wayne was sweating profusely because the van's air conditioner had died somewhere in South Dakota. Pulling off onto a low-maintenance road, he nestled the van in a copse of large pine trees covered by the low hanging boughs. Wayne removed his shirt, allowing the slick river of sweat to roll down his torso into the waistband of his jeans. The lining of his stomach felt on fire. Pushing the seat back, he rubbed his itchy eyes and leaned his head back onto the headrest. Staring through the filthy windshield, his left eye twitched, and Wayne Winckowski fell asleep with his chin touching his chest.

chapter
thirty-nine

Thursday, June 7, 7:30 a.m.

Two Streams, Minnesota

The morning edition of the *Blanchard News* blazed with the headline: "FOUND ALIVE: ONE MEMBER OF THE MURDERED WINCKOWSKI FAMILY!" The byline indicated it was written by Muriel Friechs.

A full spread reported all of the gory details of the murder, repeating the same story from the previous days. Friechs then accused the hospital of a lack of care for poor Annabelle Winckowski. The ten colored pictures of the little patient were shocking. Blood saturated Annabelle's gown, her long, matted hair spun around her face, and dark-rimmed eyes were terrified as she sat in a blood-soaked hospital bed.

Roger was furious. Grabbing his cell phone, he called Ron, who answered and snapped, "What?"

Roger assumed Ron had already seen the headlines and let his rudeness pass. "It's me. Can you find a law that was broken so we can charge both Jeff Whalen and Muriel Friechs? Anything to get them behind bars and out of my town!"

"Absolutely! I'm so frickin' pissed right now, but this will give me something to pound on. Whalen and Friechs were surely in on this together; apparently, neither one had enough compassion not to put that poor child in immediate danger! Gotta go and talk to Belinda." Ron hung up.

Roger looked at his phone for answers. *Belinda?* Anyway, Roger was confident Ron would find something that would put Muriel, Jeff, and possibly the mayor in jail. Roger slammed the newspaper with his fist.

chapter
forty

Thursday, June 7, 9:00 a.m.

Dignity Christian Hospital,
Two Streams, Minnesota

Annabelle sat on the side of the bed, her feet dangling while she waited for Kathy to bring the wheelchair. Her funeral clothes felt odd. She had never had a new dress, and unfortunately, it was black. The price tag hung between her shoulder blades, and each time she moved, the swinging label itched her back. Afraid of breaking the law, Annabelle didn't pull it off. After all, many pillow tags had that warning that it was a crime if it was removed.

Kathy had bought Annabelle her dress and black patent leather shoes for the funeral. Having never had a haircut, Annabelle had asked Kathy if she could have it cut, especially after the raging nightmare the night before. The night terrors had changed from sounds of her family being killed to being trapped, tangled in a spiderweb. Struggling against the sticky web, she would see Harley reaching for her, but he couldn't save her. She would wake to find herself caught in a cocoon of her long, sweat-drenched hair.

Kathy had called the beautician who worked in the hospital, and she was kind enough to come in early to wash and cut Annabelle's hair. The cut was just below her shoulders, and Annabelle liked the way it swung.

When the beautician held up the two-foot length of hair that had once hung past her butt, Annabelle felt a twinge of regret. The nice beautician suggested it be donated to the Children's Cancer Center for those who had lost their hair from chemotherapy treatments. Annabelle readily agreed, knowing it was a much better plan than seeing it tossed into the trash. The morning's small act of kindness made her feel good, and the orphan treasured it, knowing that would be her only bright spot for the day.

Kathy appeared, dressed in a soft black pantsuit that nipped in at her waist. Pushing the child-sized wheelchair into the hospital room, she stopped next to Annabelle. They looked at each other's sad expression, both wondering how they would get through the devastating day.

Kathy leaned over and gave the brave little girl a hug and said, "How are you doing?"

"Fine, just wish it was over. Is it okay if we remove the tag from this dress? I think it's against the law, but it is really itching my back."

Kathy held back a frown, acknowledging that she was giving too much credit to this naïve child who had never experienced real life. Annabelle had missed fun moments most nine-year-old girls had already had: new clothes with itchy tags, riding a Ferris wheel, going to a movie, shopping, vacations, eating well, and living without fears. Kathy had to remember this and try to anticipate what experiences she was lacking. She clipped the tag off from the back of Annabelle's dress.

Yesterday had been a long day of discussions. Dr. Joe, Kathy, and the Dickens had prepped Annabelle as to what to expect at the funeral for her two brothers, two sisters, and mother. Annabelle teared up upon learning that the town of Blanchard had donated the five coffins and flowers. The local funeral home provided their free services, and the burial plots were purchased by the Two Streams Police Department. The service would be held outdoors on the massive lawn to the left side of the Church of the Nazarene. Annabelle was overwhelmed with the thoughtfulness of her hometown. The little girl needed a lot of comfort during those long talks.

Annabelle had not been in church in weeks, and today she was going to the funeral of her family. It couldn't get much worse.

When her dad was on the road, her mother used to bring the family to church in her little red car. Wayne would never have allowed the family to go to church if he had known. Her momma managed to keep many secrets from Wayne. When he was away, they would also find Wayne's bag of cash and use it for the offering at church, ice cream cones, and lots of food, and they would laugh with abandon, as a family should. Letty never bought her children any clothing; Wayne would have noticed and punished them.

Pastor Henry's sermons at the Church of the Nazarene were her momma's favorite. He had always given them extra attention, even though none were dressed very well, but they were always washed and combed.

Still sitting on the edge of the bed, Annabelle felt numb and didn't want to shake it off. Kathy helped her into the wheelchair as Shelly stepped into the room wearing a black dress that fluttered around her knees. All three were quiet, not finding words to fill the void.

Kathy stepped back as Shelly quickly untangled the IV lines from the bed rails, removed the attached needle from Annabelle's hand, and promptly slipped on a Band-Aid. Giving Annabelle a couple of pain pills and a glass of water, Shelly then adjusted a small pillow to protect the tender wound on Annabelle's back. The nurse was noticeably quiet but continued to smile her way through.

Annabelle asked Kathy, "Am I supposed to wear sunglasses?"

Kathy asked, "Why?"

"I saw it on TV one time, and I figured you didn't want people to know you were crying."

Kathy took her little hands, and with a smile, said, "The people that attend a funeral have feelings for those that are being laid to rest. If you wear sunglasses, you won't be connected to those folks that are hurting. Today will be a tough day for everyone, but we all have to feel this loss; it's our way of showing respect for the departed and their lives. Honoring those in death is part of living a good life and respecting those memories.

"Those mourners on TV with sunglasses are just trying to hide their crying faces, not wanting to appear less than their glamorous selves."

"Oh." Annabelle only half heard what Kathy's point was. Besides, the only sunglasses she had were Hello Kitty, probably not appropriate.

Shelly and Kathy were escorting Annabelle to the church. The mighty little patient had fought for her right to go to the funeral when Dr. Phalen said she couldn't attend. Having a nurse come along was the only way he would allow Annabelle to leave the hospital.

Dr. Phalen argued because Annabelle had a long way to a full recovery, she was to be returned immediately back to the hospital after the burial at the cemetery. His major concern was having to remove the girl from the intravenous antibiotic drip, her fresh surgical wounds, lack of sleep, and the stress of the day. Finally, he acquiesced to Annabelle's loudest advocates, Shelly and Kathy.

Annabelle's numbness was dissipating, and the familiar slithering of colliding emotions was returning. Gripping the armrests, Annabelle was on her way to face the inevitable. She had fought the good fight for her right to go to the funeral but wished she didn't have to go.

chapter
forty-one

Thursday, June 7, 10:30 a.m.

Blanchard, Minnesota

The day offered sunshine, casting its rays throughout the crystal blue sky. Annabelle could smell the fresh air spiked with the scent of pine trees that surrounded the church property. Looking up at the massive church, she admired the intricate architecture with its soaring, stained-glass windows. To the left of where the services would take place was an elaborately designed wrought iron fence surrounding the cemetery where thousands of gravestones stood rigid.

The turf tires on Annabelle's wheelchair allowed a smoother ride over the expansive lawn surrounding the Church of the Nazarene. She felt a slap of pain in her back and chest when Shelly dipped the wheelchair into a hole accidentally.

"Sorry, sweetie."

Guarding the funeral were several policemen and women. Annabelle caught a glimpse of Hilde, who watched as two cops escorted an old woman with big gray hair into a gold car, which promptly left. Annabelle wasn't sure, but she thought it might have been the reporter from the night before.

Shelly, Kathy, and Annabelle made their way down the aisle to the front row of folding chairs, past several seated funeral-goers. Having never attended a funeral, Annabelle noticed some odd things. Even though they were outside, the mourners were talking in low whispery voices and walking very slowly. As Annabelle was wheeled down the aisle, some mourners showed surprise seeing her presence, while others offered warm hands, reaching out, gently touching her shoulder. She wasn't sure why they did that, but it felt good.

Annabelle felt strange and isolated in this crowd of people as she was wheeled down the center aisle. Kay Larson, her best friend's mother, played a keyboard in front of the congregation. Kay usually played on Sundays inside their church on a much larger organ. Music always touched Annabelle, and now all she wanted to do was listen and avoid the immediate thoughts of her lost family. Her loneliness for them never seemed to cease.

Moving to the right, the three entered the first row, and Shelly helped Annabelle move into a chair while Kathy rolled the wheelchair out of the way. The women sat on either side of Annabelle, with Mr. and Mrs. Dickens to Kathy's right. Once the three were seated, Jim and Doris stood and came over to Annabelle to hug her. Annabelle wanted to climb into their laps, but they returned to their chairs. A tear moved slowly out of the corner of her eye, unattended. Kathy passed a tissue into Annabelle's hand and used another one to attend to her own tears.

Streams of neighbors, strangers, friends, Dr. Dill, classmates, teachers, Roger, and police officers filled the many rows of chairs. The soft music continued to play, and the sun warmed the morning. Pastor Henry walked down the dewy aisle, and at the front row, he turned to step in front of Annabelle. He knelt before her. The pastor picked up her hand, giving a slight smile as his ivory robe pooled around him on the grass. Touching his fingers lightly upon his heart, he prayed for her as Annabelle studied the elegant gold stitching on his purple stole and slowly closed her eyes in prayer. Standing, Pastor Henry placed a white, child-sized Bible on her lap with a white rose protruding from the top.

He glided up the steps of the plywood stage to his pulpit. Annabelle felt her world shift as the earth stood still. The music stopped, and a hush graced the congregation. The quiet scared her at first, but then Annabelle felt a soothing calm wash over her.

Pastor Henry raised his palms, and the congregation rose. Quietly, the five coffins were rolled down the aisle of freshly mowed grass, filling the air with its delicious scent.

The caskets were positioned side by side in front of Pastor Henry, and the twenty pallbearers took their seats. Five different colorful quilts adorned the top of each coffin, and bouquets of colored flowers splayed over the tops. The quilts would later be tucked around each family member inside their coffin.

The first row of mourners stayed seated. Annabelle's cold hands were shaking, and Kathy softly took one hand, and Shelly the other. Mrs. Dickens stretched her arm behind Kathy's shoulder and placed her warm hand on Annabelle.

The pastor said to the congregation, "Please be seated. We are here today to ask our Heavenly Father to bless this family. Lord, may you welcome them through Heaven's golden gates and embrace them with your loving arms.

"Letty Winckowski, a gracious mother, alone raised five loving children despite living with an evil man. Her oldest son, Mattson, used his strength of will and courage to protect his family. Candy, the oldest daughter, was a virtuous child. She was twelve and the guiding counsel for her younger siblings. Our own little Gail, eleven, sang off-key loudly to the joy of this congregation and lovingly held hands with anyone who offered a willing palm. Harley was Annabelle's best friend and a champion of many things. He may have been mute, but his expression of love was undeniable throughout his short life.

"They have left our world to enjoy the golden glories of Heaven. They as angels will guide and protect us when we are in need…"

Pastor Henry continued without Annabelle's attention, as she had begun to shudder from crying. Her mind drifted off to the sounds of laughter and distant memory.

One dark rainy day, Mattson had started a conga line, grabbing each of his siblings, and they threaded their way through the house, laughing and giggling. Annabelle thought back to the nights when they would catch fireflies in their hands for just one glowing moment before releasing them. She remembered swinging on the old rope swing, flying into a peaceful world of time as Annabelle sang loud and clear.

Her mind snapped to a scary time. Dad was beating Harley, who lay over on top of Annabelle, protecting her from the belt.

Her mind flipped again to a bittersweet memory.

Reading with my brothers and sisters in our upstairs bedroom with the sun shining through the windows. How will I learn to live alone, without them? How will I grow up without Momma?

Annabelle wondered if the constant fear that still slithered through her would be forever, or would it leave her? Feeling sorry for herself, Annabelle was riddled with guilt for thinking about only herself, especially now sitting at her family's funeral. Unselfishly, they had loved her unconditionally, and Annabelle needed to give them her respect now. She stopped crying and winced as she straightened her back, bringing her attention back to Pastor Henry.

"Everyone here has paid homage to this beautiful family, and their memories shall reign in our hearts. They died courageously protecting one another while trying to save their own lives. The character and courage of this family are enviable."

Pastor Henry took a deep breath, pausing to regain his composure. He looked out over the mourners, hearing their soft cries of lost emotions. The pastor began again as he turned a page in the Bible.

"Annabelle has been rewarded with the best characteristics of each member of her loving family. She is a survivor, a child of faith, ingenious, courageous with a fierce love of life. Annabelle, too, was the defender of her family and blessed by God to have had such a strong family unit.

"One day, she will grow into a strong and beautiful woman and find a loving husband who will cherish and love her, giving her babies, creating a new family of her own. Their children will be rewarded with those unique characteristics given to Annabelle by her mother, Letty, and her siblings, Mattson, Candy, Gail, and Harley."

Silence covered the congregation.

"Let us pray. Dear Lord, please keep Annabelle Marian Winckowski, this child of God, safe. Please allow for healing, and may she be blessed with your grace forever. Amen."

Pastor Henry stepped down from the pulpit and walked past each draped coffin, placing his hand upon each, murmuring a blessing. When he had finished, Pastor Henry stood facing the congregation, raised his hands, and said, "I ask our Lord to bless this mother and her children as they ascend into Heaven. Amen."

Annabelle reflected on those important words said about her.

Can I grow into a woman who will have her own family? Will I find a husband who will love me without the pain from his anger? But I can't grow up alone. I'm just a kid. What will happen to me?

Her worries began slithering again through her chest.

Just then, a sunbeam broke from the opposite side of the church, piercing the enormous stained-glass windows and cast its prism over the lawn. The beam danced upon the family's caskets in a vibrant array of colors. Then it was gone. Annabelle gasped, feeling her face soften. It was a sign, and it was then she decided to believe that God would figure it all out for her. Her future was in His hands, and she would trust.

Sitting back in her chair, not realizing she had been leaning so far forward, she suddenly felt exhausted. A small smile played inside her, and she knew she would be okay. A daily reminder of her family's memories would give her joy, along with strength and courage. Annabelle knew today her life would be different; it would be a less fearful life. She wouldn't have her family, but their love was a part of her. That would have to be enough.

Five ushers approached the caskets, each removing the spray of flowers and placing them onto a metal stand behind the altar. Daneen Nelson and Doris Dickens joined Pastor Henry, and together they walked to the first coffin, Letty's. Doris removed the quilt from the top and held it while Pastor Henry opened the casket. Accepting the quilt, he placed it around Letty. Pastor Henry bowed his head, prayed over her, and closed the lid. They stepped to the next one, Mattson, and Daneen held the quilt, passing it to the pastor as he laid it over Mattson. This was repeated three more times until all five were tucked in.

Annabelle sat staring at the coffins, feeling a comforting release that they were safe and ready for their journey to Heaven. She tapped her heart, kissed her fingertips, and waved it off to her family.

The pallbearers returned and slowly guided each of the coffins down the grassy aisle. Annabelle was helped back into her wheelchair as Shelly released the brake and began pushing her down the path following the caskets. Annabelle passed two rows of mourners and then stuck out her feet.

Shelly leaned over to the side of her and said, "What is it, honey?"

Annabelle tucked her new Bible behind her, pushed down on the handlebars, and stood. Not sure what she was going to do, Annabelle looked over the enormous number of people who were now staring at her. They had come to honor her family. Shyness reddened her face, spilling down her neck, and then Annabelle opened her mouth, but nothing came out. With a deep breath, she tried again. Raising her head, looking over the congregation, she said in a strong, unwavering voice, "Thank you."

Carefully sitting back down, she looked forward. Shelly returned the Bible to Annabelle's lap, and they continued their descent.

As they wheeled past the rows and rows of people, Annabelle saw Amelia, her forever friend, who used her shoulder to stop a tear and waved a small puppet wave. Annabelle smiled shyly, returning the wave.

Passing the many rows, Annabelle spotted the boys from their math class, and they were crying and waving to her. Annabelle returned their greeting; they were nice boys. She liked them.

chapter
forty-two

Thursday, June 7, 1:00 p.m.

North of Clinton, Minnesota

The air inside the van had gotten so hot it jerked Wayne awake. The vehicle was still tucked under the pine boughs where he had parked the night before. His stomach no longer hurt, but it was growling. Wayne stepped outside to relieve himself, stretched, and ducked back into the car. A grin slid over his face as he realized he was in Minnesota and would be home soon.

He felt more focused despite the intense headache and started driving again. Hours later, Wayne had finally passed the midway point of the long state, heading northeast. It wouldn't be long before Wayne reached his destination, but he needed to stop and rest, not feeling up to driving any longer.

Up ahead, Wayne saw just what he needed, but not what he wanted. It was another abandoned farm. A couple of brown shutters were hanging from their pins, swinging against green clapboards: no cars, no equipment, no activity. It had probably all been sold off at a foreclosure auction. This home had been long forgotten, except perhaps by some banker who was constantly reminded that the deserted house had left his accounting books unbalanced.

Wayne parked behind the empty corncrib and walked toward the house. The back door had a padlock, which Wayne was ready for, and he plucked the Leatherman off his belt, removing the lock with a pick. Pushing the door open, guarded Wayne entered the kitchen, guiding his steps with his flashlight. One chair next to the kitchen table declared there had only been one person living in the house. The house smelled closed in but not as nasty as some of the other places he had stayed in.

Flipping the knife out from the Leatherman, he searched the house for animals or vagrants. There was no electricity. The house was furnished and surprisingly untouched by vandals.

The small main floor bedroom had a single bed completely made up with sheets, a pillow, and a blanket. A small tube TV in the living room sat on an end table close to an overstuffed beige recliner and a couch. He could see around grease stain on the back of the chair where someone's head had rested for years watching TV. Wayne finished the search and found comfort in the deserted house.

Needing something to eat or drink, he went back to the van and searched. In luck, he found a partial whiskey bottle and a pack of peanut butter crackers hidden behind one of the back seats. The van's clock read 9:30 p.m. The lost white loaf of bread was green with mold, and he chucked it past the side of the barn.

Wayne searched the yard and spotted a red water hand pump just to the side of the house. Hopefully, there would be water. That would be tomorrow's project.

Walking back into the house, he carried his small supplies. Again, feeling pissed for leaving everything back at that campsite and having spent all that money for nothing. He chugged the whiskey, gasped, and then licked the rim.

chapter
forty-three

Friday, June 8, morning

North of Clinton, Minnesota

Wayne woke slowly at sunrise. Remembering where he was and not in any hurry to leave the comfortable bed, he turned over and almost immediately began to snore.

A real nightmare darkened his sleep. It was mid-July, and he was a young boy sitting in the closet, feeling claustrophobic among the hanging winter clothing. He was sweltering. Once again, Wydell, his mother, was teaching him a lesson. Wayne's stomach growled, and tears came to his eyes when the good cooking smells from the kitchen wafted under the door. She was a fantastic cook and morbidly obese at six feet tall. When she finally opened the door to the closet, she

262 / Donna Graham

held her nose, avoiding the stench of her son, and released him until the next time.

Years passed inside the dream, and he had grown to a full-sized man at the age of thirteen. He and his mother were arguing on the landing at the top of the stairs. Screeching, Wydell swung her silver hairbrush, smacking Wayne's head again and again. When she pulled back for another swing, he shoved his mammoth-sized mother. Watching as if it was a movie reel in slow motion, he looked at his mother who seemed in control of her crashing down the stairs.

She didn't utter a word and landed in the corner before the last three steps turned. Her upside-down gaze was on him, seemingly unharmed, but then she struggled a little. His mother had fallen with her full weight on top of her twisted neck. Her mouth opened and shut like a fish gasping for air. Her bulging eyes turned fearful and pleading. Wayne casually sat on the top step, resting his chin in his hands. When she turned quietly blue, he climbed down the stairs, sidestepped her body, and called the police from the kitchen wall phone.

The coroner ruled the death accidental. His mother's father, Wydell Winckowski, Senior, was notified of his daughter's death but refused to accept the responsibility of raising his grandson. Wayne spent the next five years shuffled around Minnesota to various foster homes. He lost count after the twenty-second home.

Waking, Wayne gasped for air, throwing the wool blankets off him, feeling the room's cool air touch his body. He struggled to sit up as the whirlies attacked his brain. Not having eaten since Tuesday night at the CCC, Wayne felt like shit. The little bit of whiskey he had the night before did not satiate his need for water. He couldn't remember when he'd last had any. His stomach felt tender, and his headache was beyond pain. How was he going to get any driving done feeling dizzy and crappy?

Deciding to stay in place until he felt better, food, or no food, he remembered the old water pump outside. Putting his dark jeans on, Wayne eased out the door and walked over and began pumping, knowing he needed to prime it first with water, but there wasn't any. He pumped and pumped until the only water he saw was the salty sweat dripping off his overexerted face.

Swearing, he gave up. Back in the house, he started checking the kitchen cabinets. Not much there. He slowly made his way down the narrow basement steps, guiding himself as he touched the stone foundation. His penlight cast a small bean, but he found the root cellar and hit pay dirt. It contained jars and jars of canned green beans, tomatoes, corn, and peaches, and he figured he could live off the food for weeks. He brought up a few green glass jars, setting them down on the table.

Wayne rooted around in the drawers until he found a Hamm's Beer bottle opener and began to pry the lid from a jar of corn. The top shot off and the jar spilled foul-smelling corn, spreading the liquid contents all over the table floor and on Wayne. The smell was surreal. Wayne projectile vomited so viciously it hit the wall before sliding down to the gold linoleum tile. Turning away quickly, he retched until there was nothing left.

Collapsing onto the lone chair, he hung his head between his knees. He did not have any idea how long those canned jars had been down there, but he figured too damn long. Carefully picking up the crock of spoiled corn, he walked to the back door and threw it out to the yard, and heaved again. Standing a long time, he rushed through the kitchen, leaving the rancid smell of corn and his vomit behind him. Walking back into the bedroom, Wayne slammed the door, collapsed on the soft bed, facing the wall, and fell asleep.

Waking with a start, he searched the room, looking for the wild animals that were growling in his nightmare, and saw nothing but total darkness. The sun had set. The growling started again; it was his stomach begging for food. He never liked feeling hungry and did everything in his power to keep himself full. He shook his head when the chilling memories from his childhood knocked. His mother's angry face floated in front of his eyes. Shuddering, he rubbed them until they blurred.

Sitting up, he felt a bit better. It was time to leave. Wayne realized his headache was gone. What wasn't gone was his profound confusion.

He stood and left the bedroom, turning the wrong way out of the door and knocking a lamp off the table. He tried to catch it, but it got away from him and crashed to the floor. His headache had been hiding, but the noise brought it thundering back. Brushing his bald head and dry washing his face, he tried to get his bearings, not recognizing where he was. Wayne fell into the beige recliner, closed his eyes, and tried to stop them from twitching.

He rested for what seemed like an hour. Wayne stood, held onto the wall, and made his way into the kitchen. The rotten corn smell met him at the doorway, forcing him to gag. Wayne saw the drying vomit-covered with flies on the floor, he ran outside to the overgrown yard and dry heaved. It was pouring rain, and he became soaked. He didn't care and stood for a long time with his mouth open to the rain shower.

Slowly walking around the corncrib, he started the van and pulled the car around to the back of the house, aiming his headlights inside. Holding his nose, he re-entered the house and searched everywhere until he found his much-needed Leatherman along with one of his dirty socks. He looked down at his boots. How did he forget to put on both socks? He'd think about that later, but now he had to leave.

chapter
forty-four

Friday, June 8, 8:00 p.m.

West Central, Minnesota

Wayne was flying down strange country roads once again when he passed the Shangri-La Motel. He looked longingly at the motel, wishing for clean sheets and an hour-long hot shower with a new package of soap. Extending the fantasy, Wayne imagined dressing in one of his freshly ironed shirts and clean black jeans. Rubbing his neck, he sniffed his hand, searching for the scent of Patchouli. His body odor was getting in the way of his favorite cologne, but the smell was still there. His black mood deepened, knowing all of what had been lost. His enormous sense of pride used to fill him up, and now the only pathetic link to happiness was finding the scent of his cologne. The life he had planned had been taken from him.

He took a quick peek into the rearview mirror, the narrow image showing dark bags under his eyes, a scraggly beard, and a shadowed, bald head. Wayne was shocked. A stranger was staring back at him. The loss of his beautiful, dark wavy hair made him feel bad.

Shit! He almost ran off the road again and knew he had to get his mind off of these depressing thoughts. Sitting up straight, Wayne repositioned his hands on the steering wheel and concentrated on his driving to get back home. Maybe tomorrow night he'd be having a little private drink with Blaze and Fabian somewhere out in a farmer's field like they'd used to do as teenagers. The three of them had some crazy history. He leered at the memories.

Slowing down as he passed a familiar landmark, he asked himself, hadn't he already driven past it several miles back? Oh, God, he was going in circles. Pulling over, he dug through the dozens of Carl's maps, finding one that guided him back on track.

Turning up the volume on the radio, Winckowski listened to the news. And then he heard it: Annabelle was alive. He knew it! Slamming his palm against the steering wheel several times, he shouted with glee.

"I'm coming home, AnnieBelly!"

Wayne listened intently for more information, but there wasn't any. Nothing was mentioned about the police hunting for him. Had he killed the deputy in Chili Con Camp? *No news is good news,* he figured. The radio announcer said that Blanchard's entire town had turned out for the funeral of his family.

Out loud, Wayne said, "Oh, yeah, I guess they would have had a funeral. Glad I didn't have to pay for that!"

Pausing in thought, he wondered how he felt about murdering his family. He didn't have any real feelings of sadness about doing it, and he didn't miss them at all. Wayne did know that he didn't want to see all that blood again. Gross.

His mind rambled back to the number of people he had killed. Six? The news report never mentioned the man he cold-cocked at Beatty Lake, so Wayne figured old man Larson hadn't been found yet. Lying there for four days, old Carl had to be dead by now. Adding in his head, he calculated the five Winckowski's, and he should include the raccoon too. Wayne's smile flashed momentarily. Larson would have been number seven, and hopefully, the deputy was dead. That would make eight gone. He was on a killing spree and maybe famous! Some chicks went for that.

He felt so powerful. He had never thought of himself as a killer, but it made him puff up with superhuman feelings. That brought his mind back to Beatty Lake, where naked, he had squatted on the shore washing his bloody clothes, feeling the surging power of supremacy and omnipotence. His decision to drive back to the scene of the crime was a great idea. No one, *no one* would guess he would do that.

chapter
forty-five

Friday, June 8, 8:30 p.m.

Barnesville, Minnesota

Relief washed over Wayne, when he saw a sign welcoming him to Barnesville, which meant it was only a couple hundred miles to Blanchard. Driving through town, he turned off ten miles outside on a low maintenance road to take a break. Wayne needed to figure out how to get gas, food, water, and booze. Standing next to a tree, he quickly turned his head left and yipped with pleasure when a new, fresh idea popped into his head. Zipping up, Wayne did a little dance as the plan developed into Technicolor. He moved the van tighter inside the trees to wait until dark.

Finally, the clock read 10:30 p.m., and the night was darker than the inside of a goat. Perfect. Wayne slowly started making his way out the old fire road and turned left, heading back toward a farm he had seen earlier. A bright yard light glowed over the sleeping homestead, and the towering bulk gas tank that stood in the middle of the circular driveway was what had captured his attention earlier. He directed the van up the long driveway.

The white house was dark, settled in for the night. Wayne pulled the mini-van behind the silo, well hidden from the road. Wayne grabbed his pistol and got out. Keeping the gun front and center, he took a look around and slowly made his way across the yard. He crept up the wide porch steps and stood in front of the door. The yard light cast a soft glow over the antique door. It had an old-style doorbell which needed to be turned to ring. A large etched floral window covered half the door. Wayne kicked the door in. The horrendous explosion broke the silence of the farm, the antique frosted glass window pulverized.

Stepping into the front room, Wayne stopped, hearing whimpering coming from the room across the living room. He switched on the lights and proceeded slowly toward the door.

Turning the knob ever so slightly, he threw it open, snapped on the ceiling light, and pointed his gun. Hunched over on the edge of the bed was a very old lady with long gray hair, dressed in a gauzy white nightgown. She peered through the lace of her hair at the giant man standing in her doorway. The woman fumbled, trying to pull on her prosthetic leg. Wayne aimed and pointed the gun as she screamed, covering her face. Moving the barrel slightly up, Wayne fired. The slug hit the wooden carved headboard blowing a king-sized nugget into the dense wood. The woman collapsed backward, spread-eagle on the bed with her eyes closed. The artificial leg tipped over.

Walking to her bedside table, Wayne yanked the phone cord from the wall, grabbed the phone and the artificial leg, and carried them out of the room. Throwing them to the hardwood floor, he heard it hit with a racket. Slamming the bedroom door, he picked up a dining room chair and pushed the top rail under the doorknob. The old woman was locked in. Not caring if she was dead or alive, Wayne thought she had better be quiet because he was a serial killer.

Wayne laid his gun on the kitchen table and opened the refrigerator. He would have sung praises to God (if he believed) as the light displayed the spectacular contents. It looked like she had cooked an entire buffet just waiting for him to arrive. There were deviled eggs, a spiral ham, whipped cream fruit salad, fried chicken, potato salad, ring macaroni pea salad, a round link of bologna, and a leftover Polish sausage and sauerkraut casserole.

Clearing out the top shelf, Wayne placed the food on the countertops, stove, and dinette table, tasting tidbits as he went. Then Wayne started loading his treasures onto the next countertop as he continued to pull out more food. With an aha moment, Wayne discovered dessert, some kind of lemon cake. Double-checking all of the shelves, he bent down and found an ice-cold six-pack of beer way in the back. That's when he started humming one of his favorites by Waylon Jennings, "Good Hearted Woman."

Wayne was salivating as he opened cupboards looking for plates and silverware. Clearing a spot, he set the table for the party of one. Then, extending his search to the dining room, Wayne saw the most impressive China hutch he had ever seen, which took up nearly the entire wall. It was filled with crystal wine glasses, china plates, teacups, and knickknacks. Squatting down, Wayne looked into the bottom cabinet and found what he had been searching for: booze! He pulled out four bottles of red and white wine and an old, nearly full bottle of scotch. Giddy, Wayne danced his way back into the kitchen and gently set the bottles down. Searching the kitchen drawers, he found a wine bottle opener and popped open a red.

Quickly taking a long pull of the merlot, he followed up with a scotch chaser. His eyes crossed, making him shudder all the way down to his toes. Wayne sat down at the table, and with a wide toothy smile, he laid a floral napkin across his lap and began to devour his feast.

Overlooking his cornucopia of plenty, he addressed the food and excused himself.

Wayne bounced his way over to the China hutch, pulled out a large crystal water goblet, and gently closed the glass door. Squeezing a place for the goblet between two platters, he returned to his seat. He snapped his napkin and carefully placed it back onto his lap.

He smiled graciously and again said, "Thank you for your patience. Oh, and thank you for feeding me after three days of no food or booze or water." Wayne filled his mouth so full of food, his jaw started clicking with each bite.

Taking a break from eating, Wayne listened for any sounds coming from the old lady's bedroom, but he heard nothing. Wayne sat back, chewing on a chicken leg, and moaned with ecstasy. The old lady was a fabulous cook, and Wayne thought he should have told her that before he scared her to death. He chuckled.

Wayne filled the elegant water goblet with merlot and gargled. He followed it up with another shot of scotch. Quickly making his way to the second level of ecstasy with the liquor, he dug into the salads with a tablespoon and choked and blew food over the table. Swallowing, he brushed the ring noodles from his shirt, leaned back in the chair, and sang "I've Always Been Crazy." Waylon Jennings sure knew how to croon a tune.

Humming with pleasure, Wayne spotted a loaf of home-made bread sitting on the counter. Leaning back on his chair, he grabbed the recycled plastic bag and dumped it out onto the table. Pouring wine into a small bowl, Wayne pulled off a hunk of the soft white bread and dunked it into the wine until it was a droopy, purple mess before plopping it into his mouth. That was not a good idea, especially not with bologna and kraut.

Continuing to eat, he looked down onto his chest at the purple wine spots, vomit, and ring noodles scattered across his shirtfront. Wiping at it with his napkin, he just smeared it all into one big stain. He promised himself to search the old lady's house for some men's clothing, and then he'd have himself a long, hot shower.

Gorging himself, he finished the last mouthful and leaned back in his chair. Burping loudly, he stood up, filled his goblet with the wine, dropped a tablespoon into the cake pan, picked it up, and stumbled into the living room. Flopping onto the couch, he was ready to finish off more wine while watching TV. He tried to carefully set the wine on the end table, but it sloshed it over the armrest. He picked up the sticky spoon and filled his mouth with the mouthwatering lemon cake.

He dropped the partially eaten cake pan onto the floor, and the utensil popped out of the pan, skittering across the floor. Leaning back onto the comfortable couch, he stretched his arm across the back. Suddenly Wayne felt a piercing pain rip his arm, and he flung himself off of the davenport, lumbering across the living room. Wayne saw small tiny red beads of blood dripping from on his forearm. Rushing to the kitchen table, he lifted his gun and pointed it straight at the couch. Sitting on the back of the sofa was a small tabby kitten with a pink nose, looking directly at him. It mewed once.

Looking down at his painful forearm, he cursed, "Shit!" and laughed at himself for becoming so afraid. Pointing the gun at the kitten, he said, "Bang."

The kitten jumped back behind the couch and disappeared.

After watching a couple hours of television, Wayne was well into being wasted but remembered he hadn't filled up the van from the bulk gas tank and wanted it done before he left in the morning. Lurching outside, he fell down the porch steps. Regaining his balance, he moved the van under the monster-sized gas tank and pulled down the hose. After filling it up and finding himself unable to rehang the nozzle, Wayne threw the hose to the ground and re-hid the van.

Stumbling back, he recalled an event he had spotted on the old woman's calendar: family dinner, Saturday, June 9, 12:00 p.m. He had spoiled her party. Oh, well. Wayne planned on leaving by 9:00 a.m., way ahead of the party. The relief of a full stomach plus lots of liquor should have made him feel terrific, but quickly consuming the feast with the combination of alcohol on top of kraut and lemon cake made him feel grossly ill. His mouth tasted like the inside of an old, soggy army boot.

It was nearly 1:00 a.m. when he walked back into the house, slamming the broken front door behind him. Without a catch, it slowly drifted open, welcoming any of the night creatures to enter the house. Uncaring, Wayne passed out on the sofa.

chapter
forty-six

Saturday, June 9, 11:00 a.m.

Barnesville, Minnesota

Wayne woke once again to a bright morning and complete confusion about where he was with his head pounding. Scared, he jumped up and drew his gun at the open front door, which was banging against the wall. Wayne dropped his shoulders in relief, recognizing the mess in the kitchen. Quickly turning to see if the old lady's bedroom door was still secure and finding it was, he stuffed the gun inside his pants and checked the pink teapot wall clock. It was eleven o'clock! Looking carefully out the battered swinging door, he was grateful there weren't any cops. Wayne tensed when he heard cars and saw three vehicles pass, heading toward town.

The living room looked like there had been a food fight, and he found the tabby kitten eating lemon cake out of the pan on the floor. Wayne advanced toward the kitchen, and the tabby skittered under the china hutch. Rustling around in the kitchen, he found a stash of grocery bags stuffed into a metal container hanging on the wall in the stairwell. Bagging up the leftover chicken in a Wal-Mart bag, Wayne quickly snapped open a paper grocery sack. The deafening sound almost made him collapse, and he steadied himself against the table, blinking his eyes. He was in terrible shape and hoping he could find his way home.

Pulling the tab on a beer, he swallowed it in one pull. Crushing the can and feeling a little more human, he released it to the floor.

Wayne carefully placed the unopened wine bottles into the paper bag, then stuffed plastic bags around them, protecting them from breaking, before adding his partial bottle of scotch and the opener. Slowly, he set it down next to the front door along with the five-pack of beer. Wayne was anxious to leave and looked around, his eyes twitching. Picking up the groceries, he kicked the front door open and slowly made his way down the porch steps.

Wayne staggered across the yard, panting with the exertion, and finally reached the car. He tossed the bag of chicken onto the floor, added the beer, and then carefully placed the bag of bottles onto the passenger seat and buckled them in. Suddenly unsure, Wayne touched the front of his jeans for his Colt and felt relieved that it was there.

Dust flew as Wayne roared down the driveway, full but unwashed, without a fresh change of clothing, heading for home.

chapter
forty-seven

Saturday, June 9, 11:30 a.m.

Barnesville, Minnesota

In their fifties, two women stood looking up to the porch at their mother's front door, which was gently swaying back and forth. Scared to go in and scared not to, they clasped their hands together and walked up the stairs. Stepping over the broken glass, they tip-toes into the living room, stopped, and faced the mess. One called out with a hitch in her voice, "Mom?" They both heard an unidentifiable sound coming from the bedroom and saw the door was locked with a chair rail tucked under the knob. Still clutching their hands together, they moved in tandem, toward their mother's door. Both called out more strongly, "Mom?"

"Girls, come help me!" their mother shouted.

Unhitching their hands, they scrambled to remove the chair. Nervous as to what they would find, the oldest slowly opened the door. The old woman screamed with relief as her daughters ran to her and hugged her with all their might, as they let their tears fall.

"I'm fine, I'm fine," the woman reassured her daughters. "Some horrible man broke in last night and scared the piss out of me! Literally."

Breaking out in raucous laughter, the daughters were relieved to find their mother alive, and with her sense of humor intact.

"Girls, I have to get out of these wet things. I don't want the police to see me this way. I need a shower. Beth, he took my leg. Will you look around for it, please? Angie, you better call the police."

Both women did as their mother told them. Beth found the discarded artificial limb and brought it to her mother, who quickly slipped it into place.

Angie reported back that the police were on their way. Their mother stood up, took clothes out of her dresser, and said as she headed for the bathroom, "I'll be out in two shakes of a lamb's tail. "

The daughters looked at each other, sniffling, smiling, and hugged. They parted, stood, and got to work. Together they stripped the bed and started the washing machine.

chapter
forty-eight

Saturday, June 9, 11:30 a.m.

Dignity Christian Hospital,
Two Streams, Minnesota

Annabelle was asleep when Kathy woke her gently. "Hi, honey, I'm sorry to wake you, but Jim and Doris are here, and they want to see you. I know you're not feeling well, but they will only stay a couple of minutes. It's important."

Annabelle whispered, "Sure." Kathy helped the feverish girl sit up. The little patient's face was bright pink, and eyes glazed with fever. Kathy gave her some water and then went to the door motioning for the Dickens to come in. They pulled their chairs close to one side of the bed, and Kathy sat on her cot.

Annabelle would not take her eyes off Jim and Doris, hoping their news was good and not bad.

Jim finally said with a croak in his voice, "We…" He began again. "We want to ask; would you be okay with staying with us to recover once you've been released from the hospital?" Jim's eyes were pleading, and Doris swiped at her pant leg, not making eye contact.

They want me to stay with them while I recover? Annabelle couldn't make a sound, but she nodded with a weak smile.

Jim stood smiling ear to ear and gave Annabelle a gentle hug. Doris looked up to each of them and said, "What? What?"

Jim and Annabelle looked at Doris's questioning eyes and, in unison, said, "Yes."

Doris sang, "Ohhhh…" and started blubbering. She moved over to sit on the bed, taking Annabelle's hands and gently bouncing them up and down. Doris' smile said it all.

Jim sat back in his seat and passed the Kleenex box around. The relief was written on Annabelle's face. "Will I go to an orphanage when I'm all healed, then?"

Doris was taken aback and said, "Oh, no, dear. We meant for you to live with us forever. We want to adopt you. Would you like that?"

Annabelle felt a boulder drop deep within her stomach, and then it surged upwards into a heaving cry. She grabbed Ollie and sobbed with abandon into his chest as her new parents hugged her.

Just then, Sally pranced into the room and instinctively knew emotions were high. She escaped from the hold of Shelly's leash and effortlessly bounded up onto Annabelle's bed and leaped onto her shoulder, licking her face and tickling Annabelle's heart.

Shelly took in the crying scene, including Kathy, and asked, "What's happened?"

Jim and Doris were both unavailable to answer, wiping their tears, laughing, and passing the ever-present box of Kleenex back and forth.

The orphan answered over Sally's whimpering, "I'm going to live with them. Forever!"

Shelly, ever the professional, sobbed outright, rushing to the side of the hospital bed, cradling Annabelle's head into her chest. Sally nuzzled her way into the hug. Pulling back, Shelly said, "I. Am. So. Glad. For. You." Looking to Doris and Jim, she asked shyly, "Could I have that box of Kleenex? I would love to visit, would that work?"

Jim said with gusto, "Absolutely!" Mrs. Dickens sat, wiping her tears, and agreed with the continuous nodding of her head.

Jim had tossed the tissue box to Shelly, who pulled out the last Kleenex, and then she tossed it to Kathy, who jammed her hand into the box, coming out empty-handed. They all laughed as Kathy went to the bathroom, grabbed the end of the toilet paper, wiping her eyes, and walked out, trailing several feet of toilet paper behind her. Unaware, Kathy stopped dabbed at her eyes, and the whirling toilet paper roll emptied onto the bathroom floor.

Shelly announced, "I'm going to get some celebratory dessert and a bigger box of Kleenex." She hustled out of the room with her sashay at full tilt, making the others giggle. Kathy followed Shelly out, with her phone to her ear and the pieces TP still following her.

The Terrier figured the high emotions were studded with happiness and tucked her head under Annabelle's arm, falling asleep.

Looking ready to fall asleep herself, Annabelle said softly, "I prayed that you would take me."

Jim replied, "Well, we just couldn't tell you any sooner, afraid things wouldn't work out. But with the exceptional help from a wonderful social worker, Kathy, we got a lot done in a very short amount of time this week. Doris and I will first be your foster parents. If Kathy approves of how things are going, we will begin adopting you as our daughter. That will be the toughest since your dad is on the run, and the state would either have to remove his rights to you or Wayne would have to agree to have us adopt you. It is very complicated.

"We spoke with the chief and Dr. Joe, and they are both just fine with this. But we weren't sure how you would feel, and we were so nervous when we came in, worried that you may not feel quite comfortable living with us."

Annabelle's voice hitched. "I want you."

Shelly came in behind a cart filled with tableware, half of a homemade birthday cake, a pot of coffee for the adults, and a cold glass of milk for Annabelle. Sally woke up, sniffed the air, and sat up, begging for the dog biscuit that also sat on the tray. The adults were silent as they ate the cake and relished the good news. The only sound in the room was from Jim, who hummed while he ate. Annabelle sipped her milk, ate a small bite of cake, and grew quiet. The adults cleaned up and left the room, leaving Annabelle deep in sleep, curled around Sally and Ollie.

chapter
forty-nine

Saturday, June 9, 12:00 p.m.

Goulash Cafe, Two Streams, Minnesota

*D*eputy Tommy Johnson was more nervous than he had been since getting the job with Two Streams police a year ago. He had a date with Shelly Rae, the most beautiful woman in town and one fine nurse. It would probably be the shortest date in history, but Tommy would not misstep. He had showered, shined his shoes, put on his best dress shirt, and had bought flowers from Two-Lips Flower Shop.

They had decided to meet at the Goulash Cafe across the street from the hospital, and their date would be forty minutes long. Shelly was on duty, and this would be her mid-day break, and Tommy would be guarding Annabelle Winckowski after lunch.

When he showed up at the cafe ten minutes early, Mattie commented on how nice he looked. The old cook tentatively leaned over and quietly said, "You smell good too." Mattie's dentures slipped and clattered inside her mouth when she smiled.

His cheeks rose to high color, and Tommy shyly nodded his thanks.

Mattie continued, "If you would like, that back booth for eight is open. It's pretty cozy." Tommy nodded and followed her. "Also, Tommy, why don't you have the steak for lunch? I'll make 'em myself. Won't take but a minute."

"But we have only forty minutes, and what if she's a vegetarian?"

Mattie chuckled and shook her head. "Believe me, Shelly is not. She's in here all the time, and I would have noticed. I'll slap the steaks on right now. Fries for sure." Mattie slowly hobbled away on her bad hip, touching each table as she went by just for a little support.

Tommy teasingly shouted after her, "Hurry up!"

"Listen, Bub, just as soon as I get my new hip, I'll be chasing that new farmer in town."

Tommy chuckled and had just settled into the back booth when he heard the front doorbell tinkle. In walked Shelly, spotting him, she immediately walked over to her date. Tommy was hustling, trying to get out from the long, curved booth when Shelly stopped in front of him and held out her hand. She said, "Why don't I scoot over to you?"

Tommy dropped a sigh and took her hand, helping her scoot. Shelly did it gracefully and didn't stop until they were thigh to thigh. He gave her his flowers, which made her eyes dance.

Looking at each other, neither blinking nor talking, they said it all with their goofy smiles. Tommy found her pinky finger and held on for dear life.

chapter fifty

Saturday, June 9, 1:00 p.m.

Two Streams Police Department, Two Streams, Minnesota

*L*iza's drawn face expressed her exhaustion when the call came in, but she was soon on her feet, running flat out. Throwing open the chief's door, she said, "Wayne's been sighted in Barnesville! He broke into a house."

Liza watched as the Chief's ears lit on fire, but he just nodded nonchalantly and picked up his phone to call Hilde.

Liza ran to the lunchroom, knocked softly, waited as her legs jiggled. Ron opened the door and said, "Hey, what's up?"

She relayed the same information to Ron, turned, and left. Klink heard them and turned back to his keyboard. His screen popped up with a close-up of a Minnesota map with several red lines that zigzagged through North and South Dakota and now headed closer than ever to Blanchard.

Rik stepped over to Ron's desk with his phone to his ear, calling the Barnesville police chief for more up-to-date information. Rik put the phone on speaker and said, "Hey, Chief Danielsson, it's Rik, and I have you on speaker. So, Mel, we got word that our man broke into a house over there. Tell me what Winckowski took and what he did. Hopefully, no one was hurt or killed."

Chief of Police Melvin Danielsson skipped the pleasantries and began speaking with his slight Minnesotan accent, overlayed with a lilt of ancestral Swedish.

"Well, Winckowski was I.D.'d as your guy by Rose Busch. She's a widow and lives alone on her farm. Wayne kicked in the front door around 11:00 last night and found Rose in her bedroom. He shot at her and missed but left a slug in the headboard. Locking her in, but not before he yanked out the landline and took her prosthetic leg.

"He cleaned out the refrigerator, and it looks like he drank a couple bottles of wine and some scotch, taking the rest of the booze with him. Rose is madder than a wet hen because the bastard ate most of the food she had prepared for today's family dinner.

"It looks like he gassed up the van from the farm's bulk gas tank. Rose heard him tear out of the yard around late this morning."

"Is the woman, okay?"

"Yeah, she's fine, but her kitten seems to be suffering from too much lemon cake. Otherwise, all is good."

Rik asked, "No other sightings?"

"No. The two daughters found their mother close to noon and called the police. No sightings since. "

"Thanks, Mel. We appreciate the information." Rik hung up.

Klink had been working on something, and he turned to them now. He stated clearly, "He was at the house for twelve hours, ate, slept, gassed the van's twenty-gallon tank, plus the ten-gallon cans of gas, which is enough for four hundred and twenty miles. From Barnesville, the slowest route and least visible would be through Grand Rapids.

"If he drove directly here, he would have only twelve gallons of gas left for his get-away from Blanchard. Has to get gas before Blanchard or W's get-away will be short-lived. His arrival into Blanchard averaging his speed at forty-five miles an hour could be at the earliest..." Klink glanced at his large faced wristwatch, "five hours and forty-six minutes, which puts it at six-forty-six. Question One: which route is W taking? Two: where will he get gas before Blanchard? Three: how fast is he traveling? Four: will W stop to rest?"

Rik piped in, "Can't imagine Winckowski would try to enter Blanchard during daylight hours. I think it'll be late tonight." Rik looked to Ron and Klink as they nodded their agreement.

Rik said to both, "I'm going to go and talk to the chief."

He left the lunchroom and walked the short distance to Roger's office. He tapped on the chief's door, and Hilde opened the door entered with his oxygen tank behind. Rik updated the two of them on Klink's theory and left them to decide how to proceed.

Roger turned to Hilde as soon as Rik left. "Talk to me."

Hilde sat down in front of Roger's desk. She thought for just a moment and began. "I agree with Rik that Wayne will not arrive during daylight hours, which would certainly have made capturing him easier. I also think Wayne will take the more isolated route. We'll need to find all the gas stations on that route and give the gas station attendants a heads up and tell them not to engage. Just let him fill with gas, pay his bill, and once he is gone, the attendants are to call us directly. We need his timeline. Where do you figure he's going to go once he's in Blanchard? It certainly won't be the Motel 6."

Roger added, "He's *got* to be coming here for Annabelle. Wayne must know by now that she's alive and in the hospital. We need to figure out how to maximize Annabelle's safety. Moving her out of that room to somewhere outside of the hospital would mean Winckowski would still go into hospital searching. This would endanger the patients, the hospital employees, and those coming to visit. I say we leave her in the hospital and move her to a floor where he won't expect her."

Hilde had already speed-dialed someone, who apparently picked up immediately. "Evelyn, it's Hilde," she said. "We have a problem. Annabelle's Dad is coming back to Blanchard. Not sure of his intentions, so we need her moved to a different floor."

Hilde stopped talking, her knee jumping as she listened to a muffled conversation on the other end of the line. Evelyn came back on the line. "Um, okay, we'll move Annabelle to neo-natal. Right now, there are no babies on that floor, so it will be safer for everyone involved. We'll have two nurses covering Annabelle. She has had a relapse."

Hilde's brow furrowed. "Serious?"

Evelyn said, "Yes, we've had to put her onto a stronger antibiotic. Annabelle's wound is infected, and she's running a high fever. It's just not what we were expecting. The funeral took the snot out of her, not to mention the scare from that horrible reporter."

"Well, she couldn't be in better hands. Move her now, please, and let us know the room number. Thanks, Evelyn."

Hilde turned to Roger, "The wound on Annabelle's back is seriously infected. They are moving her to neo-natal, no babies there currently."

Roger said, "Damn. The stress is really getting to that sweet thing. We need to get Winckowski behind bars before anyone else gets hurt," he paused for a moment staring at the floor, and then continued. "Our plan needs to strategically position our deputies in places around Blanchard where Winckowski may go, maybe Blaze or Fabian's house, or his own home, although I doubt that, or an abandoned house. There are over a hundred deserted houses around here, not to mention the empty downtown storefronts. So, let's get Pinpoint working on it. We have just hours before Winckowski arrives, and we have a tremendous amount of work to do. You coordinate with the Pinpoint guys, and we'll talk, and then I'll have that planning session with our team as to how we are going to proceed." Unconsciously, Roger tapped his heart.

"Yes, sir." Hilde sprinted out of the room to her office for a five-minute confab with her brain.

chapter
fifty-one

Saturday, June 9, 5:00 p.m.

Two Streams Police Department,
Two Streams, Minnesota

*B*elinda was in the lunchroom, staring at a computer screen when she jumped, hearing the chief hollering. Flying out of her chair, Belinda almost bumped into him as they met in the hallway.

"What are you doing in there?" he demanded, pointing to the lunchroom.

Stuttering, she over-explained, "I, I've been helping the Pinpoint boys with background information. I've done a lot of this type of work at the school as an information tech. I've—"

Roger had both hands on his hips, in a loud whisper, asked, "Why aren't you working on Muriel Friech and Jeff

Whalen, finding out how to get rid of them? Did you *not* see the article in the paper? Did you help Muriel with that?"

Jerking her head back, surprised at his screaming anger but standing her ground, she said, "I did see the article and already promised you that I would not contribute without your approval. The report you are referring to is finished and lying on your desk. I was nervous about emailing the report, as it is pretty damning."

"How long ago did you put it on my desk?"

"Two minutes."

Looking sheepish, Roger said, "Oh, all right then, come with me."

Belinda followed him out, tapping her pits, wondering if she would ever find a deodorant that would stop her from perspiring around him.

They walked into his office, and Roger sat hard into his desk chair, rolling up to the desk. Deputy Jackson shut the door quietly and took the chair in front of him.

He read her report in silence as Belinda crossed her legs, imprisoning her hands between her knees, and rocked back and forth.

"How accurate are the facts in this report?"

"All have been verified."

The furrow in his forehead softened, and a smile creased his hardened face. The police chief sat back and said, "How the hell did you get this information?"

"Snooping. I am a good digger. Research is my forte. Muriel and her alcoholic mayor of a husband are stupid and have made so many mistakes. I found that several people knew what the mayor and Friechs were doing, but they had been threatened and unwilling to confide in me. Pushing the folks who were concealing information wasn't fun, but I promised them anonymity, and the witnesses finally told me everything. I had to promise them they wouldn't have to testify in court, which also helped get their cooperation."

Roger was amazed at the work she had done, and the report seemed flawless, but his brow furrowed. "May I ask you why you would promise the witnesses that they wouldn't have to testify?"

"I have a cousin who is a prosecutor in Chicago, and she assured me that I had garnered enough physical evidence that no one would have to face the Friechs or Whalen in court. The mayor and his wife are going to jail. Ron also found an obscure law that will throw Jeff Whalen into jail for a very long time. Plus, he'll have to pay for all the restitutions, which means selling his home. Too bad, so sad."

The chief snickered and quickly covered it, embarrassed that Belinda had a way of making him loosen up more often than not. "Exactly. Let's see here, you got the mayor and Friechs on forgery, theft of public funds, aggravated identity theft, embezzlement, and grand larceny. I can't believe they stole an impounded new Humvee and sold it and kept the money. Wow, this was a hell of a lot deeper than I gave them credit for. Well done. Get those arrest warrants ready, and we'll serve them tomorrow. We have enough on our plate for tonight with Winckowski coming to town."

"Will do, sir. Is there anything else I may do for you?"

The chief's mouth went dry. Roger pretended to be absorbed in the report and hoping Belinda wouldn't see his thoughts, Roger turned around to the credenza behind him and said, "Nope, good job."

Saying to the back of his head, "Thank you, sir," the deputy left quietly, with a quick peek over at him before leaving.

The chief stared out the window, thinking, *Oh, no! Belinda works for me. Would I need to fire her to date her? No, no, no! Crap.*

He could not and would not cross that line, but he sure wanted to.

chapter fifty-two

Saturday, June 9, 5:15 p.m.

Remer, Minnesota

Wayne stopped outside Remer for gas.

Entering the small office he came face to face with a giant man behind the counter, sporting a sour, potato-like face. It wasn't the man's bulk that stopped Wayne in his tracks, but the size of the Smith & Wesson Magnum lying on the counter within reach of the attendant.

Wayne muttered, "I need gas."

"Leave two hundred dollars."

Wayne's eyes went wide, and he started to argue but thought better of it when he saw the man's eyes grow dark. "Okay, okay." Wayne peeled off two one hundred–dollar bills and watched the man flip the gas pump on. Feeling nervous at having the man watching him out the window, Wayne tried to pump faster, but it was impossible. Soon enough, the van's tank was full, and he began to pull the empty gas cans out from the back of the minivan.

The attendant filled the doorway and shouted, "Hold it, you got enough. Get out of here!"

"But—"

The man raised his Magnum and pointed it at Wayne's head.

"Okay, okay." Wayne threw the empty cans back inside the van, scrambled into the driver's seat, and tore off, away from the ogre.

The attendant kept the gun trained on him until the bald man was out of sight. Then the potato-faced man called the number listed on the Two Streams Police Department's email, which included a picture of the man who had just stopped for gas.

Rik answered the phone, "Pinpoint."

"Hey, this is Dale. I run the big gas station outside of Remer. Your guy on the email was just here... wanting gas. My Magnum and me had our eyes trained on him the whole time. And he bolted."

Rik thought, *Shit, "Dirty Harry" has unwittingly warned Wayne that we're onto him.*

"Did you let him fill up?" Rik asked with clenched teeth.

"Yup, but he was going to fill his gas can, and I told him no, and pointed my gun at his head."

Rik's anger was increasing but pleased the extra gas cans were empty. "How many gallons did he put in?"

"Eighteen."

"Which direction did he go, and what is your address?"

"North, and my address is PO box twenty-six—"

"No, no, no, the physical address of your gas station!"

"Hehe, sorry, I'm still a little nervous seeing that killer face to face. My address is 6794 Minnesota Six, Remer. Hey, is there a reward?"

"For playing hotshot and intentionally disregarding our command of 'no engagement'? No!" Rik violently stabbed the red disconnect button three times in anger. He knew better than to throw it against the wall. Rik's wife had threatened him with a flip phone if he destroyed one more phone during a temper tantrum. His pride in wanting the latest and greatest iPhone made him keep his temper under a slow rolling boil.

Rik slipped on his cannula, took a couple of deep breaths, grabbed his tank, and rolled the Minnesota map over to Klink's desk as Ron followed him. Rik said, "We now have Wayne probably diverting his route to Blanchard because an idiot at a Remer gas station threatened Wayne with a gun." Rik filled up with oxygen and started again.

"There are several small two-lanes he could take, but they all end up back on Highway Six. But then, after Grand Rapids, there are so many back roads that we'd never be able to figure out where he is at any given time. We'll have to tell the chief and Hilde."

Good luck, Rik," Ron said.

"I was hoping you'd tell them. Shit, no sympathy for the guy on oxygen?"

"Nope."

Muttering to himself. Rik gathered his gear and wheeled his tank and bulletin board into the chief's office, getting the wheels stuck on the threshold. Both Hilde and Roger were on their phones but hung up when they saw Rik struggling and helped him into the chief's office.

"Bad news, guys. In Remer, we had a cowboy that threatened Winckowski with a gun, but he let him fill the van but not the cans. This is good because he only has a tank of gas, but now Winckowski is suspicious and probably will be changing his route to Blanchard or changing his plans altogether, and that may include not coming to Blanchard."

"Shit," Hilde and Roger said in unison. Rik went over the possible routes that could be taken by Winckowski. They soon realized it was too challenging to try to stop him before he got to Blanchard.

Roger spoke up. "What time did he get gas?"

"Five fifteen."

Roger looked down at his watch. It was 5:25.

Rik continued, "The cowboy mentioned that Wayne said he was almost out of gas. The distance direct from Remer to here is about two hours, one hundred and eleven some miles, using about a third of a tank. Winckowski can only divert so much because he won't have enough to get out of Minnesota again with only about one hundred seventy miles of gas left."

Roger studied the map. "Order all the officers off the road and bring them to Blanchard. We'll meet at 6:30, Goulash Café. They have a backroom where we can meet and eat. It's gonna be a long night." He saw Hilde on her phone, assuming she was already contacting the café to reserve the room. "The plan is that we'll have our guys strategically placed all over town.

"I don't think Winckowski would come into Blanchard until after dark, possibly between nine-thirty tonight and five a.m. tomorrow. Hilde, have Liza add double guards on Annabelle and in the hospital stairwells. Rik, you guys have to figure out where Winckowski is going to land in Blanchard. It's critical."

Rik dropped his head, thinking, then brought it back up and said, "I know. I know. We'll get on it. By the way, how is Annabelle doing?"

Hilde said, "Unfortunately, the funeral took a toll on her. An infection has set in, adding a fever, so she's on a more substantial dose of antibiotics and bedridden. Annabelle was moved to the neo-natal floor, with double nurses. "

Rik's face became taut when he thought of Annabelle possibly dying. He had lost his parents when his crazy cousin, Benji, killed them, thinking they were devils. Rik's wife, Rosita, had insisted they leave Colorado Springs and move to Two Streams. A change that would help her husband recover from his debilitating depression from the guilt of not recognizing Benji's schizophrenia.

Rik cleared the emotion from his throat and said, "Shit, she needs this thing over just as much as the rest of us do. You know, something keeps Winckowski from getting caught. It might be just drunk luck, but tonight his luck is going to run out. Guaranteed. I feel it in my gut."

Roger shook his head and said, "God, I hope you're right."

chapter
fifty-three

Sunday, June 10, 12:10 a.m.

Dignity Christian Hospital,
Two Streams, Minnesota

Screaming, Annabelle fought her dad, hitting him again and again. A female voice said, "Annabelle, wake up, wake up, honey!"

The person was trying to pin her arms down, but Annabelle would not allow it and continued to fight like an alley cat.

Kathy had pressed the nurses' call button and continued trying to restrain the little girl, but it was impossible. As a last resort, Kathy threw a glass of ice water into Annabelle's face. The little girl gasped and stopped fighting.

A nurse ran into the room, holding a syringe but saw that maybe it wasn't needed. Annabelle fell back onto her pillows, drops of water mixing with her tears and sliding off her face onto her gown. Heaving, Annabelle looked around the room, realizing it had all been a nightmare. Giving Kathy a shuddering smile, she said, "Dad was taking me again."

Sitting on the wet sheet, Kathy pulled Annabelle to her chest as the child seemed to grow smaller as she held on for dear life.

The nurse took Annabelle's blood pressure and shook her head, unhappy with the results. The somber nurse asked, "Can I get you a glass of milk or maybe some juice? You could use a little nourishment.

Annabelle shook her head.

The nurse looked at Kathy and noticed swelling around her left eye and scratches on her forearms. In the same tone she used for Annabelle, the somber nurse asked, "Can I get you a beer, or maybe some whiskey?" The two women laughed a little, releasing the adrenaline still hammering away at them.

Kathy continued to rock Annabelle, wondering if the night terrors would ever leave the poor child, her recovery questionable.

chapter
fifty-four

Sunday, June 10, 12:10 a.m.

Near Blanchard, Minnesota

Outside of Blanchard, tucked behind a deserted farm Wayne sat hidden, struggling to stay awake. He had been using diversionary tactics all day, crossing back and forth on every road possible and then hiding every few hours. The gun-toting giant at the last gas station had really shaken him up. Apparently, the police were onto him, but they couldn't possibly have figured that he would be driving home.

The hot, sticky weather was nearly intolerable, adding to his beating headache and shaky hands. Wayne tried to avoid the shakes by periodically sipping a little wine to keep his head clear, but it didn't seem to be helping in the eighty-degree heat. Scratching his arms until they bled, he felt the imaginary bugs continued to crawl over and under his skin. Wayne knew it must be his imagination, but then he wasn't sure. Deciding to sleep, he stepped to the back of the van, ignoring the onslaught of the imaginary infestation of bugs.

Wayne woke up two hours later, ready to combust from the heat and gasping for air. He had left the windows closed to keep the bugs out and nearly killed himself in the hot van.

Scrambling outside, heaving for air and light-headed, Wayne removed his shirt, wishing he had water. He pulled out the open bottle of wine and chugged it. He walked to a tree and leaned on the trunk, trying to cool down as he looked around. No moon, complete darkness—that was good. From the passenger seat, he removed the bag of chicken and ate it with a vengeance. It wasn't nearly as good as it was the night before, but it satisfied his growling stomach. Wayne felt a tiny bit better and slipped his shirt back on, swatting at the thousands of bugs that had zeroed in on his blood vessels. Jamming his pistol back into the waistband of his jeans, he finished the last gulp of wine and threw the bottle as far as his pitching arm could throw. He heard the glass bottle break in the distance, sending up a scattering of noisy birds.

Back in the van, he put it into gear, driving into Blanchard, arriving at 2:00 a.m. He cut the engine, coasting into a driveway, directing the car to the back of the yard until it was hidden from the road. He turned to look back at the house. Nothing to see; it was dark.

The red house stood looking abandoned. He silently patted himself on the back for being so smart. No one would ever figure he would go back to Carl Larson's house. Carl *couldn't* be there because he was indisposed. Wayne yucked at his morbid humor.

Looking out the windshield and side windows into the dark night, he saw nothing moving in or outside the home. It seemed as if nothing had changed since he was here Monday night. Dropping his head back against the head-rest, Wayne closed his eyes. He had finally made it. Wayne was back home in Blanchard, where he would start over again with Annabelle.

Wayne flicked at the invisible worms crawling up his thighs. His mind strayed, thinking of what it would be like. He would unpack his few possessions, putting them away in his new home. Then Wayne would go to the QuikStopHere, a short distance down the road, and buy some snacks. He was confident; no one would recognize him because his looks had changed dramatically. Back at the little house, he would watch a little TV.

After a little rest, he would make his way to the hospital to pick up Annabelle. He knew where the pediatric wing was, so it wouldn't be a problem. Wayne shivered, feeling tiny hairs tickling his ear canal. "Come out, you stupid cockroach." Poking his finger into his ear, trying to pull out the bug. With his eyes twitching, he furiously scratched his head and pulled at his ears.

Wayne continued to toss around ideas. He would bring Annabelle back to their new place. It would be just the two of them, with Annabelle cooking and cleaning for him. No interference from the rest of the family. They would have to hide out for a while until Wayne came up with an escape to another country.

He sure would like to have drinks at the Break it Open Bar with his buddies. Winckowski missed the great times he had had at that bar, but as much as he tried, he couldn't seem to make plans past picking up Annabelle. Forget it! His mind was too tired to plan; he'd figure it out as he went.

Grabbing the yoke of his leftover beer, he quietly closed the van door as the beer cans clinked together. Wayne slowly crossed the yard to the front door, feeling giddy with his accomplishments.

Knowing the door was unlocked, he tried to walk in, but it was stuck. He held onto both sides of the doorjamb and kicked it open. The door slammed so hard against the wall; the doorknob plunged deep into the sheetrock.

Giggling, he stepped in and sang out, "AnnieBelly, I'm home!"

A command came out of the dark. "Stop right there! Put your hands on your head. Now!" Just then, a light went on from the back of the house, casting a pale light on the intruder.

Winckowski was stunned but automatically went for his gun.

His movements were cut short when he saw several flashes, then heard gun blasts, shocking him. Standing stock-still, he smelled burnt gunpowder. A thought blinked, *grab your gun*, but Wayne couldn't.

Suddenly, excruciating pain seared through him as he screamed out. Reality rushed at him: he had been shot! Wayne twisted against the crushing pain, flinging the beer through the air. The full cans crashed to the hardwood floor, spinning and spewing the yeasty smell throughout the living room.

The deadweight of Wayne's body crumbled silently until his head hit the oak floor with a resounding *thwack*. Wayne's eyes rolled up into his head, no longer seeing. With a final jerk, his heart burst as he felt the violent pain, the last feeling of life.

A loud yelp came from the back bedroom. Carl Larson shouted from his bedroom, "What's going on out there?" Throwing the sheet off, he jumped out of bed with his chest bare, wearing cotton pajama bottoms. Stumbling toward the darkened living room, he said, "Pete! Pete? Tommy, what happened?"

Tommy shouted over the receding echo of the blasts. "Easy, Carl, easy. It's okay. Pete is not here. Remember he's at the hospital with the security team? Turn on the lights, please."

The light switch snapped on, scorching the white living room walls with the ceiling's one-hundred-watt bulb. Its suddenness made the men squint. Their eyes adjusted and traveled down to the floor, where their eyes zeroed in on the dark bullet holes seeping red onto the man's dirty white shirt. The brilliance of the ceiling light cast a bluish hue across the steady stream of blood pooling onto the floor.

Tommy was still kneeling in his shooting position as Carl began to move into the room. Holding up his hand, the deputy said firmly, "No, Carl, no further. Please sit down."

Carl gladly obliged, pulling out a dining room chair, and collapsed into it. Breathing hard, he gingerly laid his head in his palm and peeked over toward the front door, stuttering his questions.

"Are you okay? Is it…is it the guy?" Carl's voice quaked as he closed his eyes against the onslaught of his fears and a fresh, raw headache.

Standing, Tommy walked cautiously, with his gun trained on the man. The man was huge, sprawled across a large percentage of the small living room. It was presumptuous of Tommy to think that the man was dead, but with two hits to the man's chest and one to his forehead, it was unlikely the intruder would be alive.

As Tommy drew closer, he could smell the man's horrendous mix of booze, body odor, and fresh blood, even catching the faintest scent of cologne. His notorious tattoos were exposed, and his bald head was shadowed with stubble. Gross flecks were stuck in Wayne's overgrown beard. The dead man's hazel eyes were open but unmoving. The high-wattage ceiling light reflected off the silver belt buckle, spinning slivers of shine across the room. With that last detail, Tommy identified the dead man as Wayne Winckowski.

Tommy holstered his gun, knelt down, and felt for a pulse in the guy's neck. "The guy's dead. Carl, do you recognize him?"

Still seated, Carl looked to Tommy. His good eye went wide, and his face paled. His healing, broken eye socket was now yellow and purple, with bright red broken capillaries in his left eye making him look even worse than he had on Monday.

Carl stood up with the aid of the table and took a couple of shaky steps over to the man. "Oh, my God, it's the guy. Is it the killer, Winckowski?"

Tommy replied, "Yes, I'm quite certain. When he walked in, he said, 'AnnieBelly, I'm home!' He might have thought he was in his own house, but who knows?"

Tommy stood and, with a low voice, said, "I'll call the chief." Tommy had shot hundreds of bad guys on paper targets at the shooting range, but shooting a living person resulted in a whole pack of different emotions, even if the man he had just put down was a murderer. Nausea interrupted his thoughts.

Roger answered his home phone, clearing the sleeping frog from his throat, and said, "This better be good."

"It is. Wayne Winckowski is lying dead in Carl's living room."

Roger flew up out of bed, stood and shouted, "What the hell? No shit! What? Did you call it into the station yet?"

"No, you're my first call." Tommy's voice had dropped an octave or two.

With one leg in his trousers, Roger stopped dressing, and sat back down onto the bed. "Tommy, you just saved the life of that nice old gentleman, and I'm proud of you. Having to kill a person doesn't feel good, but this is the reality of the job, son. It had to be done. Otherwise, Winckowski might have killed both of you and possibly Annabelle."

Tommy's voice cracked as he said, "Yes, sir. Thank you for that."

Roger stood up and said in a firm voice, "Have Carl put on the coffee pot, turn on the outside lights, and you two stay in the kitchen, okay?"

"Yes, sir."

"I'll be there soon." Roger quickly dressed and shouted out a quick "thank you" to Klink for the suggestion of having an officer at Carl Larson's house. Roger sent a text to Hilde, who was on duty.

Forty minutes later, Roger arrived at Carl Larson's house and found it lit up like a Christmas tree. Hilde had further to travel and arrived much later. The group's excitement over the demise of Wayne Winckowski had lost its thrill, and the topic of conversation had turned to sports.

Stepping through the back door, Hilde slipped on a pair of paper booties over her best leather boots. Walking cautiously into the living room, she squatted down next to the dead body, who laid ignored after everyone got their first look.

Studying Winckowski, Hilde smelled the faint scent of cologne beneath the repugnant smell of days old sweat. It was the same scent from the day in the barn, when she had a reaction to it. Hilde began blinking rapidly, slammed her eyes shut, and grabbed a table leg behind her while her gut pinched as the lost memory moved forward.

Hilde's mind wandered through the fog as the scene played out from so many years ago. Each detail clicked into place like a dark puzzle. She remembered hitting the giant man with her steel baton and the fury on his face when he charged at her. The man lifted her high and spun her around, as the sweet vile odor of sweat and cologne wafted from the man's skin. Her last thought was brushing the kitchen ceiling and then flying to the floor.

The gauze, coating her memory vanished, and the truth glared back at her. Wayne Winckowski was the man who assaulted and raped her.

He was the dead man lying before her. Looking around she swiped at the tears. The shock subsided, and a sense of relief filled her, but then and there, Hilde Crosby decided it would be her secret, never to be shared. Wayne Winckowski would not be identified as Hilde's rapist. She needed to protect her daughter, Tillie. What child needed to know she was a product of rape, especially by a man who was a murderer.

The chief deputy stood, looked down at the bastard, snapped her wrist, and rolled her shoulders. For years that dark hole inside her messed her up, causing her years of sleeplessness. But she and Tillie had made a good life, and for that, she was grateful knowing the black hole would mend. There would be leftover emotions, but she would deal with that later. Taking a quick peek around, not seeing anyone, she reared back her foot, and Hilda Mary Crosby kicked the shit out of the dead body.

Straightening her shirt, she wiped her sweaty palms on her pants, and the deputy chief began to analyze the crime scene.

A reporter, June Beacon, from the Blanchard News showed up at Carl's house. She had graciously accepted the newspaper position of the lead reporter, replacing the crook, Muriel Friechs.

June's main concern was having enough space to squeeze in the double headline on the Sunday evening edition "Wayne Winckowski Shot and Killed," would be the first headline. And under that, her subheading: "Friechs + Mayor + Whalen = Arrested!"

chapter
fifty-five

Sunday, June 10, 7:30 a.m.

Dignity Christian Hospital,
Two Streams, Minnesota

Annabelle woke as the sun just crested the horizon. She was feeling better, having slept soundly after last night's nightmare. Lying motionless, she stared out the window as the dew gave the window an opalescent look, and droplets raced each other down the glass. The sky was pink and blue, girl and boy colors. It was her favorite-colored sky.

At 8:00 a.m., the morning duty nurse on the neo-natal floor brought in her breakfast tray while Annabelle and Dr. Joe finished their card game of Vermilion Rummy. Dr. Joe had never arrived before breakfast, so it was a pleasant surprise. The nurse took her temperature and checked her vitals. Annabelle's temperature had broken during the night, and it was obvious she was on the mend.

Gathering up the cards, Dr. Joe set them aside and sat back in the wing chair with his finger tapping on the armrest, which Annabelle tried to ignore. Watching his mannerisms during the week she had figured out that when he fidgeted, he was worried. Being famished, she ignored him and dove into her breakfast. There was a small double tap on her door, and Annabelle responded, "Come in."

Chief Roger Jorgenson walked in, holding his hat. Joe didn't seem surprised to see him, and the doctor tipped his head to the chief. Annabelle felt like a cold eel had slid down her spine, and she dreaded what was coming. Sitting up straight, she smoothed her white blankets over her lap. The chief looked at her with his brown puppy eyes, hesitating. Finally, Annabelle said, "What?"

Clearing his throat, Roger said quietly, "Your dad was shot and killed very early this morning in Blanchard."

Annabelle heard what he said, but her mind locked in on the name of her hometown. Wayne was in Blanchard to get her. She rolled her hands into fists and stiffened.

Looking up, she asked, puzzled. "Where was Wayne?"

"In a house, not far. We think he thought it was empty," Roger said. "It actually belonged to a man your dad assaulted Monday night. Deputy Tommy was standing guard at the man's house when your dad broke in."

Annabelle's insides felt like they shrunk. She felt no joy, no sadness, just numb, except for the resounding beat at the top of her chest. Her mind was flying through a variety of appropriate phrases she could say: "I am sorry," or "Good job!" or "Too bad, so sad." But she didn't want to make nice.

Annabelle's thoughts turned to the years of fearing her father and the pain he had caused her and her family.

Wayne had disposed of the family she most dearly loved, leaving her alone, a stranger in her own world.

With that thought, her anger burst out of her, pitching to an anguished electrified scream, making Dr. Dill jump. The pain in her back ratcheted through her as she wailed for her momma, Matson, Candy, Gail, and Harley. Annabelle's fists clenched tighter, beating her blankets as her face turned bright red. She shook her head like a wild beast until every part of her body was in motion.

Roger started to go to her, but Joe stopped him. Just then, Shelly peeked in her eyes wide, but Joe quickly shook his head at her, and she backed out, placing a "Do Not Disturb" sign on the door.

Screaming even louder, Annabelle shouted out, "You son of a bitch! I hate you! I never ever loved you. I hated you, and I will never forgive you! Go to Hell, you, BASTARD!"

Wild with rage, Annabelle began throwing anything she could get her hands on plates, books, tissue box, TV remote, and then a water glass. The glass shattered against the whiteboard on the wall, blasting glass over the floor. The blankets were tossed, her table pushed over, and then she pulled at her hair, continuing to scream.

I can't stop screaming!

Annabelle felt the pain from all the beatings, all the fearful feelings inside forcing her to pretend outside, and the times she trembled so hard she thought her limbs would fall off. The constant tap, tap, tap of the worries and responsibilities of always being 'on'.

Annabelle would no longer have her momma to comb her hair, lavishing that slow, final stroke. Who would she go to without her best friend, Harley? She wanted to taste life with her family without Wayne. But now Annabelle's world would feel smaller, lonelier, strange, and scary.

I need your help, God, please!

314 / Donna Graham

She continued to scream feeling helpless, as her emotions and bad memories collided. Her hands covered her hot, steaming face, suffocating her. Suddenly, Annabelle felt Dr. Joe lay his hand over hers. A quiet peace settled her shuddering, and she was able to pull a full breath. Her colliding emotions softened.

Deep inside her, she heard a powerful voice, *I got this. Let it go.*

Falling back onto the pillows, Annabelle slowly lowered her hands, hiccupping and shuddering. Looking over to the two stunned men, worry etched onto their faces. For the very first time in her life, she couldn't smile, not even a fake one.

Annabelle whispered with her raw throat, "Sorry. I guess I was holding in some stuff." Pausing briefly, Annabelle said, "I'm glad he's gone, but I hoped that I would have had a chance to holler at him. He's in Hell, right?"

The big men looked to each other, talking over one another, "Yup, oh for sure." "Uh-huh. Oh, yeah, forever."

"Good. Will there be a funeral for …him?" Her temper ramping up again, "If there is, I'm not going! He doesn't deserve one. I won't go!"

The doctor leaned over and took her hand, and Roger spoke up, explaining, "The St. Louis County will bury him in one of their cemeteries somewhere near Duluth, several hours away from here."

Chilled again, Annabelle shuddered and said, "Tell me how it happened."

Dr. Joe rose and said, "Just one second." Stepping out into the hall, he asked Shelly to bring in a warm blanket or two, along with a cup of hot chocolate, a broom and if there was a dog available, bring it in.

Both men pulled up chairs, and each quickly crossed their long legs, bumping the other's foot and mumbling apologies to each other as they shifted their chairs further apart. Shelly stepped in with a couple of soft blankets and wrapped them around Annabelle teepee style. Pat, the male nurse placed a cup of hot chocolate and a handful of marshmallows on the bed table, and both nurses slipped out the door. A housekeeper came in and quickly cleaned up the water and broken glass, and she too left. Apparently, there were no dogs for comfort.

Roger started, "We knew Wayne was heading back here, but we weren't sure why or where he was going. We tracked him all over North and South Dakota. Eventually, he started heading to northern Minnesota and then veered northeast toward Blanchard."

Wrapped in white, Annabelle asked, her voice quivering, "Did he kill anyone else while he was running away?"

"No, but he scared a few. Wayne thinking that he had killed Carl, went to Carl's house, assuming it was empty and would make a perfect hideout."

Annabelle stared at Roger, and he continued, "When Wayne walked into Carl's house, it was after midnight. Carl was asleep, but Deputy Tommy was on duty. After your dad kicked in the front door, Tommy heard Wayne shout, "AnnieBelly, I'm home!"

Annabelle's hand flew to her open mouth as her body burrowed down into the blankets.

"I hate to tell you this, but Tommy was the one who shot your father."

Annabelle, with only her eyes showing above the edge of the blankets, muffled out, "Is Tommy okay?"

"Yes, he is. We have to follow procedure, and Tommy will be placed on administrative leave, which is time off from work with pay until the investigation is completed. Tommy will also have to attend some counseling." Annabelle looked over at Dr. Dill, but he didn't respond to her silent question about whether or not he might be the therapist.

The chief asked, "Do you have any other questions for me?"

Annabelle shook her head.

The chief stood and said, "You call me on my cell phone if you do have any questions. Promise?"

She nodded. The chief placed a card with his number on the table, patted her hand, and left the room.

Annabelle threw off her covers, apparently warm enough, and looked over at Dr. Joe. He had changed his seat position three times while Roger was talking. The doctor said, "I'm going to ask, you know?".

"You don't need to, 'cause I know what you were going to ask. I feel numb with some tingling. That's how I feel."

"I was surprised by your rage."

"Yeah, well, me too, and it scared me. I've always had to hold in all of my feelings and pretend to be happy for everyone else. It felt good to let it out, except my throat hurts."

Dr. Joe smiled, passing her a glass of water, and said, "Well, maybe next time you might want to stay away from anything breakable."

Talking inside the glass, she said, "Do ya think?"

Dr. Joe laughed. She loved to hear his deep, baritone laughter that made his eyes sparkle.

"Was my dad drunk when he walked into the guy's house?"

"From what the chief told me earlier, Wayne reeked of booze, so probably. Inside the van that he had stolen from Carl, the cops found a canvas bag with lots of money."

Annabelle shrugged, nodded, and said with a knowing look, "Oh, that was from his vending machine business. He would hide it on the farm when he was traveling. Somehow Mattson always found it and would take a little bit of money so Dad wouldn't notice and give it to Momma. So, the money will pay the police for their work?"

"Oh, no, they'll put it into evidence, but then all of it will be returned to you, which would be for your college education, your future..."

"College? Ha! Not me." Annabelle gave him an "as if" look.

Dr. Joe shifted forward in his chair, further explaining, "The money is yours. Even if there wasn't any money, you're smart enough to get a scholarship to any college and finish with a great degree. Set your sights high because you can achieve them.

"Also, we'll find a good financial guy who will invest that money for you, which would actually make it grow to an even larger amount. When you're an adult, you could use it for a new home, graduate school, travel, anything you would like. The farm will probably be yours as well."

Annabelle was still stuck on something Dr. Dill had said. "College? I just never... thought..." She looked doubtful.

Dr. Joe said, "But why not?"

"Well, Dad always told all of us how stupid we were. He said that we girls would probably get knocked up like our mother. I never thought I would have any kind of future, maybe different but the same.

Dr. Joe's face flushed and became taut. "I'm sorry he lied to you and made you feel worthless. I know for a fact that you are very smart. I've talked to your teachers, and they are very impressed with your intelligence, your grades, and your writing skills."

Annabelle confirmed, "Well, yeah, they always told me that too, but I just thought they told everyone that. I figured Dad knew more about me than my teachers, just a stupid dumb girl."

Dr. Joe cracked his knuckles. "Nope, your dad was not only cruel, but he was the stupid one. My opinion counts, and I know you are smart. Who else but a highly intelligent person would hide in a nasty, old, scary garage and voluntarily smear smelly dead dinosaur grease all over her?" His look said, 'right?'

Annabelle looked away, taking to heart what she had just learned. Dr. Joe, the man she most admired, just told her she was smart. A small smile touched her mouth. Annabelle would have to work on believing that, and boy, did she want to believe it.

She sat back, enjoying the warmth of the moment and the calmness that enveloped her. One day she would be a college girl, wow. Annabelle suddenly felt great comfort in the fact that she had no one to fear. A hiccup escaped her throat, and she had to pinch her nose from the rising emotions. A good thought grazed her mind, of her new family, Doris and Jim.

Annabelle dug under the covers and pulled out Ollie, and hugged him. She said, "I'm going to live with Doris and Jim, and I am so triple dipled excited!"

Laughing his big, barrel laugh, Dr. Joe uncrossed his legs and leaned forward putting his big hands onto his knees and lifted himself into a standing position, looking at Annabelle with pride. Bending way down, he gave her a huge hug, kissing the top of her head.

He said, "I'll be back later today. Enjoy this delicious day."

Annabelle giggled, shrugging her shoulders up and down. "I will! I will!" Her emotions bounced, cloud-like. And that felt good.

Dr. Joe strolled down the hospital hall, thinking to himself, and decided that he would tell Annabelle his other great news later. During this horrendous week, Dr. Joe had decided a major change was needed. *You can never have too much frosting on a cake,* he thought. *Impossible.*

Annabelle crept out of bed, adjusting the tubes, and started walking to the window, but stepped back to pick up Ollie. Feeling giddy, sad, afraid of the unknown, and good, she closed her eyes, letting the sunlight wash her face. Lavishing the soft, warm glow, she was grateful for not having to fear her father any longer. In the same breath, Annabelle wished he had been killed before he had murdered her family. A large sigh of regret escaped her.

Sorry, God, I don't mean to disrespect Your plan.

Annabelle knew she had a lot of work to do to become a better person. The fear of the consequences of telling the truth made her a seasoned liar. Unwinding the shallow, entertaining court jester role she played for three years was going to be tough. She would also not have her momma around to kiss her with her special Italian kisses: a kiss on the left and then on the right. It would leave a hole in her nighttime routine. Missing her brothers' and sisters' love would be a deep loss. She wanted to be proud of herself, learn how to trust, and have a family to love. Her tears were released when she opened her eyes. Closing them again she let the sunlight dry her face, and Annabelle Miriam Winckowski prayed for guidance.

chapter
fifty-six

Saturday, December 15, 11:00 a.m.

Church of the Nazarene,
Two Streams, Minnesota

Annabelle was jittery, waiting for her turn. It had been months since the aurora. The days that had followed were not anything close to what she could have ever imagined, lots of good days, in-between days, and of course, several bad days. And now she was extremely giddy.

After being released from the hospital, she moved in with Jim and Doris Dickens. They were and had always been generous and kind. She was their foster child, and their plan was still to adopt her. The only thing holding them up was, as Jim put it, "legal red tapeworms."

Annabelle loved living at their big clean house on the farm. She could run and run over their vast property. Annabelle was close enough to Amelia's house to bike there, but Mom—Doris—insisted on biking with Annabelle and then coming to bike back with her. Annabelle loved that she cared so much, even though she may have been a little overprotective.

Her bedroom upstairs was cute, and Annabelle was thrilled that it had real walls. She helped paint them with a soft yellow, almost the same color in her hospital room. Her new, comfy bed had a quilt that was made just for her by Doreen Nelson. The original penguin quilt was ruined with black grease, but she made Annabelle an even prettier one, red and black, with yellow penguins all over it. Annabelle melted each time she walked into her room.

Annabelle and Poppa—Jim—had finished the flower garden labyrinth. The healing labyrinth was a wide, circular walking path bordered with flowerbeds. The trail was wide to accommodate wagons, strollers, and even wheelchairs, and it could be used all year round. In the center of the circle was a weeping willow tree with an aqua bench hidden underneath. They planted a variety of perennial flowers that would grow year after year.

Poppa put in some special surprises along the way, too. Mom told Annabelle he worked for days digging a trench from the stream to put in a little bubbling waterfall near the daylilies. The crabbiest woman in town had given Annabelle a special gift, a sundial, and Poppa put it in front of the hydrangeas.

The sadness from the aurora hit Annabelle hard sometimes. She would lean on her new parents, but sometimes being alone helped more. This was when she walked the labyrinth or worked in her Mom's vegetable garden. During those times, especially, Annabelle made sure to thank God for what she had.

Talking to Poppa about opening the labyrinth to others who needed to heal, his eyes welled, and he said it was a good idea. Annabelle was elated.

Annabelle felt loved, not just by her new parents, but by her hometown. The small town reached out not only to her but to others who needed help. Somehow the aurora changed Blanchard, and it had become kinder, more responsible for others.

Annabelle struggled with shyness, or it could just be that she was embarrassed that everyone knew her dark secrets. She made it hard for friends to get close, but they kept trying. Dr. Joe was always available to talk it out.

Now, concentrating on not rushing, Annabelle heard the rustling of her pink organza skirt as she slowly walked in tune with the organ music. Her smile felt like it would crack her face or worse that she might giggle. She was a bridesmaid for Miss Kathryn Cleveland, who was marrying Dr. Joseph Dill, and the wedding had begun.

Reaching the top of the altar stairs, she was met by Janet, Dr. Joe's sister, who smiled as Annabelle lined up next to her.

The organ music stopped, and the congregation stood. The wedding march began, and Kathy, holding onto her father's arm, began to walk down the aisle. Annabelle looked down the aisle and gasped. Kathy was so glamorous her new highlighted hair-style softening her face, as her wide smile made her the most beautiful bride. Her foamy white bridal gown and veil were sprinkled with tiny pink crystal beads. Kathy never took her eyes off Dr. Joe, nor did he take his eyes off his stunning bride.

Annabelle wanted to take a peek at Poppa to see if he was crying. But she wouldn't because she already had pools of tears in her own eyes. Realizing all of the bridesmaids were either sniffling or wiping their tears away, she let her tears fall. Annabelle rocked back and forth on her heels, feeling the tickling emotions running through her. She nicknamed them happy.

epilogue

July 7, three years later

49 Calico Fields Road, Blanchard, Minnesota

Without a family, the abandoned Winckowski farm continued its downward spiral rotting from the inside out. The interior of the house had become damp from the leaky roof, as the squares of siding continued to drop off the house. Struggling to hang onto the header board, the burnt-out sunroom lost the battle, and the room collapsed into an unrecognizable heap of charred timber. The dilapidated white garage where Annabelle had hidden lost the war with the pushy trees. The big barn with its red knotholes continued to stand strong and purposeful, seemingly untouched by life, wind, or rain.

It was Annabelle's thirteenth birthday, and she had grown into a tall thin pre-teen with a healthy tan and lots of freckles. Jim and his daughter came in for lunch after working on the farm and sat down with Doris. Once seated, her parents opened the difficult subject of tearing down Annabelle's abandoned farmhouse. Their sole purpose was to rid their daughter of the aurora's memories. Jim added, "I know you want to keep the house, but it is almost beyond repair, I'm sorry."

Resisting and not able to explain her rationale, she knew she did not want it destroyed. She needed to take a couple of days to think about it, and her parents agreed to wait to make a decision.

Two days later, Annabelle approached her parents, telling them she was ready to discuss it again. They settled around the table and Kitty was on Annabelle's lap.

Taking a deep breath, she looked at her parents with pleading eyes. "I would like to try to keep the house or maybe I could find a small memento. I can see it's almost collapsing, and I know there is so much work that would have to be done to make it livable, but maybe we can fix it up just enough for it to stand until I finish college. With the money leftover from the cash bag, I would have it rebuilt and have a new huge sign built to hang over the driveway, Calico Fields Organic Farm. The farm acres have been untouched for years, would be perfect for crops." Annabelle's hazel eyes sparkled with the anticipation of learning not only about organic farming but applying the principles to her own fields.

Annabelle's smile curled down. "I can understand why you want to get rid of the house, but not all the memories in that house were bad. When Wayne was around, we would all be scared to death, wondering what the next minute would mean for us, but my family was warm and loving when he was away. Alone, we played cards and games, we caught up on our sleep, danced, blasted music from the radio, and took care of each other.

My family loved me just as much as I loved them. I want to keep those memories alive." Annabelle swiped at a runaway tear. "I want to re-create the feeling of what I have here at your house, my home, and make new, happy memories. I don't know if I will ever be ready to leave you... but if I choose to, it would be into a new house on the farm or the old farmhouse. Then, I would be just across the field." She gave a small smile, unsure of their response.

Jim scratched at the vinyl tablecloth. Doris swallowed several times and took her mother's linen handkerchief, and wiped her mouth. Clearing his throat, Jim said, "Honey, we as your parents will do our best to make you happy. That old house is in such tough shape, it could have already collapsed while we sat here. But, the best thing to do is analyze its structure and figure it out. But understand memories are in your soul, not in a house. Have you been inside since aurora?"

Annabelle shook her head and said, "No. I don't want to go inside."

"Well, okay then, before it completely collapses, let's go treasure hunting and take some memories with us. Grab the camera and flashlight, girls!"

Annabelle leaped at Poppa and squeezed him. Then she turned to Doris and sat on her lap, hugging her. Giggling, Annabelle led the way and headed across the field to decide the future of her abandoned house, 49 Calico Fields Road.

As the three of them stood in the front yard, looking at the house, their concern deepened, noticing the dormer had fallen through the roof and into the living room. The happy memories she kept so close to her were not in the house as Jim had said. Annabelle looked at her home and unconsciously rubbed her arms as goosebumps trailed up and down. The broken-down house scared her.

Jim and Doris looked to their daughter for a sign when Annabelle started walking down the driveway to the back of the property. Jim and Doris followed. Annabelle stopped in front of the mauve-colored barn, with its red knot holes and stick straight walls. Touring all the way around the barn, she studied it up and down, viewing the miles of scenery surrounding the barn. The nearby trees grew with abandon. Volunteer seedlings produced magnificent maple and river birch trees, plus giant lilac bushes. Peeking out from behind the barn Annabelle waved, and said, "Come here. Hurry I found my momento."

High-stepping through the tall, prickly weeds, Jim and Doris followed their daughter around the corner. As soon as Annabelle saw them, she began prattling and pointing up to the second story. "If I turned this beautiful barn into my new house, can you imagine the views from huge corner windows up there? The barn looks straight and I would paint it Coca-cola Red. What do you think?"

Doris said, "Oh, it would be such a cool house."

Jim tagged onto what his wife had said, "And I think it would be fabulous, bright and modern. The stone foundation is nearly perfect. What a fun project."

Annabelle was standing on her tiptoes and clapping her hands, "This would be a fresh start without *any* bad memories. You were right, Poppa, the other house scared me, and this one ... makes me, um I love it."

Their smiles wide, they all began talking over each other about Annabelle's new home. One day.

That night, for the second time in its lifetime, lightning struck the Winckowski home setting it on fire. The raging inferno fed on the dried tinder until the house collapsed into a pile of smoldering timbers. The powerful thunderstorm extinguished the remaining flare-ups and soaked the debris.

The fire was fast, but went unnoticed.

The following morning, Annabelle looked out the window and was shocked to see her old house was gone. It was like in the movie, The Wizard of Oz, and Dorothy's house was blown off its foundation, flying into another world. Gone.

In her pajamas and flip flops Annabelle raced to the scene through the field of peas, hopping periodically to remove a green vine wrapped around her sandal. Stopping short at the edge of the scorched yard, Annabelle stared at the cold timbers.

Shock dropped her mouth open, and her hands shook. The fire was confined to the house, leaving the surrounding trees untouched. No longer obstructed by the house, the big red barn stood behind the rubble, unharmed. Annabelle was relieved knowing her barn would be her home one day.

A slow, deep smile warmed her face. She raised her palm and kissed it five times. Turning her hand outward toward the charred ruins, Annabelle said, "Thank you Momma, Mattson, Candy, Gail and Harley for your sweet gifts of love. I will always love you, and will never forget."

Annabelle Winckowski turned and made her way back home to her Mom and Poppa.

"Never let the sadness of your past and the fear of your future ruin the happiness of your present."
by Peter Cole

I'd be honored if you would leave a review after reading Silenced to Death. The review area is on the book page inside Amazon.com. Thank you. *Donna Graham*